THE MUMMY

UNIVERSAL PICTURES PRESENTS AN ALPHAVILLE PRODUCTION A STEPHEN SOMMERS FILM

BRENDAN FRASER "THE MUMMY" RACHEL WEISZ JOHN HANNAH ARNOLD VOSLOO

JONATHAN HYDE KEVIN O'CONNOR MUSIC BY JERRY GOLDSMITH CO PRODUCER PATRICIA CARR EDITED BY BOB DUCSAY PRODUCTION DESIGNER ALLAN CAMERON

DIRECTOR OF PHOTOGRAPHY ADRIAN BIDDLE B S C EXECUTIVE PRODUCER KEVIN JARRE PRODUCED BY JAMES JACKS SEAN DANIEL

READ THE BERKLEY BOOK   SCREEN STORY BY STEPHEN SOMMERS AND LLOYD FONVIELLE & KEVIN JARRE

MAY 7 SCREENPLAY BY STEPHEN SOMMERS   A UNIVERSAL RELEASE

DIRECTED BY STEPHEN SOMMERS

www.themummy.com

THE
MUMMY

A novel by

Max Allan Collins

Based on a screenplay by
Stephen Sommers

Screen story by
Stephen Sommers and Lloyd Fonvielle & Kevin Jarre

Based on the motion picture screenplay by
John L. Balderston,
story by Nina Wilcox Putnam & Richard Schayer

BERKLEY BOULEVARD BOOKS, NEW YORK

THE MUMMY

A novel by Max Allan Collins, based on a screenplay by
Stephen Sommers. Screen story by Stephen Sommers and Lloyd Fonvielle
& Kevin Jarre. Based on the motion picture screenplay by
John L. Balderston, story by Nina Wilcox Putnam & Richard Schayer.

A Berkley Boulevard Book / published by arrangement with
Universal Studios Publishing Rights, a division of Universal Studios
Licensing, Inc.

PRINTING HISTORY
Berkley Boulevard edition / May 1999
Berkley Boulevard Special Sales edition / July 1999

ISBN: 0-425-17381-x

BERKLEY BOULEVARD
Berkley Boulevard Books are published by
The Berkley Publishing Group,
a division of Penguin Putnam Inc., 375 Hudson Street,
New York, New York 10014.
BERKLEY BOULEVARD and its logo
are trademarks belonging to Penguin Putnam Inc.

PRINTED IN THE UNITED STATES OF AMERICA

For Bill Mumy
(*not* pronounced mummy)

"Death is but the doorway to new life—
We live today, we shall again,
In many forms shall we return."

—Ancient Egyptian prayer

THE
MUMMY

·❮ PART ONE ❯·

The Mummy's Curse

Thebes—1,290 B.C.

·❮ 1 ❯·

The Painted Paramour

As straight and shining as a well-burnished sword, the river that would one day be known as the Nile slashed through the verdant valley in the midst of a vast sand-swept bleakness that in time would be called Sahara. Any boat or barge gliding down the wide river's smooth surface would eventually be greeted by the shining golden nubs of temple flagpoles, hundreds of them, catching the sunlight to wink at the cloudless sky. Shortly thereafter, the river would widen to a harbor and an army of colorful linen pennants, shimmering against purple cliffs, would announce the city that was the crown jewel of the pharaoh's domain.

Thebes—the City of the Living—sprawled upon the east bank, a crowded, thriving metropolis of riches and poverty; in the shadows of its vast limestone palaces, tiny brick houses huddled, and wide avenues befitting the grandest royal procession were within a stone's throw of narrow alleyways, where rats and drunks made their homes.

On the west bank, symmetrical waterways fed the silty black soil, green fields edged by the paint, plaster, and pennants of grand temples. Behind these temples and fields stretched a strip of desert where the dead of Thebes, in their fine white linens, occupied burial chambers below ground. It was said that the dead rose from their underground city, on certain sundowns, and stood in the blue dusk striped by the orange dying sun, looking longingly across the water at the City of the Living.

Even as Pharaoh Seti had ruled over the living citizens of the bustling, vital city, so did Imhotep, the High Priest of the green-eyed god, Osiris, prevail over the decaying bodies of those who awaited the afterlife. The towering, sinewy Imhotep—head shaved, copper-skinned, intense eyed, and as well-chiseledly handsome as any idol—was one of the most powerful men in the City of the Living: he was the Keeper of the Dead.

And now in death, even the pharaoh—murdered by his favorite mistress, the ethereal beauty, Anck-su-namun—was under Imhotep's dominion. Seti had regarded Imhotep as a loyal servant, prized advisor, and—as much as a potentate could be said to have one—a trusted friend. So it now fell, in due course, for Imhotep to fulfill one last duty for his fallen friend: to curse the body of the woman who had betrayed the flesh-and-blood man who had worn the robe and crown of the pharaoh.

Under the starry dome of the sky, a torchlit procession of slaves, soldiers, and priests wound through and around the desert dunes. The bare-chested Nubian slaves bore the linen-bandage-wrapped mummified body of Anck-su-namun, the sinuously feminine curves of the woman apparent even in death; five more of them carried the jewel-encrusted canopic jars that held the dead paramour's vital organs, and another two lugged an unpretentious wooden coffin. White-helmeted, bare-chested soldiers in full shields-and-spears battle array accompanied the slaves, protecting the jeweled jars, if not the worthless remains of this traitorous wench. At the rear, a contingency of Imhotep's priests, as calm as the soldiers were stern, seemed to float in their dark linen, holding in their arms cats as white as the purest sand, strange cats with eyes that glowed like hot coals in the darkness, their bodies so limber they might have been boneless.

At the head of the parade of death, his own torch held high, Imhotep—his long dark face devoid of expression, but his eyes jumping with firelight, his robe black with threads of gold, muscular bare chest pearled with sweat—directed the group to a site of his own choosing, where a hole had been dug that afternoon.

Imhotep carried in one hand a massive book fashioned from purest gold, heavily hinged in brass, its cover, and the hinges, too, decorated with the letters and images of their language, which Imhotep's people called the Words of God.

The exquisitely carved book weighed as much as a man, and that the high priest betrayed no strain at bearing such a burden indicated both his emotional self-control and immense physical strength. Surrounded by dunes, in a dip of the desert, the high priest gave a barely perceptible nod and the slaves placed the mummified body, not into the grave, but on the sand several paces away, and arranged the five jeweled jars around her, in preparation for the ceremony Imhotep so dreaded.

And now, appearing as if frightful mirages, the pharaoh's elite palace guards popped up, to watch from the dunes. The Med-jai (as these ominous spectators were known) had skin interrupted occasionally by a puzzlelike patchwork of tattoos whose meaning was known only to the secret cult into which they had been born. The fervently faithful ''guards'' were here, Imhotep supposed, to honor their dead master by witnessing the curse that would be dispensed upon the treacherous paramour who had slain their liege.

The only other possibility, the high priest knew, was that the Med-jai harbored certain dangerous suspicions—suspicions that would be allayed only by Imhotep's reading of the sacred incantations from the golden pages of *The Book of Amun Ra,* condemning Anck-su-namun as evil, and sending her on a journey to the underworld where her soul would be eaten by Ammit, monster of the dead.

He would sooner send himself there.

Imhotep—like the late pharaoh—was a man of flesh and blood under his priestly vestments; and—like the late pharaoh—he had dearly loved this woman, loved the spirit of

5

her, the nimble mind of her, and most certainly the pliant flesh of her. The high priest, who had seemed to those around him as much a man of stone as any statue in any temple, had some forty nights ago—the mummification process was a slow one—stood on the balcony of the house of the pharaoh's mistress, feeling the gentle fingers of the desert breeze wafting across the slumbering river to caress him, to kiss his bare chest, in gentle foreshadowing of delights to come.

Delights she would bestow upon him.

On that night, Imhotep's contingent of priestly guards had positioned themselves in and around Anck-su-namun's palacelike residence, keeping watch. Their heads shaved, their bodies tattooed with their own cult's secret markings, their skin withered from desert ritual, their strength rivaling their master's, the priests of Osiris were devoted to Imhotep, whom they considered a god walking among them. Of course, the pharaoh, too, was said to be a god; but these priests served Osiris, and as Imhotep was his high priest, he commanded their loyalty.

The pharaoh was not expected—he was said to be attending a dinner of state—but precautions, in so dangerous a liaison, were always necessary, and never to be taken for granted.

In the many-pillared, high-ceiling anteroom, barely distinguishable from the ornate statuary, the priests of Imhotep followed with their eyes the mistress of the house as she entered through the tall golden doors and passed among them wordlessly, gliding over the marble floor with a dancer's lithe grace, crossing to part the sheer curtains of her bedchamber. No sign that the olive-skinned goddess affected them as men could be detected; nor was any anxiety apparent in their cracked-stonelike faces.

But they were not stone, these men who were priests, and they had just witnessed the sight of the most beautiful woman in Thebes, regal in the elaborate, bluntly cut human-hair headdress.

Anck-su-namun's lovely catlike face twitched a smile as she gestured to her painted skin.

"This is the final indignity, my love," she said, in a voice nearly as low as his. "Now I am truly Pharaoh's possession—with fresh coats of paint applied each day."

The lovers stood facing each other near the silk-draped slanting bed of the gilded bedchamber.

"But when Seti dies," Imhotep said, cupping her face in his hands, avoiding her painted skin where the design climbed her throat, "his son takes the throne, and you are set free. . . ."

He kissed her, greedily, and she returned the kiss, with equal passion. They both knew that upon the pharaoh's death, his mistress would receive this house, a considerable annual stipend, and the full rights of a citizen. And while they could never marry, a high priest could keep his own mistress; a high priest in Thebes could do almost anything.

"He's an old man," she said, reaching a painted hand out and stopping just short of caressing his cheek, "but healthy. He has many years left."

"Does he?"

Her eyes narrowed, dark jewels in the oval mask of her face. "Are you willing to take the necessary steps?"

His answer was a smile, and he kissed her again.

"For the love of you," he said, nuzzling her throat, "I am willing to risk death itself."

"Death itself," she echoed, and her lips found his.

They had no way to know that even as they began hatching a plot to take his life, the pharaoh was barreling through a nearby plaza, driving his chariot so hard that the phalanx of royal guards could barely keep pace with him.

They would do it—the murder—here in this chamber, tomorrow night; Imhotep would himself do the deed, with a Hittite dagger, which would remain in the pharaoh's breast, placing blame on a known enemy.

But the plan for the terrible act they contemplated was not complete when the heavy gilt doors Imhotep's priests guarded burst open with the force of an explosion.

Unaccompanied by his usual contingent of royal guards, the Med-jai, whom he had outrun in his zeal to discover the identity of his lover's lover, Seti charged into the anteroom, as Imhotep's priests—startled and dismayed by the pharaoh's presence—backed away.

Face made longer by his high, caplike serpent-embossed gold crown, Seti—his square goatee like a black stain on his chin—scowled at the cowering priests, growling, "Why are you here?" Then without waiting for a response, he strode past them, sandaled feet sending echoes off the marble floor like deep drumbeats.

And the priests watched in helpless horror as the formidable figure in leather-and-gold breastplate, muscular arms and legs bare, jewels glittering at his wrists and at the hilt of his sword, went swiftly to the curtain that separated anteroom from bedchamber, his sheer cloak trailing after him like a ghost.

Anck-su-namun, apparently alone in the chamber, stood at the foot of her bed, arms behind her, head lowered submissively, but gazing up at her longtime lover with the sensuous smile that had won her this house and so many riches.

"What a wonderful surprise, my lord, my love," she purred.

Seti sneered. "So the rumors were true."

"My lord?"

"Who has touched you?" he asked. Then he demanded: *"What man has dared touch you?"*

Stepping from the shadows of the balcony behind the pharaoh, Imhotep answered Seti's question by reaching around and withdrawing the pharaoh's heavy sword from its scabbard.

Spinning, sheer cloak trying to catch up with him, Seti faced his own raised weapon in unexpected hands; the ruler's dark eyes widened in shock. "Imhotep? My priest . . ." And then the eyes narrowed in contempt. "My friend . . ."

Those words froze Imhotep, momentarily, and he did not bring down the blade.

But in back of the pharaoh, her eyes and nostrils flaring like those of rearing horse, Anck-su-namun raised a gleaming dagger, and her small hand with the big knife came swiftly down.

8

them. The pharaoh's royal guards had their attention fixed upon their fallen leader and the beautiful, sword-wielding woman who stood over the bloody slashed remains.

"My body is no longer his temple!" she snarled at them.

And as Imhotep screamed silently into the palm of his protector, Anck-su-namun turned the sword on herself, both hands on its hilt, and plunged the blade into her heart.

Now—forty days and nights later, the mummification process of Anck-su-namun's remains complete—Imhotep stood under the starry sky in the flickering orange light of torches, in the company of Nubian slaves and Pharaoh's soldiers and his own priests of Osiris, under the wary gaze of the Medjai high on surrounding dunes, and read from *The Book of Amun Ra*, intoning the sacred incantation of damnation over the linen-wrapped body of his beloved. . . .

And the massive metal book held open in Imhotep's hands began to emanate a golden glow, as if the sun were rising from its pages; like golden lightning it flashed, sending the muscular black slaves to their knees like whimpering children.

Washed in the golden glow, as if the book in his hands were aflame, Imhotep, his voice a rumbling emotionless baritone, continued the fearsome incantation.

And now the golden lightning was accompanied by an impossible wind which whipped at the clothing of those gathered around the mummified mistress, and soldiers who had fought in ferocious battles now cringed like frightened children, hiding behind their shields as their skirts fluttered in a wind that caused not a grain of sand to shift.

Imhotep, unaffected by the lightning and the wind, read on, uttering the ghastly malediction as his faithful priests—holding their white cats in front of them ceremonially—remained as calm and unaffected by the lightning flashes of gold and the lashing wind as their high priest himself seemingly was.

As Imhotep neared the final words of the incantation, the linen-wrapped mummy began to tremble, as if coming back to life. As gold lightning intermittently flashed, a whirlpool of wind seemed to find the woman's body and, at first slowly, then with dramatic quickness, raised her into the air. The eyes of the terrified slaves, the frightened soldiers, the calm priests, followed her ascent, watching mesmerized as the mummified woman floated there, eerily, Imhotep's deep voice rumbling through the concluding passage.

Then, in one last all-pervasive golden flash, and a blast of wind that should have (but did not) created a sandstorm, the mummy fell back to earth, where Anck-su-namun's remains suddenly revealed themselves as no longer shapely, but shriveled, twisted, and grotesque, as if even the final few vestiges of beauty had been siphoned from her.

Silence draped the desert like a suffocating cloak. No wind. No one spoke as the priests of Osiris gathered up the gnarled mummy and deposited it in the wooden coffin; the canopic jars were placed within the box as well before the lid was shut. The Nubians carted the coffin to the grave and dropped it in, then began shoveling sand in on top of it with their hands. On the surrounding dunes, many of the Med-jai turned and drifted away into the night, satisfied, apparently, that their late master had been avenged. Anck-su-namun would soon be in the underworld, her soul devoured.

When the sand had been smoothed over, the grave disappearing into the desert floor, the Nubian slaves looked toward Imhotep for their next order. But the next order Imhotep issued was not for the slaves. . . .

The high priest nodded to the soldiers, who raised their spears and hurled them at the Nubians, whose cries of pain and surprise broke the unearthly silence. Within seconds the area was littered with the dead, sand stained dark with blood.

The soldiers, now unarmed, looked toward Imhotep for permission to retrieve their spears. Instead, Imhotep nodded again, and the priests of Osiris—their cats deposited on the ground, where they looked on with bland indifference—descended upon the soldiers with daggers, hacking at the startled men in a darkness relieved only by the flickering of torchlight and, shortly, the blood of dead men was again seeping into the sand.

A few Med-jai remained, watching from the dunes; they knew they were in no danger, for they—like the priests of Osiris—were holy men. Only common people—slaves, soldiers—had to be killed; no unholy person could ever know the exact location of the burial site.

And the handful of Med-jai who had stayed to watch the inevitable slaughter now slipped away into the night as well. The priests of Osiris rose from the corpses they'd created, their holy knives dripping rubies, and—at Imhotep's nod—climbed the dunes to watch the Med-jai depart.

When his priests reported back to him that the final Med-jai had vanished over a distant dune, Imhotep nodded one last time.

Then he and his priests raced to the grave of Anck-su-namun and began digging at the sand with their hands, urgently, furiously, as if the most valuable buried treasure in the world awaited them.

Which, in Imhotep's eyes, it did.

·❦ 2 ❧·

City of the Dead

The starry sky conspired with the scimitar-slice moon to turn the desert a blue-tinged ivory, its dunes undulating sinuously, sensuously, like reclining concubines beckoning their lovers; no more peaceful landscape could be imagined, no silence more still, more complete . . . only to dissolve under the sand-stirring hooves of the whinnying horses bearing chariots whose mighty wheels carved grooves in the desert floor.

Whip cracks split the night, horses straining forward, men straining forward, as the priests of Osiris followed their highest, most holy master on the lowest, most unholy of missions.

Imhotep led the charge, racing against time, against discovery, against the gods themselves. He was the general of a small army of black chariots steered by bald muscular men with desert-withered flesh who served their smooth-skinned master unquestioningly, willing to follow him even into hell. Which, on this lovely desert night, they were.

The chariot just behind Imhotep served as the hearse of the twisted, shriveled mummy that had been Anck-su-namun. The curse Imhotep had leveled upon his beloved must be cast out, must be reversed, and in this land there was only one way, one place, one book that could dispense such a forbidden mercy.

Just as *The Book of Amun Ra* had sucked the soul from Imhotep's lover, so could that other book, that volume of which even to speak was blasphemy, restore Anck-su-namun's spiritual essence. Moreover, this book, which in the rites of his religion must never be opened, this blackest of books . . .

. . . *The Book of the Dead* . . .

. . . this book alone held the incantations that could bring his beloved back to life, and in her perfect earthly state.

To do such an unholy thing was to defy the gods; as high priest of Osiris—god of the underworld—Imhotep understood this as few living men could. And yet had not Osiris himself risen from the dead, due to the love of Isis, his own beloved? As the loyal high priest of Osiris, should Imhotep be denied any less for the woman he loved? No matter—for the return of Anck-su-namun, Imhotep would willingly risk not just his life, but his soul.

So that no sacrilege might ever disgrace their kingdom, *The Book of the Dead* lay in the care of the god Anubis, at Hamanaptra, that unspeakable place known in whispers as the City of the Dead. Not a city in the sense of the City of the Living, Thebes, Hamanaptra was the temple of the god Anubis, and like many temples in the kingdom, it was not a single structure, rather a walled complex of buildings and courtyards with the honored statue of Anubis—who "lived" in the temple—in its midst.

No one lived at Hamanaptra but the warrior priests of Anubis, and the real "City of the Dead" lay below ground, carved into the rock under the dunes—rock-cut tombs having replaced those impractical pyramidal monstrosities of the early pharaohs—an underground maze of tunnels, staircases, corridors, mausoleums, and elegant underground rooms, booby-trapped with false doors and blocked passages to bedevil grave robbers.

The small army of chariots raced up the sloping sand and rumbled onto the stone ramp rising to the massive wooden gates of the temple complex, where a company of warrior priests, their shields bearing the skull-like design of Hamanaptra, stood guard. But these fierce soldiers of Anubis did not question the entry of such holy men, particularly with Imhotep himself at their head. This place was guarded from thieves and heretics, not the high priest of Osiris.

Soon Imhotep—on the pretext of paying a visit to the god who lived in this place—was alone in the grandly pillared chamber of the central open temple that looked out on the sandy courtyard of the complex. Kneeling at the feet of the enormous jackal-headed statue of Anubis, the high priest of Osiris might have been praying before the great god; but in fact Imhotep was finding the small trip lever that would open the hidden compartment at the base of the statue.

The small heavy stone door swung open with an accusing creak and Imhotep removed an ornately carved and painted chest. He opened it, lifting out a big heavy brass-hinged book which in size and shape and, to some degree, form and ornamentation mirrored that of *The Book of Amun Ra*; however, this intimidating volume was not fashioned of gold, but carved from pure obsidian.

Imhotep stared upon the black face of *The Book of the Dead*, and in the smooth stone surface, his own face looked back at him. For a frozen moment, his tortured expression questioned what it was he was about to do.

Then he returned the chest, now empty, to the base of the jackal-headed statue, closed the compartment, and went swiftly—massive stone volume held in one hand, slipped under his flowing black robe, hidden away from the eyes of any stray warrior priest—to gather his followers for the ceremony.

Into the catacombs that were the underground necropolis of the City of the Dead, the high priest—now bearing *The Book of the Dead* before him like an offering—led his black-robed followers, again with torches in hand. The procession—which included two priests solemnly conveying the mummy of Anck-su-namun—descended a stairway carved from the rock into a cavernous chamber; black hairy rats the size of small dogs scurried as sandaled footsteps echoed through the ampitheaterlike area, its cavelike walls painted orange with torchlight. At the periphery burbled moats of black muck that might have been tar, but was instead the decayed residue of human remains mingling with what had once been water, a soup of despair in which skulls bobbed like onions.

In the center of the open area was a strange, twisted altar of heavy dark stone adorned with golden decorative touches—winged scarabs, cobra heads, rams' horns—and onto its smooth surface the priests carefully placed Imhotep's mummified beloved.

Then Imhotep's followers gathered in a circle around the mummy on the altar, and began to chant, eyes hooded, faces lifeless, bald heads rocking, bodies swaying. The eerie hum of their chanting filled the chamber as, one by one, Imhotep received from five of his priests the five precious canopic jars, placing them around the altar, around his loved one, in the precise position the incantation required. Had more time passed than a mere forty days, the concubine's vital organs would not have remained fresh enough for this unholy procedure, and a human sacrifice would have been needed to replace the contents of the canopic jars.

Imhotep opened the immense pages of the obsidian book and began to read. The withered, gnarled mummy shuddered, and then shimmied and shimmered and blurred, as it magically resumed the shapely form of Anck-su-namun. The high priest's eyes were wide and his teeth were bare in something like a smile as he began to unwrap the linen bandages, pleased to find young, vibrant flesh beneath, the naked form of the woman he loved, her physical state restored.

The first stage of his sorcery, this reversal of the spells he'd previously cast, was successful. What must come next would make every other incantation he had made on this horrendous night seem like the rhyming of a child at play.

Imhotep began to read from *The Book of the Dead*, as the monotonous chanters circled around him and the beautiful dead woman on the altar, droning on. The foul black pools at the edges of the chamber began to roil, like a pot brought to a boil; bubbles popped, globules spattered, and the concentration of the priests, a few of them at least, was broken by the bizarre simmering around them. The priests, pale from fright, closed their eyes and resumed chanting, even as the bog at their periphery began to brew and gurgle and seethe, boiling bubbles bursting, snapping, until the pools began to overflow their rocky banks.

Like a living thing, a black slime slid over the cavern floor; from every dark corner it came, crawling, slithering, inexorably seeping, a thin layer of ooze that closed in on the chanters, finding its way to, and around, their sandaled feet, rising just high enough to touch their flesh, hot but not burning, a shallow fetid nasty coating that soon was all around them, even creeping to the squat sculpted ox-head statues that were the legs holding up the altar.

Imhotep, lost in the incantation, his deep voice rumbling through the cavern, seemed not to notice the black ooze gleaming at his feet. One of his priests, the youngest of them, looked down into the shining black liquid mirror that touched his toes and the reflection that looked back was that of his own mummified corpse.

The priest's scream of unearthly terror, shrill at first, then an echoing wail in the cavernous chamber, followed him as he broke from the circle and ran, splashing through the thin layer of hot black liquid, running for the stairs but losing his balance and sliding, shrieking, skidding, stumbling into the steaming mire, which swallowed him, filling his screaming mouth with slime, pulling him down into its festering stew.

This barely registered to Imhotep, who continued his incantation, though he did watch as the black slippery slime seeped around the canopic jars, slithering up them, coating them, covering them, finally invading them. . . .

The black-coated jars shuddered. Shook. A steady drumlike throb began to emanate from one of them.

Anck-su-namun's heart, beating again!

Imhotep spoke the forbidden words, the whites of his eyes exposed all around, teeth bared like a grinning animal, watching aghast, yet elated, as the black fingers of ooze crawled up the legs of the altar, trickling up over the decorative icons, painting the scarabs and cobras and rams' heads a glistening obsidian, like *The Book of the Dead* itself, until it had risen to glide up and over the naked body of the beautiful dead concubine, covering her, encasing her in slippery shining black liquid, heightening and highlighting the exquisite dunes and valleys of her body, making a gleaming black statue of her. . . .

And then, miraculously, hideously, the liquid, moving like quicksilver with an intelligence, scurried about her body seeking entrance, the ooze finding its way inside her, and it was as if the corpse was drawing the liquid into itself, sucking the slime inside her, through the nostrils, ears, open mouth, every orifice, sucking every drop inside of her until the cavern floor was clear, clean, as if the bizarre black flood had never occurred.

The beautiful naked body, stretched out upon the altar, into which—impossibly—so much foul liquid had entered, lay still, as well might be expected, of a dead woman. Then the corpse trembled.

Imhotep's eyes widened further.

The body shuddered, and jerked, in a spasm that could only mean the regenerative incantation was working its dark magic.

"Come back to me, Anck-su-namun," Imhotep said, and this was not part of the incantation. "Come back to me. . . ."

With a suddenness that made even Imhotep gasp, and his priests choke on their chanting, the eyes of Anck-su-namun snapped open!

Wide.

Alive.

Imhotep touched her cheek; the eyes met his, but she did not speak. She could not speak. Her soul had come back from the dead, but for her full return, her physical return, her organs must be transferred from the canopic jars to their rightful place within her body. And this required one last terrible step.

"There will be no pain," he told her tenderly.

Though her face held no expression, her eyes spoke to him: *Do what you must, my love, do what you must....*

Imhotep shifted the massive *Book of the Dead* into his one hand, holding the heavy volume open there, a feat his priests could only marvel at. Then, steeling himself for what he must do, the high priest of Osiris withdrew from under his black robe a sacrificial knife, its long blade wide at the hilt and narrowing to a point so honed that to test it with a touch was to bleed.

And now Imhotep, face clenched with an intense display of emotion his followers had never suspected him to possess, raised high the gleaming blade, fist white around the knife's hilt, its serpent's tooth hovering high above the perfectly restored body of his beautiful beloved, her eyes alive and granting him absolution for the vicious penetration he must perpetrate upon her tender flesh.

Anck-su-namun would, upon replacement of her vital parts, be again pristinely restored to her natural, magnificent physical state; there would be no scar, no sign of the invasion of Imhotep's blade, nor for that matter of the blade with which she had ended her life, forty days before. The foul boiling liquid within her would work its strange sorcery, its mystic healing powers....

Around them the droning chant of the priests continued; the beating of her heart in its canopic jar grew louder, as if the organ were anticipating its own return to the home in her lovely breast, providing a drumbeat to their tuneless song. Imhotep's eyes fell on the obsidian pages of the open volume in his left hand; knife poised to plunge into his beloved's breast, he began to read the final incantation, almost shouting to be heard about the rising volume of the chanting and the anxious, beating heart....

Down the stairway, flooding all around the chamber, they came, rushing, two and three and four steps at a time, bolting down, barreling down, storming the ampitheater, screaming as they made their charge, a tattooed horde: *the Med-jai!*

Like locusts they descended, and before his hand could come down, Imhotep had been seized, arms clutching him, banding around him, wrist squeezed in a grip, the knife blade frozen in air; his scream echoed through the cavern, and intensified as he saw the leader of the Med-jai raise a foot and bring it down hard, as if stepping on a huge bug: smashing, shattering, crushing the jar with the beating heart.

Silencing it.

As the tissue of the vital organ oozed like rotten fruit beneath the sandal of the Med-jai leader, something occurred that was so fantastic, and took place so quickly, that those who were to be alive, after this night, would never be sure it had really happened, would never be positive that their eyes in that dark, dank chamber hadn't played tricks on them.

From every orifice of her body, Anck-su-namun expelled the black slimy fluid; it flew from her, and scattered in the air around those gathered about her, touching none of them, as if the flying black lake that had somehow been within her, and now somehow found its way outside of her, was a beast that could maneuver around them and avoid them. The black fluid found its way to the outskirts and corners of the chamber and rejoined the black boiling brew of human detritus from whence it came.

Anguished, Imhotep, straining as the Med-jai held him captive, looked down upon the face of his beloved, sought her eyes; her eyes sought his . . .

. . . and closed.

And again, the high priest of Osiris screamed, a scream of agony that shook the stony chamber: *He had lost her again!* He had lost her again. . . .

All that remained now was for the Med-jai to take their retribution.

"You have condemned yourself, Imhotep," the Med-jai leader said, the eyes a peculiar mixture of melancholy and ferocity. "But you have also condemned your faithful priests. Before you receive your punishment, you must witness theirs, to carry that guilt with you into the judgment of the underworld."

So it was that in another chamber of the City of the Dead, in flickering torchlight, restrained by embalmers masked, like Anubis, in jackal heads, Imhotep was made to watch as his loyal followers were embalmed and mummified alive.

The embalmers were as calm as if the men they were using their knives and needles and thread upon were corpses, not screaming, squirming, living men. The final step in the process was to wedge the head of each priest—screams sealed inside sewn-shut mouths—within two strongboards so that a red hot sharp poker could be shoved up the nose, to cut their brains into small pieces before removal through their nostrils.

Insanity preceded death in every case.

Imhotep tried to look away, but his jackal-headed captors would turn his face toward the torture, and hold open his eyelids when necessary. This went on for hours, until all twenty-one of his loyal priests were before him on the chamber floor, squirming within their wrappings, wriggling like caterpillars trying to escape from their cocoons; their brains extracted, this was presumably reflex action—or were they still, somehow, experiencing pain? Yet as unimaginable as the pain his priests had suffered might have been, Imhotep could not fathom any pain worse than the emotional suffering that wracked his body, his spirit, as he was made to view this dreadful sight.

That was when the embalmers pried open his mouth and cut out his tongue, changing his opinion.

It was possible, though difficult, Imhotep discovered, to scream without a tongue, and the pain blinded him, sparing him the sight of the rats scurrying from their crannies to gather up his discarded tongue, scuffle over it and then eat their fair share of it.

When he could scream no more, held forward by his captors so that he would not drown in his own blood, Imhotep heard the voice of the Med-jai leader, informing him, "You are to enjoy a rare honor, Imhotep. You will be the first upon whom the curse of *hom-dai* has ever been bestowed."

That worst, most horrible of curses, an ancient curse no one who had walked the earth had yet sinned severely enough to earn. A rare honor, indeed.

Like his priests, Imhotep was wrapped alive, holes cut for his eyes, nostrils and mouth. His bandages were slimy with muck from a boiling cauldron whose contents had been scooped from one of the ponds of human black detritus. As he squirmed within his bindings on the cavern floor, Imhotep's bandages were patted down with the fetid slime by the embalmers, who made sure his bandages were drenched with the foul liquid.

Then the jackal-headed embalmers lifted him like the object he'd become and dropped him into a simple wooden coffin; that coffin was then placed within a granite sarcophagus. Numb from pain, barely conscious, Imhotep stared up at the high rocky ceiling and waited for the lid to be placed over him; the darkness, and the death it would bring, would be almost a relief.

But there were more pleasures awaiting him first.

A jackal mask looked down on him. A large jar was in the embalmer's hands; one last indignity to be rained down upon him—more muck, maybe?

The jackal-headed embalmer began to pour the contents of the jar down upon the living mummy, and it was not muck.

Beetles.

Living, wriggling scarabs, rancid dung beetles that scampered upon him, like a living vest, scurrying across his chest and up across his throat and onto his face to cover it like a black writhing mask, many of them vanishing into his tongueless mouth and up his nostrils.

Imhotep would have laughed if there hadn't been beetles crawling in his throat: He was eating them, and they were eating him; by so doing, Imhotep would be cursed to live forever . . . and the bugs were cursed the same. They would go together, through eternity, companions forever.

And now the coffin lid was slammed shut. Imhotep, in the darkness, invaded by beetles, of course did not see the Med-jai leader step from the darkness to lock the coffin lid tight, with eight gold keys connected as one. The embalmers lifted the heavy sarcophagus lid and set it into place, sealing it airtight with a *whoosh*; the Med-jai leader again used the strange eight-sided key, locking the sarcophagus lid.

"Here you will remain," the Med-jai leader said softly, (*and yet Imhotep, within the sealed coffin heard these words, echoing within his small world*). "Sealed within, undead for all of eternity."

The deed complete, the Med-jai leader folded the many-sided key into a small, octagonal, golden puzzle box.

As his followers gathered about him, the Med-jai leader said quietly, "We must take all precautions that He Who Shall Not Be Named never be released from his imprisonment, for he would be a walking disease, a plague upon mankind, an unholy eater of flesh with the strength of ages, power over even the sands themselves, with the glory of invincibility."

Around him, the Med-jai priests nodded gravely; they knew—*even as Imhotep himself, trapped with his beetle friends within the slime-sealed sarcophagus knew*—that such was the price of that most horrible of curses, the *hom-dai*. That was why, never before, no matter how severe the infamy, had any villain ever been so punished.

Using many ropes, into a pit where the black slime boiled and roiled, the embalmers lowered the heavy sarcophagus, the muck splashing up over it, then streaming down its sides like melting candle wax, only to be sucked into the seams of the granite casement, until—as when the black liquid had vanished into Anck-su-namun's mummy—the sarcophagus had drunk the pit dry of the viscous fluid, its sides clean, *all of it* clean and dry, not a bead of dampness remaining.

The embalmers, pulling upon the many ropes, withdrew the sarcophagus from the now parched pit and, at the Med-jai leader's bidding, carted the granite casement to its chosen burial site.

Within his cold hell, the skittering beetles upon him and within him, Imhotep knew the ramifications of the portentous curse his burial carried with it, the *hom-dai*. If he were to raise himself, and his beloved Anck-su-namun, from their respective places in the underworld, they would together be unconquerable; they would unleash upon the world an infection so vile, so indomitable, that a cataclysmic ending would come to all living things . . . all but Imhotep and Anck-su-namun.

Perhaps, like his priests before him, Imhotep had been driven insane by the torture of living mummification.

And yet the muffled, tongueless screams that emerged from the living mummy in the coffin within the granite sarcophagus, onto which sand and dirt were rudely being shoveled, seemed to threaten revenge and were tinged with a chilling promise of inevitable triumph.

They buried him in the temple courtyard, near the base of the looming statue of Anubis (*The Book of the Dead* returned to its hiding place), where the jackal-headed death god could look sternly down on He Who Shall Not Be Named. For many hundreds of years Anubis, and armed generations of Med-jai, watched the grave of Imhotep, until the sands of time and the Sahara had all but hidden the ruins of Hamanaptra, the decayed head of Anubis barely visible above the shifting desert's dry tides.

And yet, as civilizations lived and died, came and went, sealed within his coffin, with his scarab companions . . .

. . . *Imhotep lived!*

·❆ PART TWO ❆·

The Mummy's Return

The Sahara—1925

·⟨ 3 ⟩·

Legion of Lost Men

Uncovered by the unintentional excavation efforts of a recent sandstorm, the ruins of the temple complex at Hamanaptra poked from the sand like the sun-bleached bones
of some unfortunate desert wanderer who had died of thirst.
Once grand, now partly crumbled pylons proudly bore the
hieroglyphic record of gods and kings; a scattering of wind-
worn stone columns and partial walls remained upright,
while others had been toppled by time. Stone statues with
the heads of lions or rams, exquisitely carved, carelessly
chipped, stood tall here, rested there, and within his open
shrine, the massive jackal-headed Anubis, swimming in
sand, seemed lonely for supplicants. The ruins were themselves the skeleton of a once mighty people, whose deeply
held religious beliefs in modern times might seem strange
and even barbaric.

And yet in a day when a telephone wire stretched from
Cairo to the pyramids, and European tourists could play
lawn tennis in the court of a hotel built near the base of old
Cheops himself, the strange and the barbaric remained a
potent presence upon these timeless sands. Just as the
screams of the tortured Imhotep had echoed across Haman-

aptra in that bloodstained golden age, so now did the shrill battle cries of Tuareg warriors.

Scampering about the ruins of Hamanaptra like children playing in the sand, a "flying column" of legionnaires sought position, a *Battalion de Marche* of the French Foreign Legion, two hundred men strong. Or they would have been "strong," had they not been outnumbered ten to one by the fierce tribesmen, who—using time-honored tribal tactics—had at a safe distance followed the legionnaires, on the march, until they were too far from a fort or a supply dump to receive help.

As wily as they were ruthless, the Tuaregs had waited until the legion's highly trained soldiers grew careless and tired from too many days under the hot Sahara sun; then the warriors emerged from behind a sand dune like a nightmarish mirage, swords and rifles waving, their long, loose robes flapping like flags as they advanced at full gallop.

The legionnaires were clumsy in their infantry-style uniforms, burdened with backpacks of spare clothing, ammo, and rations; in this climate, only the black-leather marching boots made sense. The sun-shielding swatch that hung from each man's kepi—round cloth caps with short leather bills— were waving like white flags of surrender from the head of each scurrying soldier.

It was times like this that made a man like Richard O'Connell, formerly of Chicago, Illinois, question his career choice.

His collegiate handsomeness made rugged by intense sky-blue eyes, a leathery tan, and an unruly mop of brown hair, O'Connell—"Rick" to his friends, "Corporal" to his men—wore his kepi at a jaunty angle. Alone among the two hundred soldiers—largely riffraff from every corner of the Western world—O'Connell, in his tan coat, shoulder-holstered revolvers crisscrossing his trimly muscular frame, cut a dashing figure worthy of a recruiting poster. *Engagez-vous a la Legion Étrangère!*

Right now, however, desertion might seem more in order, if self-preservation hadn't edged it out.

The muffled thunder of hoofbeats on sand merged with

the chilling war whoops of the advancing Tuareg horde as O'Connell stood atop what had once been the protective outer wall of the Hamanaptra temple complex. He had been using binoculars, but he tossed them aside.

No need for them now.

"I've had better days," he said to no one, hefting his rifle—a sad example of the outdated Lebel bayonets he and his men were encumbered with.

Perhaps this would be a fitting end, not so much ironic as just. Greed had brought them here—not honor. Their colonel had found a map showing the way to the fabled Hamanaptra, and the promise of ancient riches had seized the imaginations of a garrison composed, after all, of thieves, murderers, mercenaries, and adventurers.

And now, with the dreaded Tuaregs upon them, this legendary entryway to untold treasures would serve only as a makeshift fort.

"A tactical suggestion, Corporal," a thin, weasely voice intoned beside him.

O'Connell glanced at the voice's thin, weasely source: Private Second Class Beni Gabor, formerly of Budapest, proof positive that not all of the legion's rabble came from Italy, England, Norway, Russia, or Spain. Narrow of shoulder, sunken of chest, with dark, close-set eyes and a pencil-line mustache in his pasty, almond-shaped face, the resourceful little scoundrel was the closest thing to a friend O'Connell had in the legion—perhaps because there was such a limited supply of worthwhile friends from which to choose.

"About the only tactic available," O'Connell said, eyeing the Arab warrior-flung horizon, "is hold your fire until they're within range."

"That's one option," Beni said, nodding, "yes it is. But personally, I would prefer to surrender."

"Give me your bandoleer."

Beni, climbing out of his cartridge belt, handed it to the corporal, saying, "Or why not just run away? There's another option. I'll bet these ruins are teeming with hiding

31

places, and what do we owe the legion? Loyalty for cold biscuits and brutality?''

"These ruins are going to be teeming, all right." O'Connell had slung on the bandoleer, which joined his own to make an ''X'' on his chest.

Working his voice above the swelling shouts of Tuaregs promising slaughter, and the pounding of their ponies' hoofbeats, O'Connell said to Beni, ''I'll take your revolver, too, since it doesn't sound like you're going to need it.''

"Here," Beni said, handing the weapon to the corporal, then following him close as a dog's tail as O'Connell moved quickly along the wall. ''You know what nobody tries anymore, Rick? And I bet it would work on these dumb savages: playing dead!''

Still moving, O'Connell sighed and broke open the revolver to check its ammunition. ''These 'dumb savages' maneuvered us into this position. But go ahead, Beni, try it—of course you'll be tortured and probably staked out in the desert to die of sunstroke.''

"It was just a suggestion.''

"How the hell d'you end up in the legion, anyway?''

Such a question was a breach of etiquette: Many legionnaires had embraced that famous motto—''*Legio Patria Nostra (The Legion is our homeland)*''—because they were wanted by the police of their former homelands. But at this moment, with the whooping Tuaregs bearing down upon them, this lapse seemed permissible.

Beni shrugged. ''They're after me in Hungary for robbing a synagogue—that's my specialty, synagogues: Hebrew's one of my seven languages.''

"Robbing churches.'' O'Connell, sticking Beni's revolver in his belt, shook his head. ''That's even lower than I'd expected.''

"Prime swag to be found in holy places," Beni said in the singsong manner of a grade school teacher. ''Temples, mosques, cathedrals—and who've they got standing guard?''

"Altar boys?''

"Exactly! How about you, Rick?'' Beni continued tag-

32

ging along as the corporal strode the wall to where he could examine their front line of defense, legionnaires kneeling at the ready, watching the approaching horde; Colonel Guizot pacing behind them, apparently contemplating his battle plan. "What did you do, anyway, to wind up in the legion of lost men, Rick?"

O'Connell turned to answer, but Beni was trailing along so close, they bumped into each other; the little Hungarian lost his balance, clutched at O'Connell in an attempt to regain it, and failed. Locked in Beni's reflexive embrace, they toppled from the wall and hit the ground in a pile and a puff of sand.

"So," Beni continued, picking himself up, offering no apology, "what'd you do, Rick? Murder somebody?"

"Not yet," O'Connell said, narrow eyed, on his feet, brushing himself off, checking his Lebel.

"What, then? Robbery? Extortion? I know! I hear it's the latest thing in America—kidnapping!"

"Shut up already," O'Connell said. He strode down a sand dune within the walls of the ruins and walked out between the front pylons onto the stone ramp where, in another time, the chariots of the high priest of Osiris had rolled up to make a fateful call.

Beni frowned. "Listen, I told you my damn story! You tell me your damn story!"

The warrior horde was half a mile out, now; the roar of charging horses and screaming men would soon be deafening. O'Connell reflected, as if time were no factor, his voice soft, musical. "It was Paris, it was spring, and I was looking for a way to impress a young lady . . . and maybe I was looking for a little adventure."

He left out the part about being drunk.

"I think you found it," Beni said, nodding toward the front line, where Colonel Guizot had panicked.

With an eerie detachment, O'Connell and Beni watched their commanding officer cut and run.

"Congratulations," Beni said with a smile. "You're promoted."

There was no horizon, now: just a blur of Tuareg warriors, shrieking, waving their long, curved swords, brandishing Lebel rifles pilfered from the bodies of slain legionnaires.

This must have been how Custer felt.

"Damn it," O'Connell said softly, to no one but himself. Then, with as commanding a tone as he could muster, he yelled, "Steady, men! Wait till you see the whites of their eyes!"

"I can't believe you said that," Beni said, standing behind the corporal.

Hooves pounded the sand; screams pierced the air. The Tuaregs knew about getting into firing range, too: They were raising their rifles, taking aim. . . .

"You *are* with me, right, pal?" O'Connell said, with a glance at his friend, still standing directly behind him.

"Your strength gives me strength," Beni said, clutching his Lebel with both hands.

The Tuareg war cry now shifted into a birdlike whoop: *"Ooo-loo-loo-loo, ooo-loo-loo-loo!"*

"That's all, brother," Beni said, backing away, and ran away so fast, his boots barely touched the sand.

O'Connell allowed himself a wry smirk, drew a deep breath, said a quick prayer, and yelled, "Steady, men! . . . *Steady*. . . ."

Steeling himself, rifle in his hands, but not poised to shoot, O'Connell waited, ears filled with the ghastly cries, the pounding hoofbeats, waited one more moment, then yelled, *"Fire!"*

And the kneeling legionnaires fired as if one, the sound of so many rifles reporting simultaneously like an explosion, a blast of firepower that blew dozens of Tuaregs off their mounts, dead before they hit the sand, their corpses becoming instant barricades over which other horses trampled and stumbled, beasts and riders going down.

O'Connell, kneeling himself now, holding fire, thought, *Good volley!*, as the legionnaires quickly reloaded, here and there a man falling as a Tuareg bullet caught him.

And O'Connell repeated his command: "Fire!"

This time O'Connell joined the volley, the sound of

which was more staggered, but again bullets yanked warriors from their steeds, and men and horses tumbled to the sand, creating chaos.

Another successful volley! O'Connell thought, but he knew, he knew. . . .

The legionnaires remained two hundred men, and two hundred men—no matter how brave, however well-trained— facing *two thousand*, were still two hundred men. . . .

And the Tuaregs began firing. The noise of their weapons was not the unified thunder of the legionnaires' two volleys, rather a rumbling, snapping, cracking, continuous hail of lead that ripped the air of the day, and the flesh of the Tuaregs' foes; the native warriors, robes flowing, were terrible apparitions moving like the horsemen of the Apocalypse through the clouds of smoke that their own gunfire had fashioned.

At least a third of O'Connell's men fell under this onslaught, choking on dust and blood, twisting in pain and death.

"Fire at will!" O'Connell shouted, retreating toward the pylons of the temple complex entry. *"Seek cover!"*

Shooting on the run, the legionnaires headed toward the temple, boots slowed by the sand, but their bullets finding more purchase, sending Tuaregs spinning off steeds, crashing to the sand, small victories, tiny triumphs, in a great defeat. The warriors were on them now, plowing into the legionnaires, wading into them, and the gunfire lessened as the nomads hacked and cleaved with their sharp, curved blades, and the screams that tore the air now were not war cries, but cries of agony, of death, as the blood of white infidels splashed and soaked the sands, as men who had lost their way in homelands they would never see again lost their lives in this strange place.

Within the walls of the temple complex now, where legionnaires were taking cover in the ruins, the Tuaregs on horseback were everywhere, charging through the front gates, leaping partial walls, storming through areas where the walls of Hamanaptra were just a memory. Their blades carved at the air when there was no flesh to cleave, and occasionally a warrior would fall under a legionnaire's bullet . . .

. . . but O'Connell, still outside the walls of Hamanaptra, throwing down his empty rifle, yanking both revolvers from their shoulder holsters, knew they'd been overrun, knew this was the Alamo, and that he would never see his family again, much less his country. He was just too goddamned busy shooting Arabs off their goddamned horses to worry about it.

He'd been too busy to find cover, as well, and as he tossed away both revolvers, empty, and yanked one from behind his back and Beni's from his belt, he got a glimpse of Beni, within the temple grounds, crawling on his belly across the sand, like the snake he was, apparently heading for the open doorway of a structure half-buried in the sand.

O'Connell, whose attention was immediately back on a pair of Tuaregs bearing down on him, did not see Beni taking time to lift a watch off the body of a dead legionnaire. Nor did he see Beni getting up and sprinting for that beckoning doorway.

But when another dozen warriors had fallen under his fire, and he was once again out of ammunition, the only legionnaires around him dead ones, O'Connell whirled, tearing ass through the front gate, looking for Beni, who was inside that temple structure now, putting all his wiry muscle behind an attempt to close its massive sandstone door.

O'Connell grinned: Beni had found his hiding place after all, and O'Connell was ready, now, to accept one of his tactical suggestions. . . .

"Beni!" O'Connell called. "Pal, wait up! Hey!"

Beni didn't appear to hear his friend, or if he did, seemed to have no intention of "waiting up."

O'Connell hurdled a huge stone column, hitting the ground running, his ears pounding with the hoofbeats of Tuareg horsemen in pursuit of him.

"Don't you close that goddamn door!" O'Connell yelled at Beni, who still seemed not to hear, though O'Connell knew damn well he did.

O'Connell, sprinting like hell for that door Beni was doing his best to close, glanced back and saw the four horsemen bounding over the huge column, charging right after him, yelling their *"Ooo-loo-loo-loo!"* war cry.

"You little bastard! Don't you close that goddamned door!"

But the door to safety closed, Beni's dark unapologetic eyes disappearing behind it, just as O'Connell slammed into its stone surface.

Little bastard closed the goddamned door!

Shoulder aching, O'Connell did a graceless pirouette, looking for another possibility, even as the horsemen closed in on him. Across the courtyard were the massive columns of an open shrine, and on the ground nearby were several fallen legionnaires whose bodies might provide a weapon or two.

He ran in perfect time to the cries of *"Ooo-loo-loo-loo!"* behind him, running for his life, weaving through the ruins, the Tuaregs getting closer and closer, the pounding hoof-beats louder and louder. In his path was the body of a dead legionnaire and he dipped down to snatch the revolver from the soldier's limp hand, and wheeled and faced the oncoming horsemen, firing the revolver. . . .

Empty.

The horsemen, yanking back on the reins, skidded to a stop right before him, stirring a cloud of sand, in which O'Connell—unarmed—stood and faced the fierce quartet, helplessly.

The Tuaregs raised their shining curved swords, and O'Connell, Chicago boy to the end, sneered at his executioners, raising his hand to his face, placing his thumb to the tip of his nose and waggling his fingers.

Suddenly the horse closest to O'Connell reared back and whinnied, eyes and nostrils flaring, and then the other horses joined in, rearing back, going bughouse, Arabian steeds transformed into Texas broncos!

The steeds screeched, they bucked, they bellowed, they snorted—and then they took off! Took off like somebody fired the starting gun, and their equally alarmed riders made no effort to rein them in; it was as if the devil himself had chased them away.

Wide-eyed, O'Connell looked at his hand as if perhaps it could explain why thumbing his nose had worked with such amazing success. . . .

Then he felt the world moving beneath him.

Later, he would wonder if he imagined it; still later, he would know he hadn't.

But right now, the sands, the earth, were shifting under him, not trembling like an earthquake, something else, something much stranger, something unmistakably evil . . .

. . . and as he glanced around him, he saw the looming ancient statue, just behind him in the remains of that shrine he'd been running toward. He knew enough about Egypt and its history to recognize a statue of Anubis when he saw it.

Was this what had stirred the horses? Or had the beasts, with their keen instincts, simply perceived the shifting sands before he had?

Decrepit, sections of it shattered, half-buried in sand, the jackal-headed statue stared at him with sinister indifference, almost as if Anubis were amused by O'Connell's startled reaction to the sands beneath him shifting and forming shapes, like snakes wriggling and writhing just below the surface.

And as those sands shifted, an artifact was revealed, a small octagonal gold box that he impulsively plucked up from the squirming desert floor and pocketed.

It was then that he realized something that frightened him more than anything this gruesome afternoon had yet leveled at him: *Not just meaningless shapes were forming in the sand, but lines, as if a ghostly finger were drawing a picture!*

He had had enough of this terrible place. If there were other riches here, beside the golden trinket he'd just tucked away, well let the desert have them.

The Tuaregs, all of them, had ridden off, leaving behind a massacre that would lead to more battles still. But Richard O'Connell would not be part of them. He ran from the ruins, knowing he would never return to the legion, knowing he'd be assumed dead, never dreaming he would return to this ungodly place.

He left without seeing the face that the sands had drawn upon themselves, a screaming face that he would not have recognized, anyway, though the group of riders on horseback high on a ridge, watching him stumble from the fragmented temple complex, would have . . .

. . . *Imhotep*.

But they did not; they saw only O'Connell, and that was enough.

These observers on the ridge were not Tuaregs though they were indeed Arab warriors, in the loose-fitting robes of their breed.

"He has found Hamanaptra," one of the riders said to Ardeth Bay, their leader. "He must die."

"Let the desert kill him," said Ardeth Bay, tall, sinewy, robed in black, golden scimitar at his waist, crossed by a gold dagger that was nearly a sword.

And the cruel dark eyes set like glittering stones in the face of Ardeth Bay—a face that might have seemed handsome were it not marked with strange tattoos—watched the legionnaire survivor stagger off into the open desert.

·❅ 4 ❅·

Another Worthless Trinket

Cairo, capital of the Mohammedan world, the majestic minarets of mosques rising above the squalor of crowded slums, was the African continent's largest city, and among its oldest. The stars themselves had changed position in the sky since the city's birth, though in all that time, one thing had not changed: the chasm that yawned between rich and poor, the only two classes into which its eight hundred thousand inhabitants fell.

In this sprawling, teeming city of donkeys and camels, this world of turbaned men and veiled women, the streets of the bazaars were too narrow for motor cars, and a pedestrian might be grazed by donkeys carrying grain or bricks or even a wealthy wife of some rich Egyptian who dwelled in a mansion behind high, solid stone walls, gates guarded by eunuchs, as the rest of the master's harem strolled a great tropical garden within.

The modern section of Cairo, with asphalt streets as wide as any in Paris and a beautifully landscaped park alive with flowers, shrubs and trees, offered electric streetcars and automobiles for hire, magnificent hotels, beautiful villas, modern apartment houses, and the Mouski, its main business street, was lined with fine European shops.

But Evelyn Carnahan, who—though schooled in her native England—had spent much of her childhood here, never deluded herself into thinking that Cairo was becoming a Christian city, that the Arab element was giving way to the European. She, perhaps more than any other white woman of her age in this city—or anywhere, for that matter—knew that she lived in an Egypt as ancient as civilization itself.

Her parents, who had died several years ago in a plane crash, had not been as wealthy as some supposed, and at any rate had left the bulk of their estate to the Cairo Museum of Antiquities, leaving her brother, Jonathan, and herself only the house and an allowance of a few hundred pounds a year each. This Jonathan greatly resented, though Evelyn did not: Her great love for this land and its history had been learned at the feet of her late archaeologist father.

Howard Carnahan, son of an English painter of birds and himself a gifted watercolorist, had joined Sir Gaston Maspero—before the turn of the century—in the Egyptian government's Department of Antiquities and made his reputation with his celebrated detailed drawings of important objects and murals found in the Valley of Kings. And, of course, his crowning achievement had been his role in the discovery of Tutankhamun's tomb in 1922.

The loss of her parents—the press had insisted upon connecting their accident to the Tutankhamun "curse"—was still keenly felt by her. In her small way, however, she hoped to follow in her father's legendary footsteps, though she had chosen archival work and had no real longing to go out on digs—she was a librarian, not an Egyptologist. She was, as might be expected, rather torn between her passion for history and a respect for those bygone people who had, with their lives, written it.

Her father had certainly suffered pangs of conscience over his work, feeling the success of the Tut dig had opened the door on wretched excesses tantamount to grave robbing. Just a year before his death, he had precipitated the firing of the curator here at the museum who had rather notori-

41

ously been selling mummies excavated in the valley of the Nile for one hundred dollars each (in cash), complete with certificates of authenticity as to age and nobility.

Evelyn felt rather in her father's shadow, and her position here at the museum—under the next curator—might have seemed obligatory, granted out of some sense of posthumous nepotism, if she were not so supremely skilled in the reading and writing of ancient Egyptian. Few could rival the young woman's ability to decipher hieroglyphs and hieratic, and perhaps no one anywhere was better suited for the proper coding and cataloguing of the vast library deep in the recesses of the museum.

Still, as much as she loved this place, she hoped to move on, and on this afternoon a month and two days after the legionnaire massacre (an event of which she had no knowledge, incidentally), Evelyn Carnahan was perhaps off her form, suffering from the disappointment of the rejection of her application by the Bembridge Scholars.

The *second* rejection, actually.

The tall, slender young woman—her Nefertiti-like shapeliness lost in a long cream linen skirt, mannish white pinstriped shirt with brown scarf, and oversize tan cardigan—was atop a tall ladder between two of the many towering rows in the "stacks," the museum's extensive collection of volumes pertaining to the history and culture of ancient Egypt. Her long brunette hair was tucked into a bun and her almond-shaped blue eyes lurked behind the eyeglasses she used for close-up work. None of this served to heighten her attractiveness, but could not wholly disguise the lovely features of her heart-shaped face, either. Her love for Egyptian antiquities was her father's doing; but her looks had come from Mum.

The glasses did cause certain misjudgments of distance, as was about to become evident. She had just discovered a book on Tuthmosis, improperly shelved among the "S"s, and was attempting to reach across to the adjacent shelf, just behind her, where the "T"s would find the volume a rightful home.

She had to stretch a little to reach it, and pulling on the

top rung of the ladder, she leaned across the aisle. *Almost there, a little closer now* . . .

And suddenly the ladder pulled away from the shelf and Evelyn, who prided herself on her composure, on her cool handling of any problem, yelped and flung the Tuthmosis book as if it had caught fire. The volume sailed, then fell, pages fluttering like a bird with too many wings, and landed with a *thunk* on the floor below—far below.

Instinctively, she latched on to the top rung with both hands, only to find herself on a ladder that was standing straight up, precariously so, as if she were standing on one stilt. Teetering there, she drew a slow, steady breath; there would be no more undignified yelps, thank you . . . and then she lost her balance.

Stilt-walking down the aisle on the ladder, Evelyn did not yelp; it was more of a prayer: "Please! God!"

Swaying, she rode the ladder across the main aisle, struggling for balance, to no avail: The ladder crashed into the next bookshelf . . . and came to a stop.

Evelyn heaved a relieved sigh.

Which preceded the bookshelf falling away from her, crashing into the bookshelf behind. This produced two results, one being helpful: The angle allowed Evelyn to slide down the now slanting ladder to plop unceremoniously, but none the worse for wear, to the floor.

The other result, however, was most unpleasant, and the term "domino effect" should suffice, here. She chose to close her eyes through much of it, and so spared herself the sight of one bookshelf toppling into another, and another, and another. But she did not think to cover her ears, so was privy to the sounds of thousands of precious volumes flinging themselves off shelves and scattering to the floor. When the last bookshelf crashed into the far wall, and emptied its books to the floor like a wagon dumping coal down a chute, the worst was over.

Almost.

When she opened her eyes—one at a time, as if that would lessen the blow—she saw not just a librarian's worst nightmare in the jumble of fallen shelves and spilled books

43

but the wide-eyed presence of her boss, the museum's curator, Dr. Bey.

She looked up at him timidly, ventured a tiny smile.

"Oops," she said.

The curator was a small round man with a small round face in a dark suit with a black string tie; his black hair sat upon his skull like a spreading spider.

"Oops?" he asked, black eyebrows climbing a high forehead, his black mustache lost in his curled-back upper lip.

"I didn't hear you come in, Dr. Bey."

"Perhaps it was the books crashing to the floor."

Quickly, she got to her feet, smoothed out her sweater and skirt, adjusted the scarf at her open collar, and began picking up books, as if implying this was a mess easily cleaned up, when it would obviously require months of her time.

Dr. Bey was shaking his head. "Give me frogs, flies, locusts! Compared to you, Miss Carnahan, the other plagues were a joy."

"I'm sorry, sir. It was an accident."

"No. Rameses destroying Syria, that was an accident. This is a catastrophe." He shook a thick finger at her. "I only put up with you because your parents were our finest patrons . . . Allah rest their souls."

She had long suspected the curator resented her presence, and knew she had irritated him with various misjudged attempts to offer him "valuable artifacts" her brother, Jonathan, had bought from barroom archaeologists.

"Dr. Bey," she said, "anyone could have made this mess. But not just anyone could put it right."

That stopped the fat little man cold.

"If you'd like my resignation," she said, "I'll gladly offer it . . . though I doubt you could find anyone within a thousand miles who could put this particular Humpty Dumpty back together."

Brusquely, he said, "Straighten this up," and stormed out.

Irritated and embarrassed, but pleased that she'd made her point with Bey, Evelyn surveyed the scene of the disaster. She would have to gather all the books, check them for damage; one of the museum assistants would have to reposition the shelves themselves, they were much too large and bulky for her—

A sound interrupted her planning: *footsteps*.

She turned to look, to see if Dr. Bey had returned, but no one was there. The silence became eerie, as it frequently could in this sprawling turn-of-the-century building where room after room was lined with the coffins of kings, their embalmed bodies often exposed to view.

There it was again!

Someone was walking, but it was a slow, ominous shuffle, as if a bad leg were being dragged; it seemed to come from the gallery across the way.

"Dr. Bey?" she called.

Nothing.

"Abdul?"

Still nothing.

"Mohammed? . . . Bob?"

She moved through the connecting room into the area where treasures from the Middle Kingdom were on display; this was after hours, and the gas lighting was subdued, flickery, throwing shadows, making a haunted house of this room filled with the plundered possessions of the ancient dead. She moved down the aisle, past a closed sarcophagus, skirting cases of artifacts.

Another noise!

Was someone was in this room—a prowler? A thief? There certainly were treasures here to steal: great cases of gold and silver ornaments taken from tombs, golden coiled-snake armlets, necklaces, girdles, chains, the sort of jewelry the Israelites had borrowed to melt into the golden calf that had so annoyed Jehovah.

She would get Dr. Bey.

Moving past a statue of Anubis, another of Horus, both staring down at her menacingly in the dim lighting, she headed out. But on her way to the exit, she caught sight of a sarcophagus, leaned against the wall, exposing its hideous, rotted mummy.

45

Not every one of these mummy cases was meant to stand open; in fact, a room upstairs was dedicated to mummies, in glass cases, and tourists were warned of the disturbing nature of the displays. Grown men had been known to go running out of there, sweating at the sight of grinning mummies.

She sighed. Was this a prank, or the careless action of some assistant curator? In either case, the footsteps she'd heard might have belonged to whoever had opened the sarcophagus; she leaned forward, peeking in at the decayed mummy, which really was quite nasty, thinking, *This one won't do for display*, and the mummy seemed to lurch at her, accompanied by an unearthly screech that sent her reeling back, and screaming!

"Quiet, Sis," Jonathan Carnahan said, slipping out from behind the sarcophagus, "or you'll attract that dreadful little man back here again."

"Jonathan! You bloody idiot!"

"Such language, sis." Dapper, dissipated, Jonathan had strong eyes and a weak chin; he was thirty, but looked closer to forty, a cheerfully indolent individual barely getting by on his yearly stipend from the family trust fund, mostly spent on bourbon, a flask of which he removed from his cream-colored jacket and sipped.

She closed the sarcophagus lid, resisting the urge to slam it. "Have you no respect for the dead?"

"Have you no respect for the dead drunk?"

Steaming, she paced. "What are you doing here? I'm already in trouble. I just made a mess of the library...."

"I heard. And I heard Dr. Bey scold you." He sipped from his flask. "Pity."

She faced him, hands on hips. "Do you really want to ruin my career, the way you've ruined yours?"

"Now that's unfair, Sis." He belched, excused himself, and added, "I'll have you know that my career is thriving, at this very moment."

Evelyn smirked. "You haven't been out on a dig for six months."

"Not true! I've been digging, my dear. Digging away."

"What, in bars again? Please, Jonathan, I'm just in no mood for your capering. The Bembridge Scholars . . ."

He sat down heavily on the edge of a display. "Don't tell me those fools had the bad sense to turn you down again."

She sat next to him. "They say I lack experience."

"Well, you're getting it here, aren't you?"

"Fine. Just fine. I'll stay on another year or two and try again . . . and what sort of reference do you think Dr. Bey will give me?"

He beamed at her. "I've got just the thing to get you back in his good graces." Jonathan began scrounging in his other jacket pocket.

Shaking her head, Evelyn said, "Oh, no, no, not another worthless trinket, Jonathan. If I bring one more piece of junk to Dr. Bey, on your behalf—"

But Jonathan had withdrawn a small octagonal golden box, obviously ancient—New Kingdom, she'd say.

She grabbed it from him; he made no attempt to stop her. "Where did you find this, Jonathan?"

"On a dig . . . near Luxor."

Evelyn rolled the box around her in hands, examining it carefully, appreciating its carved surface, mumbling to herself as she translated the hieratics and hieroglyphs decorating it.

They began tapping their feet together in nervous unison as she inspected the box.

"I've been such a poor excuse for the son of Howard Carnahan, Evy . . . never came across a damn thing worth finding. Is it . . . is it something? Please tell me I've finally found something, old dear."

The box had tiny little slats on it, which she began to shift this way and that.

"What is it, Evy? Is that a puzzle box?"

As if in reply, the thing seemed to unfold itself, blossoming into an eight-sided key; and sitting within the open box was a folded piece of papyrus. Carefully, Evelyn unfolded it into what was clearly an ancient map: the Nile was obvious, as was a representation of the jackal-headed Anubis;

47

an eagle and various other drawings, and hieroglyphs, indeed dated it to the New Kingdom.

"Jonathan?"

"Yes, Sis?"

"You've found something."

Seated behind his desk in his cluttered, cubbyhole office, the curator used a jeweler's eyepiece to examine the box. Evelyn, standing alongside Dr. Bey, demonstrated how to open and close the object, and pointed out the cartouche on its surface.

"That's the royal seal of Seti the First," she said.

The curator shrugged. "Perhaps."

"No 'perhaps' about it, Dr. Bey."

"Which pharaoh was Seti again?" Jonathan asked, smiling, seated across the desk from the curator. "Afraid I've forgotten. Was he rich, by any chance?"

Evelyn could never be sure when Jonathan was joking. "He was the second pharaoh of the nineteenth dynasty. Some historians speculate he may have been the wealthiest of all rulers."

"What a splendid fellow, this Seti. I like him very much." Jonathan's grin, as he leaned into the dramatic glow of a candle on Bey's desk, was rather mummylike; though the museum had electric lighting, the curator often kept an aromatic candle burning.

On the curator's desk lay the golden map, stretched out as if the trio were planning a trip. Dr. Bey lifted it nearer the candlelight for a better look.

"This map is almost three thousand years old, Doctor," she told him. "And the hieratics over here indicate exactly what is being charted. . . ."

Dr. Bey looked up at her.

With a nervous grin and a little shrug, she ventured into dangerous waters. "It shows the way to Hamanaptra."

The map trembled, or rather Dr. Bey's hands holding it did; he seemed rather shaken by her statement, but only for a moment. Then he smiled and laughed, shaking his head.

"My dear girl, don't be ridiculous," Bey said. "I'm surprised at you, a scholar of your qualities, of your serious-ness. That's a myth, Hamanaptra—told by ancient Arabs to amuse Greek and Roman tourists.''

"Let's not confuse the myth of Hamanaptra, Doctor,'' she said, "with the very real possibility that the temple, and its necropolis, may have existed. Of course, I don't take that silly blather seriously—a mummy's curse, a place of evil—pure nonsense, obviously.''

"Hold on, there,'' Jonathan said, candlelight flickering on his suddenly keenly interested face, "you're not talking about *the* Hamanaptra? City of the Dead sort of thing? Hiding place for the wealth of the early pharaohs?''

Evelyn was amused. "Amazing how your Egyptology has improved.''

"Where treasure is concerned, dear girl, I'm a bloody expert. Anyway, every schoolchild knows of Hamanaptra and its wonderful big underground treasure chamber. You suppose it's true that the pharaohs had it rigged so the whole place could disappear under the dunes, flick o' the switch?''

"None of it's true,'' Bey said, chuckling, but still ex-amining the map, holding it closer to the light. "As the Americans would say, it's bunk . . . hooey . . . hokum.''

"Are you sure that's English, old man? Say! Watch it!''

The corner of the map had touched the candle's flame . . . and now the map was on fire! Bey bolted to his feet and tossed the burning papyrus off the desk, onto the floor, where Jonathan dropped to his knees and patted it quickly out with his hands. Then Jonathan held the smoldering pa-pyrus up and the left third of the map was gone.

"Oh dear,'' Evelyn said, fingers touching her lips.

Jonathan's frown was more like a pout. "You burned it! You bloody fool, you burned off the best part!''

"I am sorry.'' Bey bowed. "It was an accident.''

"Rameses destroying Syria,'' Evelyn said coldly, "that was an accident.''

"Perhaps it's for the best.'' Bey sat back down, shrug-ging. "We are scholars, not treasure hunters, after all. Many men have wasted their lives in pursuit of foolishness like

49

this. No one has ever found Hamanaptra, and many who've tried failed even to return.''

Evelyn arched an eyebrow. "My research indicates the temple city may have existed."

Jonathan was holding up the map, staring at its charred edge with the expression of a child who has just broken his first toy, Christmas morning. "You burned off the lost city," he said accusingly to the curator, who merely shrugged again.

"I'm sure it was a forgery, a fake. Really, Miss Carnahan, I thought better of you than to be fooled so easily. . . . However, as for this box . . ."

And the curator reached toward the golden octagonal artifact on his desk.

"... I may be able to offer a modest sum."

Jonathan's expression perked up, but Evelyn snatched the box from Dr. Bey's grasp and glared at him.

"No thank you, Doctor," she said. "Suddenly, it is not for sale."

And she quickly exited, with Jonathan—scorched map in hand—trailing bemusedly after.

·«5»·

Gallows Humor

Jonathan Carnahan may have been a bit of a dilettante where Egyptology was concerned, and an utter fraud as an archaeologist, but one thing he did know: every watering hole in Cairo. From the plush cocktail lounges of the Continental and Sheapard hotels to waterfront dives few cultured Englishmen had dared enter (and fewer still had ever exited), Jonathan—and his thirst, and his money—were welcome guests.

This gave him access not only to alcoholic libation, but information; so it was that he knew a certain Richard O'Connell was a guest at the most dreadful lodgings possible in a city noted for its dreadful lodgings: the Cairo prison.

So, too, was Jonathan able to arrange—at rather short notice, with a handful of phone calls—an audience with the host of the city's worst hellhole, Warden Gad Hassan, a thickset greasy man whose porcine features were distinguished by glittering dark eyes, a mustache flecked with the memories of several meals, and black-stubbled cheeks that apparently crossed paths with a razor no more than once a week.

The warden, his rumpled cream-colored suit stained with sweat, food, and other substances quite unimaginable, had taken Evelyn's arm in a fashion at once gentlemanly and lascivious as he ushered the Carnahans across a small, pen-like courtyard in a sprawling stone structure from which moans of agony and ghastly smells emanated. It was Jonathan's theory that close proximity to the smells might be creating the moans.

His sister, hugging an alligator purse, looked rather lovely in another cardigan-and-dress ensemble, topped off by a large flat-brimmed hat that sat at a sun-shielding tilt. Perhaps, Jonathan thought, *too* lovely to be visiting a pigsty like this. . . .

"Welcome to my humble home, Miss Carnahan," the warden said. "It is a rare honor to have a woman of your elegance step across my lowly threshold."

Despite the musical accent so common when Arabs spoke English, the warden's command of Jonathan's native language was impressive. But then again, a man this gross—the chief difference between Hassan and his worst prisoners was that Hassan was in charge—did not achieve so prominent a position without brains.

As they walked, the warden's palm cradling Evelyn's elbow, Hassan gestured with his other hand about the crushed-stone area. "This is our visitors' area. . . ."

"Charming," Evelyn said, the sarcasm so faint even Jonathan couldn't be sure of it.

Evelyn still seemed to be pouting. She had been irritated, even accusatory, when she learned that her brother had found the puzzle box not on a dig near Luxor, but in an establishment known as the Sultan's Casbah, a dump catering to European rabble in one of the less reputable corners of the French Quarter.

"You lied to me!" she had said, sounding wounded.

Why did that surprise the silly girl? It was hardly the first time. Lying to one's family, after all, was where the art of fabrication began; if one couldn't deceive the gullible sods who loved one, how could one hope to pull the wool over a stranger's eyes?

Jonathan had explained that he'd lifted the box from the pocket of the unconscious O'Connell, who had been involved in a drunken brawl, after which he (O'Connell) had been arrested. Evelyn—following the requisite expression of shock that her ''own brother'' could commit such a horrendous act—had insisted the box's previous owner be interviewed at the prison (but said nothing about *returning* that box).

This had seemed a less than smashing idea to Jonathan, having stolen the box, knowing that in Cairo the penalty for picking pockets thereafter made scratching one's nose (or anywhere else, for that matter) a physical impossibility.

The warden ushered them toward a barred cage that would not have been out of place in a monkey house at a zoo; the heavily barred pen was attached to the prison wall, where presumably a prisoner would be brought out to meet with visitors.

Evelyn asked Hassan, ''Why is Mr. O'Connell in custody? My understanding is he was arrested after behavior that might be termed 'drunk and disorderly.' ''

The warden shrugged. ''Why don't you ask him? His only excuse is that he was 'looking for adventure.' I will say this: Your visit is well timed. I saw his name on the list today.''

''For his trial, you mean?''

''Trial?'' The warden laughed explosively; his teeth were that shade of green so attractive in jade jewelry, less so in a smile. ''How very droll, Miss Carnahan. So seldom does a woman of your grace and beauty have so keenly developed a sense of humor. . . .''

They had reached the cage when the interior doors on the wall of the prison burst open and four Arab guards dressed in khaki dragged in a handsome, unshaven young white man, heavily shackled at the wrists and ankles, in what had been a white shirt and jodhpurs, before they had become filthy and torn from a week in captivity.

''Ah!'' the warden said. ''Here's your friend, now.''

The guards hurled the young man against the bars; the

53

prisoner struck the steel with a nasty clang, but his face registered no pain.

"I say," Jonathan said to Hassan, "was that necessary?"

The warden beamed greenly at Evelyn. "I see your brother's sense of humor is also well developed. This is Mr. O'Connell, formerly of Chicago, Illinois, and more lately, the French Foreign Legion. He's a deserter, your friend."

Evelyn was looking O'Connell over; he was doing the same to her, from (it seemed to Jonathan) a slightly different perspective.

She asked her brother, "Is this him? The one you stole it from?"

Jonathan laughed nervously, glancing at the warden. "My sister and her sense of humor. . . . Yes, dear, this is the blighter who *sold* it to me."

O'Connell wedged his face between two bars, frowning as he studied Jonathan. "Sold what to you?"

"Warden," Jonathan said, "would it be possible for us to have a few minutes alone with our friend?"

"What friend?" O'Connell asked.

Jonathan extended a hand with a pound note in it to the warden, for the man to shake, and take.

"Certainly, sahib." Hassan bowed. "I'll leave you now . . . you have five minutes."

"It won't be the same without you," O'Connell said to the warden, and blew him a kiss.

The warden did not smile, greenly or otherwise; he waved a finger in the air. "A sense of humor in prisoners I do not appreciate."

O'Connell laughed. "What are you going to do about it, fatso? Not change my sheets?"

The warden nodded to the scruffy, sleepy-eyed guard standing behind O'Connell, and the guard slammed the prisoner into the metal bars again, where his face bounced like a rubber ball off pavement. But O'Connell still registered no pain, though he did toss the guard a glare.

"Unwise, sir," the warden said, and began walking away, adding to himself, "most unwise."

Jonathan, watching Hassan go, said to O'Connell, "You

might not want to get on his bad side, old man.''

"Where have I seen you before?'' O'Connell asked Jonathan.

"I'm just a, uh, local missionary spreading the good word.''

"And who's the dame?''

Evelyn frowned. "Dame?''

Jonathan gestured. "This is my charming sister, Evy.''

"Evelyn,'' she corrected.

O'Connell glanced at her and shrugged. "Yeah? Well, maybe with her hair down she wouldn't be a total loss.''

Evelyn's eyes widened. "Well, I never!''

"That wouldn't surprise me,'' O'Connell said. To Jonathan, he said, "You look mighty familiar. . . .''

Jonathan laughed giddily. "I just have one of those terribly common faces, old boy.''

"No, I know you from somewhere.''

Evelyn said, "Mr. O'Connell, allow me to explain why we've come.''

Face striped with the shadows of prison bars, O'Connell half-smirked. "Till I heard your British accents, I was kinda hoping you were from the American embassy.''

"Sorry, no,'' she said. "We're here about your box.''

"My what?''

"Your puzzle box. A little gold knickknack with eight sides? You see we, uh, that is my brother . . . *found* your box. . . .''

"Now I remember,'' O'Connell said, nodding, smiling, and, shackled or not, the prisoner managed to throw a short, sharp right jab into Jonathan's jaw. Pugilism had never been a long suit of Jonathan's, and the punch dropped him to the ground. He sat there rubbing his jaw, not quite unconscious.

"At any rate,'' Evelyn continued, "we found your puzzle box and we've come to ask you about it.''

O'Connell was looking at her with renewed interest. "I just decked your brother, you know.''

"Yes, well, and I'm sure he deserved it. He is my sibling; I would know.''

O'Connell half-smiled at her. "I guess you would at that, Evy."

"That's 'Miss Carnahan,' if you please. Now about the box—"

"Don't you mean, about Hamanaptra?" White teeth flashed in the unshaven, deeply tanned face.

Jonathan, finally getting to his feet, brushing himself off, replacing his hat which had been knocked off, said, "Keep your voice down, man! The walls have ears."

Actually, it was the scruffy hood-eyed guard standing in the cell with O'Connell who had ears, and while English may have been foreign to those ears, the word "Hamanaptra" might be all too familiar.

"What an interesting thing to say, Mr. O'Connell," Evelyn said, coyly. "Whatever was it about that box that brought, uh, that mythical place to mind?"

"Maybe it was because I was at that mythical place when I found it."

She blinked. "You were there?"

"Yeah, and if a caravan of diggers out of Cairo hadn't stumbled across me in the desert, I wouldn'ta lived to tell the tale."

Jonathan, jaw aching, feeling irritable toward the chap, snapped, "How do we know this isn't a load of pig swallow?"

"Well, for one thing, I have no idea what pig swallow is. And for another, step over here near the bars again. . . ."

"No thank you," Jonathan said, taking a step back.

But Evelyn had no compunction about stepping near the bars, closer to the filthy prisoner. She asked, "You were there? At Hamanaptra?"

He flashed her another big grin. "I sure as hell was, lady. Seti's joint. City of the Goddamned Dead."

"You swear?"

"I'm afraid so—every goddamn day."

She frowned in frustration. "No, no, what I mean to say is, do you take an oath that—"

"I know what you mean. I'm just pulling your leg. Or anyway, I'd like to. . . ."

Her chin lifted, her gaze traveled to him down her fine nose. "You're hardly in a position to make flirtatious remarks, Mr. O'Connell. This is strictly business."

"Is it, now?"

"What did you find?"

"Sand. A lot of sand."

"Well, then, what did you see?"

"Death. Lot of that, too. They aren't kidding when they say that place is cursed."

"Superstition, Mr. O'Connell, is the hallmark of the small mind. My interest is in research. My brother and I are Egyptologists."

"Really? Well, then—I bet you'd like to go there. To Hamanaptra, I mean."

Jonathan crossly said, "Will the two of you keep your voices down?"

Evelyn was very near the bars of the cage. "Could you tell me how to get there? The exact location?"

"Better than that. I'll take you there."

"But Mr. O'Connell—you are rather indisposed."

"That's one way to put it."

"Couldn't you just tell us how to get there? Give us the exact location?"

"Have you opened the box?"

"Well, uh . . . yes we have."

"Then you have the map."

Evelyn glanced at her brother, who shrugged.

"About the map, old boy," Jonathan said, keeping his distance, "I'm afraid there was a slight mishap—a portion of it was burned away . . . the, uh, portion including the particular site of interest, shall we say."

"Come closer, Jonathan," O'Connell said, crooking his finger, smiling tightly, "I can't hear you. . . ."

Jonathan stepped back a pace.

Evelyn said to the prisoner, "You've been there. You can point the way."

O'Connell nodded. "I can take you there."

"How?"

57

"Well, you might start by, oh, I don't know, maybe by . . ."

She leaned closer. "Yes? Yes?"

"Getting me the hell out of here!"

Evelyn reared back. "Well, you needn't be rude, Mr. O'Connell."

"Forgive me. A man loses all sense of propriety in a place like this. Would you really like to know the way?"

"Oh yes."

He nodded to her, to come closer, his eyes indicating he didn't want the guard to hear. She leaned in to him and he kissed her full on the lips.

Then he grinned at her, rakishly, and winked. "Get me the hell outa here, honey, and we'll both go on an adventure."

The guard had witnessed this forbidden physical familiarity with a visitor, and as O'Connell was speaking to Evelyn, the scruffy fellow was stepping forward to throttle the prisoner again.

But this time O'Connell was ready: He grabbed the man and yanked him head first into the bars and let the guard's face slam into steel for a change. In an instant, other guards were hustling into the pen, grabbing O'Connell and dragging him out.

O'Connell shouted out, "Nice meeting you!"

Then he was gone, disappearing around the corner, into the fetid darkness of the prison, hauled away by angry Arab guards.

Suddenly the warden was back at her side.

"Oh dear," Evelyn said. "Will they beat him?"

"No, no, Miss Carnahan," the warden said pleasantly. "There's no time for that."

"No time?"

"Yes, he's being taken to be hanged."

"Hanged?"

"He's a deserter from the Foreign Legion, as I told you. That's a hanging offense."

Jonathan said, "But the French Foreign Legion have no jurisdiction here. This isn't Algeria, for heaven's sake. . . ."

"We've civilized people, Mr. Carnahan, Miss Carnahan—we have . . . what is the word? A reciprocal arrangement with the legion—for fifty of your pounds, we waive them the trouble of extradition. And now, I'm afraid, my presence is required at the execution—a formality, but I am so a stickler for doing things right."

"Let me go with you," Evelyn said.

Groaning, Jonathan said, "Oh, sis, why?"

The warden said, "That's out of the question. No women are allowed at hangings in my country."

Her chin up again, she said, "In your country, women wear veils. Do you see a veil on my face? I'm an English-woman, after all."

Hassan shrugged. "So be it. Unlike your face, hanging is not pretty, my dear."

Soon Jonathan, Evelyn, and the warden were stepping out onto a balcony overlooking another courtyard, where from barred windows all around, inmates could look down at the gallows that had been erected. These gallows had no lower apronlike enclosure to keep onlookers from seeing the strug-gling and kicking of a hanging man. The warden was no sadist: he obviously felt the need to provide his prisoners with a little entertainment.

And Evelyn's presence was providing entertainment, as well: From every barred window, bulging eyes in horrible faces took in the presence of Jonathan's lovely sister. There were no catcalls or wolf whistles: These sorry counte-nances—displaying a remarkable collection of scars, scrag-gly beards, missing eyes, and rotten teeth—had gone dead silent at the sight of her, starving jackals staring at fresh meat.

"A woman without a veil," the warden said, lifting an eyebrow in an *I-told-you-so* manner, "might as well be sit-ting here unclothed."

Evelyn ignored the remark, her eyes on the prisoner be-ing ushered into the courtyard.

O'Connell was led up onto the gallows by the same guards who'd manhandled him in the visitor's pen, and positioned on the trapdoor. A hangman in a mask, with a bare chest and loose-fitting pants, draped the noose around the prisoner's neck, then cinched it tight. O'Connell noticed Evelyn and Jonathan seated in the balcony nearby, and at first frowned, then smiled.

The warden took his seat and Evelyn sat next to him; Jonathan preferred to stand.

Evelyn said to Hassan, "I will give you fifty pounds more to let him live than the legion's paying you to kill him."

Jonathan could barely believe his ears. One hundred pounds for that lout? Of course, if he could lead them to Hamanaptra . . .

The warden's nose twitched like a big dark bunny's. "I would *pay* one hundred pounds to see the insolent pig hang."

"Two, then," she said.

"Two hundred pounds?" Jonathan asked. Now he sat down, heavily, next to his sister.

"Two hundred pounds," Evelyn said, nodding curtly.

The warden shook his head, dismissively, and raised a hand. "Proceed!" he called to the hangman, who stood near his deadly lever. O'Connell's forehead was tensed and beaded with sweat; he could hear every word of the negotiation between the warden and Jonathan's sister.

"*Three* hundred pounds!" Evelyn said.

Jonathan clutched his sister's arm, whispering, "Are you mad? A year's stipend for that blackguard?"

Evelyn looked daggers at her brother and her mouth formed, but she did not speak the word, "Hamanaptra."

The warden, however, did not even reply to this latest offer. Down on the gallows, the hangman was saying to O'Connell, "Any last request?"

"Yeah—could we do this tomorrow, instead? That fish-head lunch just isn't settling."

That stopped the hangman cold—he'd never had such a request—and he turned, and yelling, repeated the plea for the balcony, though the warden and his guests had heard every word.

Interrupting, the warden said, "No, he can't wait until tomorrow. Get on with it!"

Embarrassed, the hangman gave O'Connell a *why-I-oughta* look, and grabbed the trapdoor lever.

"Five hundred pounds," Evelyn said firmly.

Jonathan covered his face with a hand.

The warden looked at Evelyn, calling out to the hangman, "A moment! . . . Five hundred pounds?"

"Yes."

Hassan placed a hand on Evelyn's leg, just above the knee. "I will consent, if you grant me some other inducement, not financial . . . a personal kindness. I am a lonely man in a difficult job."

Evelyn plucked his greasy paw from her leg with the thumb and middle finger of her right hand, as if removing a particularly odious bug. She turned away and made a sound in her chest that conveyed her revulsion.

The warden had his pride, which was wounded by rude, crude laughter from the windows where prisoners had witnessed the rebuff. In the thumbs-down gesture that had been good enough for Nero, Hassan cued his hangman to pull the lever.

Which the hangman did.

The trapdoor fell away, under O'Connell's boots, and as Evelyn screamed, "Nooooo!", the former corporal of the Foreign Legion dropped through the hole, the rope jerking tight.

O'Connell's body snapped at the end of the rope . . .

. . . but he was clearly alive, struggling, kicking!

"Ah!" the warden said, and touched the fingers of his hands together playfully, "a rare treat: His neck did not break. We have the pleasure of watching him take his time strangling to death."

The audience in the barred windows gave the show mixed reviews: Some were amused, and hooting with laughter; others were angry, possibly outraged that the prisoner should be tortured so slowly, or was it annoyance over having the fun of seeing a neck broken denied them? Jonathan certainly took no pleasure in seeing the beggar turning various shades of red, struggling so piteously.

Evelyn was whispering in the warden's ear. Surely she wasn't telling him about . . .

"Hamanaptra?" the warden said, eyes wide. "You lie!"

"Never! I'm a respectable woman."

Hassan frowned. "This filthy godless son of a pig knows where to find the City of the Dead, and all its treasures?"

"Yes . . . and if you cut him down, we will give you five percent."

O'Connell, strangling and eavesdropping, managed to croak out, "Five percent?" His eyes were bugging out, in part due to Evelyn's cheapness, Jonathan supposed, but also because he was choking to death.

"All right," Evelyn said, "ten percent."

"Fifty," the warden said.

"Twenty."

"Give it . . . give it to . . ." O'Connell was saying, as he twisted and turned redder.

"Forty," the warden said.

"Thirty."

"I'm . . . I'm dyin' here!" O'Connell called.

"Twenty-five," the warden said.

"Done!" Evelyn said, and they shook hands.

The warden flashed his green smile, yelled a command in Arabic, and a scimitar slashed the air, cutting the rope, sending O'Connell crashing to the ground.

He rolled on the gravel, half dead, still gagging; but he'd won the crowd over: the captive audience at the barred windows was cheering and clapping and whistling, though O'Connell was in too much agony to appreciate his celebrity.

Jonathan didn't feel much better himself. Twenty-five percent! That City of the Dead better bloody well be out there. . . .

Evelyn stood and leaned over the balcony railing and smiled down at her new partner.

"Nice meeting you, too," she said.

And O'Connell passed out.

·⟨ 6 ⟩·

A Night on the Nile

The Nile—with its two branches, the White and the Blue—was the longest river in the world and the only one Richard O'Connell ever heard of that flowed north. Everyone in this damn-fool country lived on the river's banks or along its canals; here at Cairo, and just south, was the widest part of the valley—five whole miles.

Under the hot, dry afternoon sun, the Nile lay like a bolt of shimmering satin, a few shades deeper than the nearly cloudless sky, spiked by pyramids across the way. On the river's placid surface graceful little boats glided, laden with passengers and cargo, sails spread like the white wings of gulls.

The peacefulness of this view was negated by the bustle of the boardwalk adjoining the docks of Giza Port, where tourists and teams of explorers were pushing awkwardly through an army of turbaned men in their nightshirtlike robes, hawkers peddling King Tut trinkets, and beggars bellowing, "Baksheesh!"

The word, which meant "Gimme something!", seemed to be a two-syllable national anthem: They all sang it. O'Connell, lugging a gunnysack, ignored them, even the child who informed him, "Fadder and modder dead, belly empty." The Chicagoan had spent enough time in this part of the world to know that pitching a quarter to one of these poor souls would bring every beggar down on him like the Norte Dame front line on a ball carrier.

O'Connell was a new man, thanks to the twenty pounds he'd talked out of his benefactor, Miss Evelyn Carnahan, to cover expenses and supplies. Shaved, hair cut and combed, boots and chinos begging to be broken in, his white shirt so new and fresh it bore no sweat circles yet, a brown kerchief covering where the noose had rubbed his neck raw, he looked dashing and handsome and damn well knew it.

He spotted them in the crowd. Evelyn, in a wide-brimmed white hat and a blue dress that might have seemed frumpy were it not traversing some very nice curves, and her brother, Jonathan, in pith helmet and khakis. They were both hauling heavy carpetbags, doing their best to hold on to their hats, dignity and money, as they moved through the horde of peddlers and panhandlers, to the steamer *Ibis* that awaited them at the jetty.

As he caught up to them, O'Connell could hear their conversation, in progress.

"How can we even be sure he'll show up?" Evelyn was saying. "For all we know, he's sitting in a bar, drinking away my twenty pounds."

"That sounds more like me, Sis, than O'Connell. He'll be here—these American cowboy types are as good as their word. It's all they have."

Evelyn continued, in a clipped, haughty manner: "Well, personally I find him a filthy, rude, impertinent cad, and I don't like him one tiny bit."

"Anybody I know?" O'Connell asked, sidling up to her.

Her eyes widened in surprised embarrassment—big blue eyes that O'Connell wouldn't have minded diving into; and that mouth, full, sensual. . . .

He caught himself, not wanting to give her the satisfaction of noticing his admiring her, and in the process he failed to notice that she had been admiring the new spit-and-polished him.

"Afternoon, O'Connell," Jonathan said, nodding toward his sister, taking the American's arm, shaking his hand enthusiastically. "Don't mind Sis—she was talking about some other cad."

"He sounds pretty bad," O'Connell said, with a little smile.

"Hello, Mr. O'Connell." Evelyn smiled nervously at him, pretending she didn't know she was being needled, as O'Connell fell in step with them, pushing through the crowd toward the waiting stern-wheeler.

All around them, beggars were bawling, "Baksheesh!"

"Ripping day to begin an adventure, what?" Jonathan said, a hand on O'Connell's shoulder.

"Yeah," O'Connell said, withdrawing himself from Jonathan's grasp and stopping to check for his wallet. " 'Ripping.' "

"Dear boy," Jonathan said, pausing to touch his heart in a gesture of wounded pride, "I would never steal from a partner."

"Nice to know you have standards. How's the chin?"

The bruise on Jonathan's jaw, from O'Connell's punch-through-the-bars, was a lovely black, blue, and orange, like an exotic blossoming flower.

"Think nothing of it, partner mine," Jonathan said cheerily. "That sort of thing happens to me all the time."

"Bet it does."

Evelyn dropped her bags to the boardwalk, where they clunked heavily, drawing the two men's attention. She cleared her throat and, with exaggerated formality, said, "Mr. O'Connell, as you well know, we have a considerable journey ahead of us—"

"One day by steamer, two by camel, yes, ma'am."

"Yes. And before we embark on this arduous adventure, and put ourselves to considerable trouble and discomfort, not to say expense . . . can you look me straight in the eye and convince me that this is not a sham designed to bilk me of my money?"

"What?"

Evelyn, lovely face blushed blue by her hat brim's

shadow, lifted her chin and looked down her nose at him—a habit she had that was not her most endearing, in O'Connell's opinion. "Despite what you might assume, my brother and I are not wealthy, nor do we have any desire to spend our meager funds and risk our lives on . . . what is the phrase?"

O'Connell lifted an eyebrow. "A wild goose chase?"

"That would seem to cover it, yes. I would understand entirely if a man facing the gallows were to stoop to deception to find his freedom. If that is the case, you have my permission, even my blessing, to—"

"Straight in the eye, is that how you want it?" O'Connell marched right up to the patronizing young woman and practically touched his nose to hers. Her eyes became huge and her lashes fluttered like startled butterflies. "Lady, two hundred men, my whole battalion, followed our colonel across Libya and into Egypt to find your precious City of the Dead. They found it, and they joined it—all but me. Now, I'm willing to go back there because those bloody sands defeated me. And I intend to win this time. I'm going with or without you . . . and, frankly, I would advise you stay here in Cairo and let your brother and me take the risks."

She did not back away, holding her ground, despite how obnoxiously, presumptuously close he was standing to her. "No, thank you. I'm going along. To look after my interests."

He took a step back, shrugging, intoxicated by the fragrance of her lilac-scented perfume. "Suit yourself . . . let me get those."

And O'Connell, slinging the gunnysack on its strap around his shoulders, bent down and picked up her bags, and headed up the gangplank.

He did not hear Jonathan whisper to Evelyn, "Oh yes, you're right, dear sister—he is an utter cad. Nothing to admire there, in the least."

But O'Connell did hear a familiar voice—a voice he had hoped never to hear again—saying to the Carnahans, "A cheery good afternoon to you."

O'Connell, halfway up the gangplank, whirled, and Evelyn asked his question for him, minus an obscenity or two.

"What are *you* doing here?"

And to the young woman, the warden of Cairo prison tipped his battered porkpie hat, a new addition to the rumpled ensemble of his vari-stained cream-colored suit.

"I have come to protect my investment," Gad Hassan said. "As my people know all too well, the English have a way of speaking politely as they steal the ground out from under you."

Then the warden bowed and, lugging a single carpetbag, moved up the plank onto the deck, smiling benignly at O'Connell, who just glared at the greasy little bastard.

"No hard feelings," the warden said.

O'Connell, bags at his feet, touched his throat, saying ominously, "If you ever want to a borrow a necktie, just ask."

The warden didn't seem to like the sound of that offer, and disappeared off toward the bow.

O'Connell carted Evelyn Carnahan's bags to her cabin door and asked to take his leave, saying he was going to have a look around the steamer.

"Do what you like, Mr. O'Connell," she said crisply. "I'm not your employer."

"Don't forget that," he said, and with a huff, Evelyn disappeared within the cabin.

"Evy's always been a headstrong girl," Jonathan said, hauling his own bags. "Pay her no heed—it only means she's fond of you."

"Funny way of showing it."

"That's true of most women, isn't it? The ones worth knowing, anyway. See you at dinner?"

"See you at dinner."

The stern-wheeler was a shabby wooden house of a boat, about twenty feet wide, one hundred and fifty feet long, a glorified passenger barge with two decks—the lower one with thirty cabins and a dining room and bar, the upper piled with luggage and crates, with an open area arranged with chairs under an awning so passengers could watch the green-and-tan scenery glide by. The pilot, a short-bearded Nubian

67

in turban and gown, set a corkscrewing course that wound from one side of the river to the other, as the steamer plowed its six-mile-an-hour way downstream, against the current.

A low barge, with a flat deck of rough boards, was towed alongside; this was for horses and camels—and second-class and third-class passengers, who carried their own bedding and would sleep on the deck.

The dining room served table d'hôte, at eight o'clock; everyone was in evening wear except O'Connell. The waiters were Nubians in white gowns with red sashes, and the service was elegant. Feeling out of place but not really caring, O'Connell sat with the Carnahans, never letting his gunnysack out of his sight. They did not speak of their mission, keeping Hamanaptra to themselves, as they shared a table with strangers, a party consisting of a pair of missionaries, Warden Hassan, several commercial travelers, and a group of big-game hunters.

The food was excellent—a clear spicy soup, boiled fish fresh from the Nile, salmi of pigeons, roast lamb with mint sauce, rice, string beans, tomato salad, pudding, fruit. . . .

O'Connell wolfed it down greedily, and at one point Jonathan said, "Good God, man—you're eating everything but the tablecloth."

"I suggest you do the same. We won't be dining like this in the desert."

Jonathan thought about that, and dug in.

After dinner, O'Connell stood at the rail on the lower deck and watched the moon stare back at itself from the surface of the iridescent Nile, the desert on either bank turned a soothing ivory. Moments like these reminded him why he'd left Chicago behind and gone looking for adventure. Then a bug bit him and he went inside the bar, at the bow.

At a central table, a poker game was in progress, four Americans and Jonathan. O'Connell stood and watched, gunnysack at his feet. No introductions were made—poker precluded social niceties—but before long O'Connell had gathered that the Americans were heading out on a dig. A small professorial fellow of perhaps fifty-five with clear blue eyes and a white wispy mustache—Dr. Chamberlin—was the expedition's Egyptologist.

The others were rough-hewn, thrill-seeking adventurers of O'Connell's own stripe, men in their late twenties and early thirties: Henderson, towheaded, loud, cheerfully arrogant; Daniels, dark, quiet, even brooding; and Burns, easygoing, in a good mood, but then he was winning, coins and dollar bills littering his side of the table.

Right now Burns was polishing his wire-rim glasses with a hanky. Maybe twenty seconds ago, Henderson had slammed the deck of cards down in front of him.

"For Chrissakes, Bernie, you see good enough!" Henderson roared, a stubby cigar in a corner of his mouth. "Cut the cards, already!"

Burns put his glasses on and said, "Gotta see 'em to cut 'em," and did.

"Join us, Mr. O'Connell," Jonathan said, waving toward an empty chair. "Sit down! We can use another player."

"No thanks. Not much of a gambler."

"Not what I hear," Henderson said, grinning as he fanned his five cards out for his personal perusal. "Only a gambler goes looking for the City of the Dead."

". . . *What* am I looking for?"

"You heard me, O'Connell. Sure you never bet?"

"Not with money."

"Pity. 'Cause I got five hundred smackeroos says our little bunch gets to Hamanaptra before you."

O'Connell twitched a smile. "Oh, so you're lookin' for the City of the Dead?"

"Hope to shout."

"And I'm supposed to be looking for this place, too, huh?"

Henderson grunted a laugh. "Damn straight."

"Says who?"

"Little Lord Fauntleroy here." Henderson jerked a thumb toward Jonathan, who smiled awkwardly, then—under O'Connell's glare—returned to the study of his latest hand of cards, whistling innocently.

Henderson flashed a yellow grin. "Well, what do you say, O'Connell? We got a bet?"

O'Connell didn't much care for the look on Henderson's sweaty, stubbly face; but the kind of man who runs off to join the French Foreign Legion is not likely to ignore the throwing down of most any gauntlet.

"You're on," O'Connell said.

The Egyptologist, Dr. Chamberlin, had already folded his hand; he was studying O'Connell like a hieroglyph he was trying to decipher.

"What makes you so confident, young man?" Chamberlin asked O'Connell.

"What makes *him* so confident?" O'Connell asked, nodding toward Henderson.

Henderson blew a smoke ring, grinned, eyes narrowing. "Maybe we got a man on our team who's been there."

"Where?"

"Where do you think? City of the Dead itself. Hamanaptra."

"I say," Jonathan said, "that is a coincidence. Why, we also have—"

But that was all Jonathan had to say at the moment, because O'Connell—swinging his gunnysack up from the floor, back around his shoulder, accidentally bumped Carnahan in the ribs with it.

Jonathan said, "Ow!" Then he quickly recovered, asking brightly, "Now, uh, where were we? Whose wager is it, gentlemen?"

O'Connell was heading out on deck.

Henderson called out: "We got us a bet, remember!"

"I'll remember, gents. G'night."

As he left, O'Connell heard Burns exclaiming, "Full house!"

"What a damn lucky streak," Henderson said.

"Can't last forever," Daniels said, finally speaking.

The desert breeze wasn't just cool, but cold, which made this a typical night on the Nile, and O'Connell discovered that Evelyn Carnahan had the whole upper deck to herself. The moonlight was so bright, Evelyn was reading by it;

hatless, wearing her glasses, sitting beside a wicker table where her cup of tea rested, she was lost in E. M. Forster's *A Passage to India*. O'Connell set his gunnysack onto the deck nearby and she jumped, startled.

"Sorry," he said. "Didn't mean to disturb you."

Chin up, she said, "The only thing that disturbs me, Mr. O'Connell, is your frightfully poor sense of decorum."

He shrugged. "I didn't bring any evening dress with me."

"I wasn't talking about that."

"What, then . . . ? Oh, you aren't miffed 'cause of that peck I gave you, back at the prison?"

"Peck, Mr. O'Connell?"

"You know—kiss."

"Is that what you call it?"

She returned her attention to E. M. Forster, and O'Connell shrugged, kneeling at the gunnysack, from which he began to withdraw various items, mostly weapons: a pair of revolvers, several hunting knifes, an elephant gun, and half a dozen carefully wrapped sticks of dynamite.

Arching an eyebrow, peering over her book, Evelyn said, "Did I miss something? Are we going to war?"

"You and I've had a few skirmishes already, I'd say. . . . Look, the last time I dropped by your precious City of the Dead, everybody with me got themselves butchered."

O'Connell sat in the chair on the other side of her reading table, with the weapons spread out at his feet. From the gunnysack he withdrew a box of oversize shells and began loading up the elephant gun.

"I suppose certain precautions are necessary," she granted him.

He looked up at her from his work. "You notice that group of Americans?"

"Those roughnecks with the little professor?"

"Yeah. Them."

She nodded curtly. "I noticed them, all right. I recognize one of them, an Egyptologist, Dr. Chamberlin—formerly attached to the Metropolitan Museum in New York, left under a cloud of scandal. Treasure-hunting riffraff, I'd say."

O'Connell smirked at her. "Guess what treasure they're hunting."

"Oh, dear—not Hamanaptra! What a terrible coincidence."

"I don't believe in Santa Claus and I don't in coincidences. . . . On the other hand . . ."

She frowned thoughtfully. "On the other hand, what, Mr. O'Connell?"

"Something *is* out there, you know."

"Pardon?"

"Under the sand."

"Well, of course there is. Unimaginable riches, which is what attracts my brother." She sighed, and shook her head. "I'm afraid Jonathan is little better than those dreadful American treasure hunters."

"What attracts you?"

She tapped the cover of *A Passage to India*. "A certain book."

"A book."

"Yes, not that you'd understand. A rare antiquity. . . . What do you think is out there?"

O'Connell gazed out at the peaceful shimmer of the Nile, the steamer slowly chasing the moon. "Something very old, Miss Carnahan, something older than civilization itself . . . *evil*."

"Evil."

"Yes—evil. Tuaregs and Bedouin think that place has a curse on it. Your Hamanaptra, in their language, is the 'Doorway to hell.' "

She arched an eyebrow. "*Ahmar isos Ossirion*, actually: 'Passageway to the underworld.' "

He began cleaning and oiling the revolvers, which he'd bought secondhand. "You can't learn about evil from books."

"Mr. O'Connell, I don't believe in Santa Claus, either, and I don't believe in curses. But I do believe that one of the most famous books in the history of mankind lies buried in those sands, somewhere: *The Book of Amun Ra*. I've been fascinated with *The Book of Amun Ra* since I was a child, when my father first told me of it."

"Why, because he told you that that book is made out of solid gold?"

That threw her. "Well, uh, yes . . ."

"And *you're* not a treasure hunter."

She stiffened. "Mr. O'Connell, my objectives are purely those of the scholar."

"Ah."

Her expression softened; he'd impressed her. "But I must say . . . for you to know that *The Book of Amun Ra* is purportedly fashioned from gold, you have a better grasp of history than one might suspect."

He grinned at her. "Maybe I have a better grasp of treasure than one might suspect."

The moon had found a cloud to slide behind. No longer able to read, and obviously disconcerted by their conversation, Evelyn stood. "If you'll excuse me, Mr. O'Connell."

"Sure. G'night."

But she wasn't leaving; she was just standing there, hesitating nervously, apparently trying to get the nerve up to say something.

"What is it, Miss Carnahan?"

"I was just wondering . . . why *did* you kiss me, back there at the prison?"

He shrugged elaborately. "Hell, every condemned man gets a last meal, doesn't he?"

She drew in a sharp breath, her eyes widening, said, "Well!" and stormed off.

"What did I say?" O'Connell asked himself, and resumed the inventory and maintenance of his arsenal.

The gunnysack was nearly repacked, and he was just examining one last weapon, a gunlike mini-crossbow, when he heard a movement, and sensed a presence. He rose slowly, stepped over his scattered weapons, then spun around and grabbed the eavesdropper out from behind a large crate.

Beni Gabor, last seen shutting the door on his "pal" back at Hamanaptra, smiled his weasel's smile; he wore what appeared to be black pajamas with a red fez, suspenders and sandals.

"You are alive!" Beni said, beaming unconvincingly, clasping his hands together. "It is a miracle! My friend Rick is alive!"

"No thanks to you, buddy." O'Connell shoved the point of the mini-crossbow in Beni's neck, and Beni backed up against the crate, hands in the air. "Why are you alive, anyway?"

"Probably managed it the same way you did, Rick—the camels of the dead milled around the ruins. When it was safe, I came out and helped myself to a couple. . . . Take that thing out of my neck, Rick, please."

"Why should I? Why shouldn't I kill your sorry ass?"

Uneasy as he was by the point at his throat, Beni could still grin—nastily. "Because . . . your lady friend might not appreciate the mess. She is attractive, in a schoolteacher way—but careful, Rick—you know the ladies are your weakness. . . ."

O'Connell shoved the point just a little harder into Beni's neck. "I should've known you were the one leading those raggedy-ass Americans. What scam do you have in mind this time? Ditch 'em in the middle of the desert, and leave 'em for your relatives, the vultures?"

Beni was sweating now. "An admirable plan, Rick, but unfortunately, impossible. These Americans may be filthy pigs, but they are smart filthy pigs."

O'Connell backed off the crossbow point, laughed harshly. "Half down, half on delivery, huh?"

Beni nodded glumly, rubbing his throat where the point had left its mark.

"That's the American way, pal," O'Connell said. "You'll have to deliver the goods—and climb over me to do it."

Beni gestured with open arms. "We should not compete, Rick—we're friends, comrades. . . ."

"Go to hell, you little weasel."

Beni's eyes glittered in the moonlight. "I've *been* to hell, Rick—and so have you. Treasure takes me back there;

what's your excuse? After all, greed isn't what makes you tick."

Below them, someone, a female someone, yelped.

O'Connell looked over the railing and saw Evelyn, who had been walking alongside where the barge was being towed, specifically near the paddock of camels and horses, moving away from a camel who was apparently craning his long neck onto the deck to have a nip at her. She yelped as the camel tried again, and scurried toward her cabin.

O'Connell returned his attention to Beni, who was grinning at him with narrow-eyed knowingness.

"Rick, Rick, Rick . . . the ladies, Rick. They'll be the death of you."

"Yeah. But what a way to go."

Beni didn't disagree with that. "So—we part friends? No hard feelings?"

"Naw. Good-bye, Beni."

"Good-bye? You mean, 'good night,' don't you?"

"No, I mean good-bye," O'Connell said, and he grabbed the little man by his pajamalike garments and chucked him over the side, where Beni went sailing and flailing and howling into the Nile, making quite a splash.

O'Connell picked up his gunnysack, and walked down the stairs to the lower deck, heading to his own cabin. Out on the Nile, Beni was treading desperately, his face distorted with rage.

His voice echoed across the water: "You will pay, Rick! Oh, how you will pay!"

O'Connell regarded Beni and his threats with mild surprise: He hadn't been aware the little bastard could swim.

That was when he noticed the four sets of footprints—very wet footprints—as if someone, four someones actually, had climbed up and over the railing from the river. The footprints trailed down the deck, and—O'Connell ascertained, with a glance over the side—a narrow skiff, tied up to the boat, awaited the return of the group that had secretly boarded the *Ibis*.

And O'Connell—seeing where these wet footsteps headed—dug into his gunnysack.

·❦ 7 ❧·

Midnight Swim

In the glow of a kerosene lamp on her nightstand, Evelyn Carnahan, who found the accommodations of her small cabin quite acceptable, was studying her reflection in the mirror of the dressing table, where she was seated, preparing for bed. The white nightgown only hinted at the shapeliness underneath, her arms and shoulders bare, the swell of her breasts providing the most telling evidence of her pulchritude, with its scoop neckline.

Evelyn did not think of herself as particularly attractive, or unattractive, for that matter: She had little interest in men. She had wanted to walk in her father's footsteps and, so, had chosen a career; she was a feminist—a New Woman.

But something was stirring within her, and it was the doing of that American cad O'Connell. He was impertinent and boorish and had simply the most divine blue eyes, and the way that lock of his hair hung over his forehead was just . . .

She smirked at herself, for such schoolgirlish feelings. But the warmth of that kiss, the soft sensual mouth of that ruffian, lingered in her sense memory. What was it he'd said at the prison? Maybe if she let her hair down she wouldn't be a total loss?

Unpinning her long brown hair, she gave her head a good shake, unleashing a torrent of tresses, which fell loose to her bare shoulders. She sat and brushed it and thought about O'Connell, and then scolded herself for doing so, then thought about him some more.

Distracted, she knocked several hairpins onto the floor and bent to pick them up. When she returned to her sitting position at the mirror, the reflection in it had changed.

Standing right behind her was a grotesque male intruder with a wicked-looking hook where a hand once had been, and flesh that wore the puzzlelike tattoos of an ancient sect thought lost to the sands of time and the desert. The hieroglyph markings could be seen everywhere skin was exposed: the narrow, angular face framed by a black sphinxlike headdress; his bare chest crisscrossed with leather straps; and even the muscular legs under the black kilt, whose waistband bore both dagger and, in a modern non sequitur, revolver.

Her surprise at having her cabin invaded was heightened by her instant awareness that her uninvited guest was a Medjai; but all of this registered in such an eyeblink that the intruder had slipped a moist palm over her mouth before she could scream, and in the mirror she could see her own widened eyes as the hook was raised, poised to strike.

But he did not strike.

He whispered, in a rough-edged voice made melodious by his accent: "The map! I will have the map. . . ."

Reflexively, her eyes went to the map, which lay spread out upon a table in the flickering glow of a candle nearby.

"Good, good . . . And the key? I will have the key."

Did he mean the puzzle box?

She would not give this up so easily, hidden under the bed as it was, the gold glint of it visible in the mirror at this moment—if one knew where to look for it. Evelyn met his eyes, in the mirror, shaking her head "no," shrugging her shoulders, feigning no knowledge.

"Tell me where the key is, or you will die."

She shook her head: no, no, no!

And hard dark eyebrows in a tattooed face lifted in a little shrug, and the hand with the hook drew back for its death blow.

The cabin door behind them exploded under a splintering kick, and there, in the mirror's reflection, was O'Connell!

O'Connell, a gun in either hand, his eyes tight, jaw firm, a bloody hero! If she hadn't loved him before, she certainly loved him now. . . .

"Hope I'm not interrupting you lovebirds," he said.

The impertinent cad!

The hooked Med-jai grabbed her by the shoulders, spinning her around, making a human shield of her, the point of his hook dimpling her throat.

For several endless moments, the standoff turned the two men and the woman into a frozen tableau promising violence. Then a candle flickered on the table, where the map lay spread out, and O'Connell whirled on a now open window, which had let in the candle-flickering breeze and allowed another of the warriors to lean in, with a revolver in hand, blasting away, O'Connell ducking as wood chips flew off the wall in a splintery shower.

Held captive by the hooked Med-jai, Evelyn watched in horrified amazement as O'Connell calmly aimed at the warrior in the window and shot twice. The warrior caught both bullets in the chest and fell awkwardly over the sill, firing as he died, one of his wild shots shattering the kerosene lantern on the wall, which was almost instantly engulfed in flames.

Her captor had been watching this with as much surprise and amazement as Evelyn had, and the point of his hook drew away from her throat just enough that she could risk reaching out to pluck the burning candle from the table beside her, which she did, and, in an action so quick and savage she could barely believe she'd done it, Evelyn jammed that candle, flame and all, back over her shoulder, into the Med-jai's face, cramming it into his right eye, and he screeched in pain, pain that so overwhelmed him, he released his grip upon her, and she bolted away, into

O'Connell's grasp, the room around them a crackling inferno of blue and orange and yellow flames.

Then Evelyn felt herself being yanked into the hallway, and O'Connell, gun in one hand, the other one stuck in his belt, pulled the splintered door shut, and began dragging her along, but she stopped and said, "Wait!"

He frowned at her. "What?"

She pulled free of him, and pointed back where fingers of smoke were finding their way around the closed door of her cabin. "The map! We need the map!"

"Relax, baby," he grinned at her, and tapped his forehead with a finger. "*This* is the map."

"How very reassuring."

"You're welcome for saving your hide."

And he grabbed her hand again, and pulled her along; but she pulled free again and said, *"Wait!"*

"Jesus! What?"

"The puzzle box is still in there! It's under the bed!"

"Why, you want to go back in after it?"

"The Med-jai was after the map and the box!"

"The what?"

"Mr. O'Connell . . ."

"No time for this, baby," he said, and grabbed her hand again, and pulled her along.

"I'm not your 'baby'!"

He ignored that. "We better find your brother. . . . There's at least two more of those bastards aboard."

"And if I'm a target," she breathed, "so is Jonathan!"

They headed out on deck, and did not see behind them, coming down the hallway from the other direction, the man they were looking for: Jonathan Carnahan.

Jonathan was saying, "Good lord, smoke!", which he had smelled, then saw, leeching out from around the door to his sister's cabin, a ruptured door that seemed to be somewhat the worse for wear.

What the hell was happening?

Still, he managed to shove it open, and did not realize that in so doing, he had slammed the door into the upturned buttocks of the hooked Med-jai, who—risking his life in the burning room, but pledged to fulfill his purpose—had been on his hands and knees, searching for the golden puzzle box.

"Evy!" Jonathan cried, looking in, seeing nothing but flames, relieved that his sister was nowhere in sight; then he noticed the golden glint of the puzzle box, just under the bed. . . .

Braving the smoke and flames, he had just bent down to pick up the artifact, when tattooed fingers snatched it from his grasp.

"I say," Jonathan began crossly, "that's mine. . . ."

And Jonathan looked around to see a hideous Arab warrior with a hook for a hand and melted-wax covering his face, whose back was on fire, like a peacock trailing its feathers.

Summoning courage he didn't know he had, Jonathan snatched the puzzle box back, and the hooked warrior howled in rage, weaving in pain. The warrior, somewhat blindly, began clutching at the pistol in his waistband, and Jonathan, who often had to be told when to leave a party, needed no prompting on this occasion.

He scrambled out of the burning cabin, bullets chewing up the hallway woodwork where he'd just been, and ran out onto the deck, portside, looking for his sister.

But Evelyn and O'Connell were on the starboard side of the *Ibis*, where the walkway along the rail was clogged with screaming, hysterical passengers—the fire hadn't spread yet, but panic certainly had.

And it had spread as well to the animals on the paddock of the barge lashed alongside the steamer. The camels and horses were restless, to say the least; the former braying and stirring, the latter whinnying, rearing, kicking, bumping against the locked gate between the *Ibis* deck and the barge. The second-class and third-class passengers were already abandoning ship, leaping into the water, swimming for shore.

"We have to find Jonathan!" Evelyn said, as O'Connell embraced her, keeping her away from the shoving, pushing crowd.

"Head for the bow," O'Connell said, nodding in that

80

direction. "He was in the bar, last I saw him!"

A gunshot cracked the air, notching the wall just over Eveyln's head, showering them with wood chips; she gasped, and O'Connell pulled her down, then pivoted and returned fire, toward the stern of the ship, where another of those tattooed devils was firing a revolver at them, more wood fragments exploding over and around them.

Then one of the Med-jai's bullets caught a kerosene lantern, hanging on the wall just above and to their left, and the wall was soon dancing with orange and blue flame.

And the Med-jai was advancing down the deck toward them, training his revolver on them.

"We're sitting ducks!" O'Connell said, glancing frantically around as he reloaded a revolver. Behind them, toward the bow, the walkway was jammed with panicking passengers, shouting, and coughing with the spreading smoke.

There was nowhere to go, not even into the water, with those flared-nostril, kicking, penned-up animals between them and the shore.

Suddenly O'Connell grinned tightly, and fired his revolver—not toward their assailant, but at the barge beside them!

Evelyn thought him mad till he fired again and she realized what he was doing: shooting the lock off the paddock gate!

The horses, driven even wilder by the gunfire, kicked the gate open and began charging forward, onto the deck, O'Connell grabbing onto that gate and guiding the stampede toward the warrior, who screamed in terror and then in pain as the hooves pounded over him, crushing him, pulping him.

The flames were stampeding, too, racing up and down and across the walls, the upper deck consumed by flames, the awning blazing like a banner in the night.

More passengers were starting to leap into the Nile, swimming for the nearest shore; the way to the bow was no longer clogged by the panicking mob. O'Connell slung his gunnysack over his shoulder and guided Evelyn in that direction.

They were not aware that Jonathan was stranded, portside, caught by three Americans who blocked the way, standing there like three idiots at a target range, blasting everything in sight, their Egyptologist professor cowering behind them like a frightened schoolboy. Their target—another of those villains, down at the bow—was returning fire, no more successfully than the Americans.

"Bloody wild West show," Jonathan muttered, pondering whether to go over the side and swim for shore. He didn't witness the Americans finally succeeding, blowing their quarry over the railing, as Jonathan—still hoping to find his sister—had turned to see if he might go back in the other direction . . .

. . . and a flaming man was advancing upon him!

A flaming man with wild eyes and a hook for a hand raised to do him no bloody good at all. . . .

"Duck!" someone cried.

Jonathan ducked and a volley of bullets flew over his head, as the gunfire of the Americans hit the hooked flaming warrior like a firing squad's barrage, sending him toppling over the railing, into the Nile, where the fire finally went out.

"Wild West indeed!" Jonathan exulted. "Jolly good show!"

But the Americans were looking at him with wide eyes, terrified suddenly, as if Jonathan were one of those dreadful scoundrels, and then the blighters were running off toward the bow like scared puppies, only their footsteps sounded like a bloody stampede of horses.

And then Jonathan realized those were indeed hoofbeats, accompanied by frenzied whinnying, and turned to see the wild beasts pounding toward him, toward the bow, and he ran.

The Americans had turned the corner and leaped from the starboard bow, but Jonathan dove in, from portside, wondering what had become of his poor sister and that American chap.

• • •

On the starboard side, where O'Connell had come upon more passengers diving into the drink, he and Evelyn bumped into their unwanted business partner, the warden of Cairo prison, waiting his turn. O'Connell turned his back to the man.

"Swim to the far bank," he told Evelyn.

Everyone else was swimming to the near bank.

"Why?" she asked.

"You *can* swim, can't you?"

"Certainly, if the occasion calls for it."

Around them were billowing smoke, leaping flames, screams, shouts, pounding hoofbeats, braying, whinnying.

"I'm going to go out on limb here," he said, "and say the occasion calls for it."

He picked her up in his arms, as if he were the groom and she the bride and the railing of the ship their threshold.

"Put me down!" she demanded.

He did—pitching her over the side, into the Nile. Then he dove in after her.

The water was freezing; it shocked Evelyn, chilling her body to the bone even as her mind wondered how a desert river could be so blasted cold. She dogpaddled for a moment, gasping for breath, looking about her, seeing all those people, and animals, too, swimming for the near shore.

But O'Connell was stroking toward the far shore.

She followed him, and soon was clambering up onto the riverbank, pleased to see her brother standing there with O'Connell, both of them dripping wet, shivering with cold—but alive.

Her nightgown clung to her, and it did not occur to her that her every physical attribute was on display, at least not until she saw O'Connell standing there, with his mouth open, river water running down his face like drool, as he drank in the sight of her.

Wringing out her nightgown, she said, "Get your mind out of the gutter! We've lost everything, you fool! All of our equipment, our tools . . ."

"Not everything," O'Connell said, and nodded toward his gunnysack at his feet.

Then Warden Hassan came crawling out of the water, like a big fish beaching itself.

"I took your advice about swimming to this bank," the warden said, grinning greenly.

"I'm so glad you didn't drown," O'Connell said.

The flaming *Ibis* was drifting up the Nile with the current, going back the way they'd come, already starting to sink. Across the way, the passengers had made it to shore, and a skinny man in a red fez and black shirt and pants was working with the Americans to round up the horses and camels; the animals were tired and wet and easily tamed.

"We lost the map," Evelyn told Jonathan, glumly.

"Ah, but we still have this," her brother said, and withdrew from his shirt the gold puzzle box. "Did I panic? I should say not."

"Nice going," O'Connell said to him, and Jonathan beamed at the praise.

"Hey, Rick!" a voice called, echoing across the river.

It was the skinny man in the red fez.

"Who is that dreadful person?" Evelyn asked O'Connell.

"Oh, he's my pal," O'Connell said dryly, as dryly as a soaking wet man could manage, anyway. "We go way back—clear to Hamanaptra."

"Oh, dear. He must be working with the Americans!"

"Yeah. Another legionnaire deserter. Maybe we can talk the warden into hanging him for us."

Beni was dancing about, calling out, "Hey, Rick! Looks to me like *we* got all the camels and horses!"

This was followed by a peal of obnoxious laughter, as high-pitched as it was unpleasant.

"Maybe so, Beni!" O'Connell called back. "But looks to me like *you* are on the wrong side of the river!"

The skinny man in the fez stopped dancing in midstep. He looked up at the stars and shook his head, and his fists, then started angrily kicking the sand, cursing in several languages, a display both impressive and ridiculous.

"What now?" Evelyn asked O'Connell.

"We try to keep warm till morning. You do know how to cuddle, don't you?"

She smirked at him, arms folded over her breasts. "When the occasion calls for it."

·❪ 8 ❫·

Camel Jockeys

The endless, sunbaked Sahara stretched out before them, a frying pan for the little camel caravan to sizzle in. O'Connell led the way, with Evelyn just behind him, keeping up nicely, trailed by her brother and the Cairo prison's absentee warden, Gad Hassan.

O'Connell found the great desert, with its sweeping vistas shimmering in the sunlight, an awe-inspiring, intimidating landscape, not be taken lightly. Right now they were moving over hard, sandy terrain littered with stones—plains not unlike the American Southwest, dotted with the Egyptian version of sagebrush, *vissigia*. But a day ahead awaited seas of fine, shifting sands, with the peaks and valleys of dunes, where at any moment the scorching winds called "siroccos" could sweep in, suffocating man and beast.

They had purchased these four, flea-bitten camels at the trading post of an oasis several miles inland, after their rescue by Bedouins who had seen the fire against the sky. Its date palms thriving along a shallow stream, the oasis was a site of bustling Bedouin commerce, and O'Connell had spent much of the night dickering over the price of the camels, some rudimentary camp equipment, and food supplies (dates, cakes and mint tea).

Jonathan, whose cash supply had survived the swim, complained about the price of the four "mangy beasts," until O'Connell pointed out that the alternative was to give the Bedouin trader Jonathan's sister.

"Tempting proposition, what?" Jonathan had said.

And O'Connell had said, "Tempting indeed," but in reference to the sight of Evelyn Carnahan emerging from a tent wearing her new dress: a beautifully sewn blue Bedouin gown that both flowed over, and clung to, her womanly curves.

At first they had trekked through the green valley of the Nile, breathing in the sweet perfume of grass and clover wafted to them by a bracing desert wind. But only a few hours later, their camels were shuffling over the flat, stone-littered desert floor, ground dry with a centuries-old thirst unquenched by rain.

Jonathan rode well enough; though a trained equestrian, he obviously resented the ungainly gait of the camels.

"Filthy buggers," he said to O'Connell. "They smell, they bite, they spit. Never seen the like."

Apparently Jonathan hadn't noticed the warden, just behind him, gobbling up dates, spitting out their seeds, unheedful of the flies buzzing about his head.

"Well," Evelyn said, "I think they're adorable."

O'Connell figured she was referring to the camels, not the warden and his flies.

Evelyn seemed to be enjoying herself, her skills as a horsewoman serving her well. She jogged up on her beast, bobbing along next to O'Connell, and said, "Don't mind Jonathan. He's just a trifle peevish. You see, his bourbon supply is at the bottom of the Nile somewhere."

O'Connell squinted at the blinding bright sun. "We're all likely to get 'peevish,' before this journey's over."

"Well, personally I think this is lovely countryside," she said, chipper. "Doesn't it just make you wonder what all the fuss is about our so-called civilization? I mean, here we are in the midst of this barren immensity. Doesn't it just put humility into your soul, and purge the vanity from your heart? Doesn't it make you ponder that the great vastness of the desert is like the universe, and we are but tiny grains of sand?''

''I was just going to say that.''

She smiled, her chin crinkling cutely. ''You're making fun of me, Mr. O'Connell.''

''Why don't you call me 'Rick'?''

''Why should I?''

''It's my name.''

She looked down her nose at him, reining back on her camel, to fall back in place behind O'Connell. ''But then Mr. O'Connell, I should have to allow you to call me Evelyn.''

He grinned back at her. ''Or worse yet—Evy.''

And she had granted him a tiny smile.

Perhaps an hour later, however, she and her camel sidled up alongside O'Connell again, and now her cheery attitude had darkened, her brow tightly troubled.

''I've been reflecting on last night's unfortunate incident,'' she said. ''Those terrible men on the boat . . .''

''The ones with tattoos, you mean?''

''It's nothing to make light of. I believe they may have been attempting to halt us in our . . . quest.''

''How so?''

''Their tattoos were ancient markings indicating they belonged to a sect known as the Med-jai, a cult thought lost in antiquity.''

''What sort of cult?''

''Well, that's why I suspect they had hoped to prevent us from reaching Hamanaptra. The Med-jai were said to be the guardians of the City of Dead. Little more is known of them.''

''So you think we might run into some more of these jokers?''

''That's difficult to predict, Mr. O'Connell—after all, the ones we saw last night were the first, to my knowledge, ever seen in the twentieth century . . . or the nineteenth, for that matter, or the eighteenth, or—''

"I get your point."

As the afternoon wore on, he detected her spirits waning further; but then so were his. It was tough going, and the endless ride on the bumpy road that was the back of every camel drained the riders' energy, and the caravan talked little amongst themselves.

O'Connell knew his tiny brood was fading. Late in the afternoon, he spotted a cluster of palms up ahead and—as soon as he'd convinced himself it wasn't a mirage—directed them to set up camp there for the night.

The flaming crimson ball that was the setting sun threw streaks of red and purple across the landscape, until the eerie haze of dusk banished them from view. The furnace of the day shut off, suddenly, and coolness descended as they made camp, at first crisp, then downright cold. An old well provided fresh water, drawn in a goat's skin at the end of a rope draped over a worn beam, which they hitched to O'Connell's camel, pulling the water pouch up by driving the camel away from the well.

"I want you all to get some sleep, now," O'Connell told them, as they gathered about the small fire he'd made of palm tree twigs and branches, eating dates and cakes and sipping the syrup-sweet minty tea. "We're going to rise again around one a.m., so we can travel without that sun beating down on us."

This meant only a few hours of sleep, but there was no argument: The idea of traveling under the stars and moon sounded inviting after so much time under the blazing sun.

The supplies purchased from the Bedouins included four little tents with four camel's hair pallets and camel's hair blankets that made for fairly comfortable sleeping conditions, though—even with the fire, which O'Connell kept going—the desert cold was brutal. O'Connell had wrangled four burnooses from the Bedouins, and the hooded robes made excellent sleeping wear in the chill climate.

Amused as he'd been by Evelyn's grandiose ramblings about the desert and the universe, O'Connell knew she was on to something. That was the lure of the desert: a sense that in the vastness of eternity, your life was meaningless, which offered a kind of freedom, a release from the need to pursue gain and glory. Under the star-studded purple of the desert sky, a man could reflect on such things.

At least he could have, if not for the thunderlike snoring of the warden. Tossing and turning, Jonathan grumbled about it, then began to snore, himself. O'Connell, amused as he lay in his tent, was almost asleep when Evelyn crawled in with him.

"I'm so sorry," she said. "But it's so bitterly cold. Would you mind, terribly?"

"Mind?"

"Cuddling. Conditions do call for it, once again."

And he held her in his arms, and spent at least an hour thinking about kissing her, lost in the sweet softness of holding her close, before he finally drifted off to sleep, not knowing Evelyn had been entertaining similar desires.

He woke just before one, roused Evelyn, bidding her return to her tent before the others awoke, and misunderstood; and she nodded, saying she quite agreed. Soon he had roused them all, advised them to leave their burnooses on for the night travel, and they pulled up stakes and mounted their camels for a ride over sands turned ivory by moonlight.

The hot tan world of the Sahara had turned cool and blue under the stars. O'Connell, as always, led the way, with Evelyn beside him, their camels loping along; behind them, side by side, were Jonathan and Warden Hassan, both sound asleep, bobbing like the heads-on-springs of carnival toys, their snoring echoing across the sands, their camels following the lead of O'Connell's and Evelyn's.

O'Connell kept an eye on the young woman, still drowsy from so short a rest, and when she slowly began to slide off her saddle, he reached over, caught her, gently pushing her back up onto her mount, without even waking her. He took advantage of her slumber to study her, to bask in the beauty of her heart-shaped face, with its delicately carved features, the fullness of her lips. . . .

Beni had been right: Women were his weakness. But this was different, somehow; he was not viewing Evelyn with an adventurer's eye, seeking conquest. He was facing the worst danger that could befall a soldier of fortune: a woman he could love.

Then his eyes rose to a distant ridge where he detected another danger: a group of riders on horseback, dark-garbed Arabs, who seemed to be following along with them, keeping pace. They were too far away for him to be sure, and with the moonlight painting the desert ivory and blue, it was hard to be sure . . .

. . . but he could swear the riders' hands, their faces, were the tattooed flesh of the warriors who'd attacked on the *Ibis* last night. Could these desert shadows be Evelyn's fabled Med-jai?

Of course, they could be desert nomads of any number of tribes, none of which were a threat to the little caravan. As if bearing this theory out, the riders disappeared from the ridge and, as the early morning hours edged their way toward daylight, O'Connell saw nothing of them again.

The coolness of night began to disappear before the sun had shown its face, and as the heat of the coming day began to assert itself, the four lone camel riders stopped to stow away their burnooses and sip some water. Jonathan and Hassan took this opportunity to bicker, accusing each other of snoring, each denying his own guilt.

Soon the caravan was under way again, the dawning sun hiding behind an immense sand dune, alongside which their camels loped.

Eveyln fell in beside him. "What are you thinking?" she asked him.

"I'm thinking we're almost there."

"How can you be sure? One stretch of desert looks much like any other stretch of desert."

"Not if you pay attention to the road signs." And he nodded off to his left, and her eyes followed his lead to what at first glance appeared to be some sort of rock formation; then she realized what she was looking at: bleached bones. Human bones, skeletons sticking out of the sand, haphazardly, looking as if they were trying to crawl up out of desert graves.

"Oh my dear," she said.

"Bloody hell!" Jonathan said. "Who do you suppose those poor blighters were?"

"Other seekers of the City of Dead," Warden Hassan said; he was shivering, though the chill of the night had long since gone.

A wooden sign on a post had been stuck in the sand, in the midst of the boneyard, bearing Arabic script.

"What does that say?" Jonathan asked his sister. " 'Keep off the grass'?"

Evelyn flashed her brother a withering look. "It says, 'Go back—stay away.' "

Jonathan shrugged. "I was fairly close, at that."

"That was recently placed," O'Connell said of the sign. Had it not been, the shifting sands might well have covered the freshly painted warning. "Advice from your Med-jai friends, perhaps?"

Evelyn said nothing, but her expression was grave. Then she turned toward a rumbling sound just behind them.

The rumbling quickly grew to a thunderous pounding of hooves as, around the far end of that looming sand dune which still blotted out the sun, came three dozen riders, kicking up their own sandstorm.

Evelyn, next to O'Connell, reached for his sleeve. "The Med-jai!" she cried.

"No," O'Connell said. "Those are native diggers— that's my pal Beni, in the lead."

"With those blasted Americans," Jonathan added.

And indeed it was: the three American roughnecks on horseback, their mousy professor of Egyptology on a mule, and Beni—leading the expedition, the man who, after all, knew the way to Hamanaptra—was astride a camel, a considerably better groomed one than those of O'Connell's group.

Beni reined his camel to a stop and the expedition drew up behind him, like cavalry waiting to attack. Perhaps a hundred feet separated the larger American party from the little caravan.

"Good morning, Rick!" Beni called. "What a small desert this must be, for friends to run into each other like this!''

O'Connell just nodded. He kicked his camel, gently, and his group began to edge along the mountainous dune, toward the rising sun which had not quite shown itself.

Beni nodded at the Americans, and they—and the native diggers behind them—followed along with O'Connell's group at this leisurely pace.

That arrogant bastard, Henderson, called out, ''Hey, O'Connell? We still got a bet, right? First one to the city wins five c's?''

O'Connell again nodded, but his attention was fixed upon the endless horizon ahead, where the sky over the sandy ridge was lightening.

''What the hell are we doin'?'' the stoic Daniels demanded of Beni.

This was a conversation O'Connell and his group could not hear.

''Patience, my good *barat'm*,'' Beni said, ''patience.''

Burns, squinting behind his wirerim glasses, asked Beni, ''On this terrain, which mount is faster? Camels or horses?''

''Camels.''

Daniels leaned in. ''Wanna make a hundred clams, Beni boy?''

''Clams?''

''Smackeroos. Bucks. Simoleons. Dollars.''

''Ah yes—a rose by any other name.''

''Well, help us win that bet, and you can have your hundred roses. You be our jockey in this little camel race.''

During this consultation between Beni and his employers, O'Connell was having his own tête-à-tête with Evelyn.

''You're a fine rider,'' he told her.

''Why thank you,'' she said, surprised.

''Obviously you're a skilled horsewoman, or you wouldn't sit a camel so well.''

''Thank you, Mr. O'Connell. Why do you . . . ?''

''Get ready.''

''For what?''

His eyes tightened and he almost smiled at her. ''We're about to be shown the way.''

93

The crimson sun was finally revealing itself, rising to flood the sands with its rays, yet a dark shape was rising too, revealed by the sun, the silhouette of a mountain, its peak lopped off . . . no—a volcano, older than antiquity, dead as the desert sands, but as unmistakable, and as majestic a landmarker as the gods . . . or God . . . had ever provided.

O'Connell glanced over at Beni; and Beni glanced over at him. As the sole survivors of the legionnaire expedition that had followed their colonel's map to this volcanic guidepost, they shared a moment, exchanged grins . . .

. . . and then simultaneously swatted their respective camels, shouting, *"Tuk-tuk-tuk!"*

As O'Connell and Beni raced toward the looming landmark, the other riders blinked a few times, gathered their wits, and took off after them. The horses were magnificent Arabian steeds, but on these sands were no match for the mangy graceless camels.

One of the camel riders, Jonathan Carnahan, amazed and delighted by this turn of events, jeered back at the Americans and damn near fell off his perch; but O'Connell and Beni were still way out ahead, neck and neck, though Evelyn was coming up fast, hair streaming in the wind.

Beni, his face clenched in a terrible smile, whipped his camel, then suddenly, viciously, used that whip on O'Connell! The air cracked twice as the whip lashed out for O'Connell in Beni's attempt to knock him from his camel. But on Beni's third try, O'Connell reached out, grasped the whip and jerked it, yanking a screaming Beni right off his saddle, slamming him to the sand in a tumbling pile, in the direct path of the oncoming camels and horses.

Stumbling awkwardly at first, then dancing nimbly, Beni got out of the way as Jonathan and all the others stampeded past him in a cloud of dust and sand, leaving him weaving, wheeling, wheezing, coughing, cursing.

O'Connell glanced beside him and saw that Evelyn was right alongside, keeping a hard, steady pace, her eyes glittering, her smile endless, her joy palpable. The volcano loomed next to them, guiding them into the valley where, up ahead, the fabled ruins of Hamanaptra beckoned.

Her laughter, her look of triumph, made him smile, and he told himself he liked this girl, when of course he already loved her. Then she bolted out ahead of him, charging toward the stone ramp up to the pylons of the temple.

And that's when he remembered the sand dune just beyond the gates of the temple, and shouted, "Evelyn! Slow down! There's a really big—"

But that was all he got out before she flew between those pylons and her camel threw on its brakes and she went flying, ass-over-teakettle, landing in an unceremonious heap in the sand dune.

"Never mind," O'Connell said, as he drew up alongside her, where she sat up, stunned, spitting sand.

He climbed down and helped her dust off—she had sand in her hair, her eyes, she was really quite a mess—and soon Jonathan and the warden had arrived on the scene, followed by the Americans and their diggers, sitting astride their horses, eyes wide with the wonder of the Hamanaptra ruins.

O'Connell gestured about him, saying, "Welcome to the City of the Dead, boys—by the way, you owe the young lady five hundred bucks."

·❨ 9 ❩·

What a Woman Knows

Within the ruins of the temple complex of Hamanaptra, uninhabited since the days of Seti the First, the rival expeditions set up neighboring towns of tents. Dozens of stray camels roamed the ruins, milling listlessly, buzzing with flies, dusty backpacks and old saddlebags slung over their humps. Evelyn had noticed O'Connell's stricken expression as he watched the beasts wander aimlessly about.

"Where did those poor creatures come from?" she inquired of him. How dashing he looked in brown neckerchief, his white shirt crisscrossed with leather shoulder holsters, chinos, leather boots.

"My fellow legionnaires," he said softly. His sky-blue eyes bore a haunted cast. "The vultures have taken their flesh, the sands their bones . . . but their camels are still waiting for their masters to return."

The American expedition, with its two dozen native diggers and full gear, had a large-scale operation going, Dr. Chamberlin setting up worktables, overseeing the turbaned, gowned diggers, with their hoes and picks and rakes, in hauling the baskets of rock and dirt from an area around several massive columns with hieroglyphs the Egyptologist considered significant. The three American fortune hunters themselves weren't doing any of the drudge work. They just sat in front of their tents, asking questions of their helpful guide, Beni, who sat smoking tobacco from a hookah.

O'Connell had dropped by to wish his competitors luck, and reported to Evelyn the following dispensation of advice by Beni: "If you get bit by a snake, just *X* the wound with a knife, suck out the venom and spit it away."

Burns, the squinty man with the wire-rim bifocals, had asked, "What if you can't reach the wound yourself?"

"That is what friends are for."

"Jesus! What if I get bit in the ass?"

"Well, *barat'm*, if the friend you come to is Beni— you're going to die."

O'Connell found this story endlessly amusing, though Evelyn could only muster a polite smile at best.

The rival groups were keeping their distance, and the Americans did not seem to consider the smaller, rival dig to be much competition. Dr. Chamberlin had been overheard saying, "They're led by a woman—what does a woman know?"

This Neanderthal attitude suited Evelyn just fine—it prevented interference and sabotage; and, anyway, she had her own ideas about where to dig.

Within the open shrine from which the upper portion of a massive, time-decayed statue of Anubis poked from the sands, a crevice in the rock had opened, tentatively revealing what appeared to be either a cavern, or a carved-out chamber, in the darkness below.

On her knees, wishing she had apparel other than the Bedouin gown, Evelyn examined the crevice and looked up at the three ignorant male faces hovering about her.

"This is an entrance," she said.

"That's a hole in the ground," O'Connell said. "It's not man-made. . . . You don't have to be an archaeologist or damn geologist to know that."

"You're right, it's not man-made, but men made use of this as an entrance," she said, brushing away sand from a shining surface that suddenly caught the sun and momentarily blinded her brother, Jonathan, who said, "Bloody hell! What is that?"

"A mirror," O'Connell said, eyes tightening. "One really old mirror . . ."

The small round mirror in its ancient hieroglyph-embossed bronze frame was affixed to the rocky edge on the left side of an area where the crevice widened enough to accommodate a man—or woman.

Standing, Evelyn said, "This was a shrine, and this crevice was no doubt covered by a floor of stone or perhaps wood. Understand that the pharaohs took advantage of natural rock formations, caves, and what have you, but they then dug their burial vaults out of solid rock. I believe that below us is a subterranean city, of caverns, yes, but also of chambers cut from solid rock."

She instructed her meager digging team, with its handful of tools purchased at the Bedouin trading post, to seek more of the mirrors along the lip of the crevice; within an hour, half a dozen of the ancient mirrors had been uncovered—on either side.

"What the hell are they for?" O'Connell said, brushing himself off.

"Ancient Egyptian lighting system." She moved along the crevice, angling the mirrors to catch sunlight, just guessing about their positioning, but excited nonetheless. "If I'm right in my educated estimations, you should soon see for yourselves."

"Ready to go down there?" O'Connell said.

"Please."

He began to tie ropes around a nearby pillar.

"According to the Bembridge scholars," she said, as her brother and the warden and the dashing adventurer listened with rapt attention, "somewhere within the statue of Anubis is a secret compartment . . . which may conceal *The Book of Amun Ra.*"

O'Connell, heavy hemp ropes affixed to the pillar, tossed its trailing coils down into the darkness of the crevice. He slung on his backpack; in his waistband were the wooden shafts of a pair of torches whose canvas nubs, though dry, were thoroughly soaked in kerosene.

"I'll signal with the torch when it's safe," he said. "I don't want to yell and alert the other team."

"Keen thinking, old man," Jonathan said.

Pausing at the edge of the crevice, O'Connell reached around into his backpack and withdrew something, which he tossed to Evelyn.

She caught it—a brown leather pouch about the size of a small book—and before she could ask, he said, "Little something I, uh . . . borrowed from my fellow Americans . . . when I dropped by to wish 'em luck."

He grinned at her, and—holding on to the rope with leather-gloved hands—jumped into the crevice, rappelling down.

"What a lovely present," she said softly, examining the gleaming archaeologist's tools that filled every compartment of the pouch.

Soon the orange waving signal of the lighted torch below told them he'd found his footing, and—at Jonathan's bidding, and after an endless *after you, no, after you* exchange—the sweat-beaded, wide-eyed warden went down the rope first.

Jonathan smiled at his sister, saying, "I guess if the pillar supported *his* weight, we're safe enough," and went on down.

Finally Evelyn, in her flowing gown, descended hand over hand into the spooky darkness, wishing more than ever she were in trousers. Her sandaled feet slipped when she touched down, and she flopped to her bottom, rather rudely.

As O'Connell crouched to help her up, his torch gave a quick tour of the chamber they were in, unveiling straight smooth walls, decorated with geometric designs, figures of gods and goddesses, carved in bas-relief out of solid rock.

The beauty of it all made her gasp.

"My friends," she said in the sort of hushed tone generally reserved for church, "do you realize we are standing inside a room no human being has entered in over three thousand years?"

"Where's the treasure?" the warden asked.

"Help yourself to my share of the spiderwebs," O'Connell said, brushing some away.

He lighted the second torch and handed it to Jonathan, who said, "What *is* that awful smell?"

Evelyn sighed.

She was sharing this special moment, at the start of what might prove to be an archaeological find comparable to the tomb of King Tutankhamun, with a trio of utter barbarians.

Jonathan had some panic in his voice, his torch held high, wavering. "I tell you, it's the stench of death!"

The warden, leaning in at her brother's side, sniffed the air. "I don't smell anything."

Jonathan's nose twitched in the direction of the sweat-soaked warden, then he pulled away, smiling awkwardly. "False alarm . . . I say, Warden Hassan, would you mind keeping your distance? I'm feeling a trifle crowded."

Insulted, Hassan sneered and backed away.

Evelyn took O'Connell by the arm, saying, "Shine that torch over here," and soon she had found what she was seeking, a metal disk affixed to the stone wall. She brushed away the cobwebs and repositioned the disc on its tiny pedestal, aiming it at a ray of light that had fingered down from above, shining in from those ancient outer mirrors she had discovered, and done her best to calibrate. . . .

The ray of light hit the disk and bounced and every one of those outer mirrors pitched in, instantly illuminating the entire underground chamber.

"That *is* a neat trick," O'Connell said.

"God in heaven," Evelyn breathed, taking in the beautifully fashioned chamber—even its ceiling was carved! Her hand was raised as she followed the hieroglyphs, her mind translating a mile a minute. "It's a *Sah-Netjer!*"

"I was just about to say that, actually," Jonathan said, dryly.

"Which is what?" O'Connell asked her, as he brandished a torch made redundant in the mirror-lighted chamber.

"A preparation room," she said, nodding toward an

altar-like pedestal in the center of the room. "For entering the afterlife."

"Good lord," Jonathan said. "It's a bloody mummy factory!"

Evelyn turned to O'Connell. "I'm afraid I've lost my bearings. . . . Can you point me toward the statue of Anubis in the shrine?"

"Sure," O'Connell said, pointing his torch, inadvertently revealing a passageway. He gave her half a smile. "Shall we?"

She nodded primly, as if accepting an offer to dance. "Please."

The tunnel, one of a labyrinth of such passageways, was narrow, low-ceilinged, and infested with cobwebs. Crouching, clawing his way through, O'Connell led as they headed toward where the statue should be, until a chittering, scurrying sound from the walls froze them.

"Sounds like insects," Jonathan offered. He was just behind Evelyn, with the warden bringing up the rear.

O'Connell drew one of his revolvers, then, lighted torch in hand, pressed onward, the light from the ancient mirrors dissipating, the passageway growing darker and darker as they went deeper and deeper.

Finally they emerged into a cavern, not a man-made area at all, into which—either over time, or perhaps as a result of some ancient earthquake—the statue of Anubis had partially dropped. At any rate, there it was: the lower half of the massive idol.

A sound of movement—*Was it that same scurrying sound?* Evelyn wasn't sure—seemed to come from the other side of the statue.

O'Connell handed Evelyn his torch, whispered, "Stay close," and withdrew his other revolver.

The sound of movement increased. The warden was backpedaling, but Jonathan seemed to have found a new resolve, standing firm and tall, drawing a derringer from his jacket pocket.

Whatever it was, whoever they were, it was almost upon them! O'Connell lunged around the base of the statue . . .

. . . around which three sweaty figures lunged toward him: the American adventurers—each of whom had his own revolver in hand.

And now the three Americans were thrusting their revolvers at O'Connell, whose two revolvers were pointed at them in what promised to be an all-around massacre.

"Stop!" Evelyn cried. "Don't anyone do anything stupid!"

The two groups froze in a dangerous poised-for-action tableau around the base of the idol. Behind the three Americans were Beni, who also brandished a revolver, Dr. Chamberlin, and a wide-eyed group of turbaned native diggers.

"Jesus, O'Connell!" Henderson said, backing off. "You scared the heck out of us!"

"Watch your language," O'Connell said. "There's a lady present!"

A swagger in his shoulders, O'Connell stepped back, lowering his revolvers; the Americans backed away a step, too, also lowering—but not holstering—their weapons.

Burns, eyes narrowing behind his wire-rims, pointed toward Evelyn, saying, "Hey! That's my tool kit!"

Evelyn hugged the leather pouch to her breast, saying, "Impossible—it was a gift from a dear friend, upon my graduation!"

"I tell you, it's mine," Burns said, and he stepped forward.

O'Connell moved between them, and raised his revolver, training it directly between Burns's squinty eyes.

"You're mistaken," O'Connell said. "But if you'd like to borrow a bullet, just ask."

Burns swallowed, smiled nervously, backing away, saying, "You know, I believe you're right—my pouch was a darker brown. These eyes ain't what they used to be."

Evelyn moved up next to O'Connell, near the base of the statue, which she rested a hand against, in a gesture that pretended to be casual, but was actually proprietary.

"Well, gentlemen," she said sweetly, "do run along, now, and have a lovely day. My companions and I have considerable work to do."

Dr. Chamberlin, face tight with controlled rage, moved up between Henderson and Daniels, saying, "Young lady, this is our dig site. Would you kindly vacate these premises, at once?"

She glared at him, her arms folded. "I would think, Dr. Chamberlin, that I would not have to explain the protocol of such matters to so eminent an Egyptologist as yourself. To put it in terms your American confederates might understand—*finders keepers*!"

O'Connell and Beni exchanged glances, and the three American fortune hunters did the same.

Then all of the men raised their guns again—and the opposing groups were right back where they started, tension mounting, violence waiting for its chance to explode.

Daniels, the stoic brawny one, shared one of his rare comments, directed at O'Connell: "That there is our statue . . . *pal*."

"Funny," O'Connell said, smiling (and Evelyn didn't ever recall seeing such a terrible smile before), "I don't see your names carved on it anyplace . . . *chum*."

The skinny, mustached, fez-wearing guide of the Americans, Beni, was pointing his revolver at his former Foreign Legion comrade.

"Rick, Rick, Rick," Beni was saying, with a quietly crazed expression that seemed to speak of wanting the worst to happen in these awful close quarters, "such bad odds you're facing."

"I've faced worse, you little bastard," O'Connell said, "and you damn well know it."

On either side of the standoff, thumbs cocked weapons, making clicks that echoed in the chamber—tiny, huge echoes. . . .

Evelyn felt helpless, wanting to stop this, not knowing how, and her gaze dropped to her feet, where she noticed, for the first time, a wide crack in the floor. She lowered her torch, as inconspicuously as possible, toeing some pebbles into the crack . . . and faintly she heard them hit bottom.

There was a second chamber, below this one!

"Boys, boys, boys!" Evelyn said, in her most charming,

chiding manner. "Behave yourselves—this is an enormous site, and you are such a large group, and we are so pitifully small. . . . We'll concede this statue to you, and press on. After all, there's plenty here to go around."

The tension eased, but suspicion still clenched the faces of the Americans, in particular Dr. Chamberlin's.

Eveyln's laughter was gentle, if brittle, as she latched on to O'Connell's arm, guiding him away, back toward the passageway, giving him a pointed look that directed him to go along with this, as she said, "If we're going to play together, we must learn to share."

Moving backward, keeping their guns trained on Beni and the Americans, Jonathan and the warden followed after Evelyn and O'Connell.

Evelyn's group did not see the Americans lowering their weapons, but heard their derisive laughter and stinging remarks about cowardice.

O'Connell was scowling, burning under that manhood-questioning onslaught, but Evelyn clutched his arm, halting him (and her brother and the warden) in the passageway. She lifted a finger to her lips, in a shush gesture, and they listened.

The voice of the Egyptologist, Dr. Chamberlin, echoed down the passageway to them: "The next step is for me to translate these hieroglyphs—they should lead us to the location of Seti's treasure!"

These words made Evelyn smile, and she motioned for O'Connell and the others to follow her back to the embalming chamber, still illuminated by the mirror-ricocheting sun rays.

"Dr. Chamberlin apparently is ignorant of the secret compartment in that statue," she told the little group. "They're searching for Seti's treasure, not *The Book of Amun Ra*."

"That's what we should be seeking!" the warden said, frustration seizing his sweaty face.

"The book she's talking about," O'Connell told Hassan, "is made of solid gold—get it?"

The warden considered that piece of information, as Evelyn informed the group of the chamber she'd discovered, below the statue.

"Let's find our way down there," she said, and they headed back into the labyrinth, with O'Connell, torch in hand, in the lead. Within minutes, he had found a tunnel heading downward, and—after another crouching, cobweb-clawing journey—they were in a vast, spare, low-ceilinged chamber, similar to the embalming room, less elaborate in its hieroglyphs.

"This is another preparation chamber," Evelyn said, "probably for the mummification of figures less important than royalty."

"Why?" O'Connell asked, guiding his torch around the room. "Don't tell me they had different levels of mummy-making?"

"Three, actually—pharaohs and princesses got first-class treatment. I'd say this room prepared the dead to travel by, well . . . steerage, you might say. Bodies would be thoroughly cleaned and soaked in salt and stored in a chamber like this for seventy days. But it's good for us—we can reach this ceiling without much effort. According to my calculations—which have been pretty precise so far, you must admit—we should be right beneath the statue."

Jonathan looked upward at the cracked ceiling, grinning. "And when those damn dirty Yanks go to sleep . . . oh, sorry, O'Connell."

"You were talking about those other dirty damn Yanks."

"Precisely," Jonathan said. "When they've called it a day, we dig our way back up there, and steal that book right out from under their noses."

"They'll have guards posted, up top." O'Connell was pacing, his torch fanning the walls in orange and blue designs. "We can't risk being seen—we have to get that book without them knowing we have it—without them even knowing the damn thing exists. . . . Miss Carnahan—you *can* find that secret compartment, can't you?"

"Yes, unless Dr. Chamberlin gets lucky and stumbles onto it."

"Good, then we're all agreed," Jonathan said, and

pointed at the ceiling. "We've got digging tools. . . . Let's find a soft place and dig up through."

Evelyn frowned at her brother. "They just might notice a fresh hole in the floor, Jonathan."

O'Connell strode across the chamber, holding his torch high, examining the ceiling. "We can dig over here. . . . The stone is fragmentary, and it should take us up into one of the tunnels."

"Do we dare start digging?" Jonathan wondered. "Or will they hear us?"

"They expect us to be digging," O'Connell said, reaching into his backpack for chisels, "and we won't be right under them. . . . I say we get started."

"I'll take one of those things," Evelyn said eagerly, referring to the chisels, loving the adventure of this.

Jonathan hefted the tool, sighed, and said, "Physical labor finds me at last. . . . At least it doesn't smell so bad in here." And then he realized why, glancing all around him, adding, "I say! Where's our fragrant friend gone off to?"

O'Connell flashed his torch around the chamber.

Jonathan was right: The warden was gone.

·⟨ 10 ⟩·

Plenty to Go Around

Gad Hassan had not risen to the high position of warden of Cairo prison by following the initiative of other men, much less a woman. Hassan had had quite enough of Miss Evelyn Carnahan's leadership, particularly since the unveiled hussy had made it clear that finding the pharaoh's treasure was not her objective.

In this underground city of boundless treasure and endless possibilities of wealth, the lady librarian was looking for a book! Yes, yes, a book fashioned of gold; but when King Tut's tomb had been found, what *hadn't* been fashioned of gold?

The woman was right about one thing, that much the warden would grant her: There was plenty of plunder here to go around.

And so it was that Gad Hassan had slipped away, and gone crawling down a tunnel of his own choosing, with Jonathan Carnahan's torch in hand. His girth made passage difficult, but not impossible, and a few cobwebs were nothing to a man who dealt on a daily basis with the worst thieves and murderers in Arabia. What danger could await him that compared to even a slow day at Cairo prison?

Within minutes of the inception of Warden Hassan's private expedition, he had made his own mindboggling discovery. Wheeling about, he took it in, gape-mouthed, his torch lighting up another of these fabulous chambers, carved from rock by ancient engineers, walls straight and smooth and dancing with geometric decoration. Then his torch stopped, held in place, and Hassan stared as the firelight glittered upon the face of a mural that combined exquisite hieroglyphic storytelling with embedded jewels. . . .

The warden, awash in greed and self-satisfaction, withdrew a pocket knife and began to pry the purple stones from the mural. Had Evelyn Carnahan been present—the woman of whom his recent thoughts had been so contemptuous—she could have told Hassan that these were only semiprecious amethyst quartz stones, and not really worthy of his effort, certainly not of defacing so elaborate and unusual a mural.

Evelyn would also have pointed out the mural's bizarre subject matter, an image that the warden was standing too close to perceive. If he had noticed, superstitious man that he was, the warden might have continued on in his treasure hunting, and let this be, this mural depicting an ancient Egyptian priest covered in scarabs, screaming in pain as the deadly dung beetles consumed his flesh.

Hassan dropped the first pried-loose amethyst into a pouch on his belt, then began carving away at the wall, loosening another. It was an awkward one-handed procedure, as he must do his work by the light of the torch in his other hand.

But he repeated this process, again and again, forehead gleaming with jewels of perspiration, his eyes glimmering with greed as he murmured to himself a song of riches and wine and beautiful women, a hymn to his own resourcefulness. He did not notice one of the amethysts missing the pouch and dropping, almost silently, to the sand-dusted stone floor at his sandaled feet.

Nor did he notice the scarab-shaped jewel begin to glow, to pulse, to transform, as something within it began to wake and wiggle and wriggle, as if the amethyst were a cocoon.

The warden's eyes were fixed upon the latest jewel he was chiseling loose, and could not be bothered with the sight of the amethyst at his feet splitting open, and a living scarab beetle scurrying out.

The hideous black bug moved as if with a purpose, as if doing the bidding of some unknown, unseen presence that sent it nestling, burrowing inside the leather sandal of the man self-contentedly prying at the face of the mural, muttering his own praises.

That muttering, those praises, ended abruptly, as the warden felt the sharp bite—not a sting, but a bite, more like a small animal than an insect—and the sensation was a burning one, as if hot lava had been injected into him with a needle, but hot lava with gnashing, hungry teeth. He began to scream, a scream of fear and agony that accompanied his every action that followed. He dropped his knife and his torch and clawed at his trousers, as the bug—somehow he knew it was a bug—crawled up his left pantleg, but no, not up the pantleg, *inside* his leg, burrowing up in his flesh, sending searing pain along the way of its excavation route.

His screaming was coming in shorter bursts now, gasps of anguish and terror, as he felt the bug making its steady, swift way up across his groin; he ripped at his shirt, popping buttons, and up the rise of his belly it came, a moving lump under the skin, and then down the hill and up under the forest of his hairy chest, like a mole rooting.

Clawing and scratching at it did no good; the bug's progress was both steady and inexorable, and his screams turned to whimpers and tears as he felt the bug furrowing up the tender flesh of his throat, and then, under his chin, it disappeared, no longer a presence just under his skin, but tunneling up inside his head.

For a man of the warden's size, the insane dance he began to perform was quite nimble; and there was an eerie music to the ascending and descending nature of his renewed screaming, as he left the torch behind, and his pocket knife, and the jewels he'd plundered, abandoned in that chamber, as he pranced into the darkness of the labyrinthian tunnels, in the company of his unseen dancing partner.

● ● ●

The warden's screams were not heard by the American expedition, who were still gathered around the base of the statue of Anubis. Dwarfed by his burly partners, Dr. Chamberlin stood staring at the base, a hand on his chin. These men of action were frustrated by their dependence on this man of science, of scholarship, and Chamberlin was aware, at every moment, of their volatility.

Still, some matters could not be rushed.

"Well," Henderson said impatiently, "is there something in the base of that thing or not?"

Using a small sable-hair paintbrush, the Egyptologist gently cleared away sand from the seams he'd discovered, seams that could well indicate a secret compartment.

"The hieroglyphs indicate that a valuable treasure is at the feet of Anubis," Chamberlin said slowly, thoughtfully.

"Then stand aside," Henderson snarled, and jammed the tip of a crowbar into one of the seams.

"No!" Chamberlin said, clutching the American's arm, a powerfully muscular arm that might have pried that compartment door off—if indeed that was what it was—in a single tug.

Henderson's eyes were tight with menace. "You better have a good reason for layin' hands on me, Doc."

Chamberlin loosed his grasp, but said, "If this is a secret compartment, consider: These hieroglyphs virtually dare a looter to attempt just what you're about to do."

Henderson thought about that. He, and his crowbar, withdrew a step. "What would you suggest?"

Beni stepped forward, with a smile as thin as his mustache. "May I offer a humble alternative, *barat'm*? You are paying good money to these men to dig." He nodded toward the half dozen turbaned diggers standing just behind the Americans, then shrugged elaborately. "So have them dig."

Chamberlin nodded. Their guide was an untrustworthy scoundrel, but his advice was sound.

"I think perhaps we should let the *fellahin* have this rare honor," Chamberlin said. "We are guests in their native land, after all."

110

"Listen to the good doctor," Burns said to Henderson.

But Henderson, crowbar in his now limp hands, was already convinced. "Yeah, sure . . . let them have the pleasure."

Chamberlin found Daniels the most mercurial of the group, brooding and dangerous. So it was no surprise when Daniels turned to the diggers and snarled, "You heard the man—get your asses over there!"

The diggers, exchanging wide-eyed expressions of alarm amongst themselves, backed away, murmuring their dissent.

"Mr. Daniels," Chamberlin said, "no disrespect meant, but you have the social skills of a drill sergeant. This is a delicate matter—one must reason with these men."

Chamberlin stepped forward and, screaming at the top of his lungs, told the diggers, in their own tongue, that if three of them did not step forward at once, he would invoke an ancient curse that would shrivel all of them, and every member of their families, to a desiccated death.

A hushed moment allowed the diggers to take that in.

Then three of the turbaned natives stepped forward, heads lowered, crowbars in hand, and lumbered reluctantly forward, while the other diggers backed away, cowering. Chamberlin directed them as to where precisely the tips of their crowbars should be inserted, around the seams of the panel at the statue's base.

As the diggers were poised to pry, Beni took several steps backward; Henderson noticed this, and followed suit—and then so did Burns and Daniels. This amused Chamberlin—the hardbitten soldiers of fortune were every bit as fearful as the simple natives.

Chamberlin stood to one side and shouted, *"Feni!"*

And the three diggers tugged back with their crowbars.

Sighing, the professor told them, in their own tongue, to put some damn muscle into it, again yelling, *"Feni!"*

The three men tugged harder, and the ancient stone panel seemed to give, somewhat.

"Feni!"

The diggers tugged at the crowbars again, putting their backs into it. The panel seemed to be loosening. . . .

"Feni!"

And this time the diggers put every ounce of strength into their effort, and the seam widened to a good half an inch . . .

. . . and an intense stream of liquid sprayed out from all around the seams, drenching the three diggers!

The three men screamed, each at a different pitch, creating a shrill chorus of anguish and horror as the acid bath stripped their clothes from their bodies, and then the flesh from their sinew, like melting candle wax, their corpses half-skeletal before they even had time to fall to the stone floor.

The remaining diggers had long since run off, their own cries echoing through the labyrinth as Chamberlin, the fortune hunters, and their guide—who had backed well away so none of them had even been touched by a drop of the deadly spray—gazed in horrified amazement at the steaming piles of bones that lay strewn at the base of the statue, whose compartment had sealed itself tightly shut, once again.

The tough Americans were white with fright; Beni was covering his eyes, trembling so severely his knees were knocking.

"Interesting," Chamberlin said, rubbing his chin. "What say, gentlemen? Shall we move on?"

O'Connell chipped away at the ceiling of the chamber with his chisel, Jonathan, beside him, was doing the same. Evelyn—who was holding the torch—wasn't quite tall enough to join in, and since there was nothing for her to stand upon, she was in the process of sharing her knowledge and enthusiasm about ancient Egypt and the practice of mummification.

"The ancient Egyptians believed in the transmigration of souls," she was saying. "The spirit might wander for thousands of years after death, and finally come back to its home on earth, looking to re-enter his or her body. Therefore, the body needed to be kept intact."

O'Connell kept chiseling. "And wrapping your body up in bandages does that, huh?"

"Oh, that's just a small part of the process. The intestines are removed through an incision in the side, then cleaned and washed in palm wine, covered with aromatic gum, and stored in jewel-encrusted jars; same with kidneys, liver, lungs. The heart was removed in the case of those who'd been . . . naughty. The body cavity was filled with cassia, myrrh, and other aromatic spices, then sewn up and soaked in, well . . . a sort of carbonate of soda for forty days. Only then would the fine linen bandages be wrapped around the mummy."

O'Connell glanced at her. "Did they leave the brain in the body?"

"Oh! Did I forget the brain? The brains were extracted by means of a sharp, red-hot iron probe . . ."

Jonathan winced as he chipped. "This is more information than we really require, dear sister."

". . . which they stuck up one's nose, cutting the brain into sections, which were then removed through the nostrils."

"That's got to smart," O'Connell said.

Evelyn smirked. "It doesn't smart at all, silly. Mummification was strictly for the dead."

"That process could wake the dead."

"It would certainly get my attention," Jonathan said.

She rolled her eyes. "You're such schoolboys. Any progress?"

And, as if in answer to her question, a big chunk of the roof fell out, right between O'Connell and Jonathan, a huge slab of stone that shattered into a thousand pieces as O'Connell dove out of its path, pulling Evelyn along with him, while Jonathan leaped the opposite way.

They were still scrambling, in their respective directions, when through this hole in the ceiling dropped a massive granite object, which—accompanied by shower of rubble—came crashing down to the floor with a slam that rocked the chamber, turning pebbles to dust that filled the air like fog.

Coughing, picking themselves up gingerly, blinded by the sudden dust storm, the three moved tentatively toward the object, O'Connell plucking the still-lit torch from the floor, where Evelyn had dropped it.

"Now that was a crash to wake the dead," Jonathan said.

"You may be closer than you think," Evelyn said, as in the light of the torch she got her look at what was clearly a man-made object, a massive granite casement.

"What the hell is it?" O'Connell asked.

"A sarcophagus," she said. The dust was clearing. "Buried in the shadow of Anubis, at the feet of the god. Whoever this was must have been a personage of great importance."

"They honored him in death, you think?"

She shrugged. "Either that, or he needed keeping-an-eye-on by the gods. Perhaps he'd been very . . ."

"Naughty?" her brother offered. "Shall we look inside and see if he's got a heart?"

"Help me dust this off," she said, and from the backpacks of the two men came rags, and soon a single hieroglyph had been revealed on the lid of the sarcophagus.

Though it seemed to O'Connell that this was a rather simple hieroglyph (not that he had any idea what it meant), Evelyn stared at the thing for the longest time, her expression developing into a sort of stricken look.

Jonathan was drumming his fingers impatiently on the stone lid. "Well? Who is he? King Somebody, or just the royal gardener?"

She seemed confused, concerned; finally she said, "It says . . . 'He Who Shall Not Be Named.' "

"Perhaps a very bad gardener," Jonathan put in.

"This looks like quarried granite." O'Connell was using a rag to clean off what seemed to be a huge lock.

"Yes," she said, "and it's likely to have a copper lining."

"If he was such an important chap," Jonathan said, "mightn't the inner coffin be solid gold, like Tut?"

"Possibly," Evelyn conceded.

"Without a key," O'Connell said, sighing, shaking his head, "it'll take us a month to crack this thing and find out."

Evelyn's eyes widened and she snapped her fingers. "That's it—the key! Don't you see? That's what the Med-jai on the boat were looking for, that fiend with the hook! He asked me for the key!''

''Of course,'' Jonathan said, brightening, ''the puzzle box! He was after my bloody puzzle thingamajig!''

Evelyn plucked the golden box from her brother's backpack and quickly unfolded the object until its jagged petals revealed themselves as an oversize key shaped precisely like the keyhole of the sarcophagus lock.

Excited smiles blossomed all around, accompanied by several long moments of breathless anticipation, as O'Connell and Jonathan, on either side of Evelyn, watched her approach the granite casement with the bulky key poised for insertion.

But the historic moment was interrupted by an unearthly, agonized scream that came echoing up to them from the labyrinth, clearly the cries of someone in desperate trouble.

Evelyn quickly folded the box back up, tossed it to Jonathan, who snugged it into his backpack, as O'Connell snatched the torch from the young woman's hand and led them into the tunnels, in search of whoever it was that needed their help.

They entered an area where the tunnel widened into a small cavern and the screams seemed to be running toward them, so they paused, waiting, and then there he was: *Warden Hassan!*

The plump warden emerged from a passageway, doing a demented dance, eyes popping, clawing at his head, literally tearing clumps of hair from his scalp.

''Grab him!'' O'Connell said to Jonathan, and soon both men had hold of his arms, pulling his hands away from where fingers of frenzy were ripping at his hair.

But the warden, crazed by pain, managed to shove both would-be helpers off, hurling them aside, not breaking stride as, screaming like an attacking horde of Tuaregs, Hassan ran headlong across the cavern . . .

. . . and smacked into the rock, like a car hitting a telephone pole.

Then Hassan just stood there, for a moment, giving Evelyn the chance to gasp in horror before he fell, flopping onto his back, staring at the rocky ceiling with wide-open, unseeing eyes.

"Jesus!" O'Connell said.

Evelyn had clasped a hand over her mouth.

"What got into him?" Jonathan wondered.

O'Connell went over and knelt to take Hassan's pulse, then closed the man's eyes, and stood.

"City of Dead's claimed another resident," he said.

Evelyn turned away, weeping, and O'Connell and Jonathan exchanged troubled glances.

Which was why none of them noticed the blood-soaked beetle slither out of the late warden's ear and into the darkness.

·☾ 11 ☽·

Night Visitors

Night's star-studded sapphire shroud had descended upon the City of the Dead, moonlight painting the partial pillars and crumbling walls of Hamanaptra a chalky ivory. The two camps set up within its fragmentary walls were as far away from each other as possible. The Americans with their larger contingency, a city of tents with a roaring bonfire, made a pitiful suburb of the four pup tents of the Carnahan group, whose small campfire consisted of brush O'Connell had gathered, *vissigia* and *siveeda*, and palm tree twigs and branches he'd loaded up on, back at the Bedouin oasis.

When O'Connell returned from burying Hassan, he found Evelyn and her brother huddled near the small, crackling fire.

Evelyn looked up at O'Connell, who tossed his shovel near his ever-handy gunnysack arsenal, and asked him, "What do you suppose killed the poor man?"

"Maybe it was something he ate," Jonathan said dryly.

The little group was well aware of the late warden's repellent eating habits.

"Or something that ate him," O'Connell said, sitting beside the young woman. This remark made both Evelyn and

Jonathan look at him curiously. "He had a wound on his foot that looked like an animal bite."

"Snake perhaps?" Jonathan wondered.

"Not sure. It was a fairly small bite, but the wound was deep—my finger couldn't find the end of it."

Evelyn shuddered, gathering her folded arms closer and tighter to her breasts. "I saw you talking to the Americans. Have we made peace?"

"I wouldn't go that far," O'Connell said. "But they're not as cocky as before. . . . They had a sobering experience of their own today, their own tragedy."

O'Connell told them of the the three diggers who'd been killed by an ancient booby trap, pressurized salt acid, apparently.

Evelyn's eyes widened. "Perhaps we're lucky we were interrupted today. We'll have to take precautions when we go back to open that sarcophagus tomorrow."

Jonathan, sipping at a tin cup of minty Bedouin tea, glanced about uneasily, and with none of his characteristic irony at all, said, "Perhaps this place truly is cursed."

As if in response to him, a gust of wind swept through the camp, sounding like a ghostly groan, blowing sand, rippling Evelyn's Bedouin gown and the shirts and trousers of the men, damn near blowing out their little campfire.

O'Connell swallowed, and as the fire flickered and came back to life, he exchanged wary looks with Jonathan.

Evelyn picked up on this and laughed at them. "You two! You're such children."

O'Connell leaned back against the rocks, arms folded. "Don't believe in curses, huh?"

"No," she said, almost snippily. "It's rubbish."

"How can you say that?" Jonathan said. "The Carnahans know all too well that such things shouldn't be taken lightly."

Evelyn waved him off, laughing a little more. "Be quiet, Jonathan. Don't pay any attention to him, Mr. O'Connell."

Jonathan, his expression gloomy all of a sudden, said, "Ask her about our parents, O'Connell. See what she has to say about that."

"Am I missing something?" O'Connell asked, confused, almost as uneasy with this conversation as he'd been with the ghostly wind blowing through the camp.

Evelyn replied, with crisp confidence, "I believe what can be seen, what can be touched, is real. That is what I believe."

"My sister is an atheist, Mr. O'Connell," Jonathan said. "A fairly recent convert to believing in nothing, actually—ask her about that, sometime, too. . . . What do you believe in, old boy? The stars and stripes and Mother and, what is it? Cherry pie?"

"Apple," O'Connell said. He withdrew his elephant gun from the gunnysack and cocked it, a metallic sound that rang in the night. "I'm an old boy scout, Jonathan—I believe in being prepared."

"As for me," Jonathan said, "I'm a worshiper in the Church of Self-Gratification." He dropped a hand down to pick up something—*the canvas pouch Warden Hassan had worn on his belt*—and unsnapped it and reached inside, fumbling.

"That was the warden's, wasn't it?" O'Connell said, the massive weapon draped across his lap.

"Yes, dear boy. Wouldn't have wanted to bury something so valuable with the poor bloke—might have incited future grave robbers to plunder . . . *ouch!*"

Evelyn, concerned, sat forward. "Jonathan! What is it?"

"Damn it, anyway," Jonathan said. "Forgot about the damn thing being chipped!"

And he withdrew from the pouch a small liquor bottle, and—sipping carefully at its broken spout—drank greedily, with orgasmic satisfaction.

"Glen Dooley," Jonathan sighed, wiping his mouth with a hand. "Twelve years old . . . For a man with such shortcomings in the area of physical hygiene, our late friend the warden had remarkably good taste in libations."

Carelessly, Jonathan tossed the pouch to the ground, and the rest of its contents—sand—leaked out.

O'Connell and Evelyn glanced at each other, shook their heads, amused by their mutual uneasiness over something so trivial. Then a distant rumbling—so distant, of the three around the campfire, only O'Connell heard it—caused the American to raise a hand in a gesture of silence. As the brother and sister watched him with alert interest, O'Connell knelt and placed an ear to the ground, listening; but a sudden pounding of hoofbeats, quickly joined by a thundershower of gunfire, rendered his effort moot.

The rain of lead was falling on the American camp: O'Connell could see it as well as hear it, how the small orange explosions of rifle fire popped against the darkness like kids setting off backyard fireworks.

O'Connell thrust the elephant gun into Evelyn's arms, startling her. Then, jumping to his feet, withdrawing a shoulder-holstered revolver with one hand, snatching up his gunnysack with the other, he told the Carnahans, "Stay put!"

And he took off running through the ruins, toward the battle, revolver in hand.

He did not realize that Evelyn—slowed by, but nonetheless lugging, the hefty elephant gun—had taken off after him. So had Jonathan, reluctantly, wielding his derringer, holding his precious liquor bottle to his breast like a baby he was protecting, calling to his sister, "I say, Sis! Didn't the man just tell us not to do this?"

Keeping low, darting about the rocks and ruins, O'Connell made his way toward the besieged camp. Through the town of tents galloped a dozen Med-jai riders, rifles blazing, picking off fleeing native diggers like tin-can targets off a fence. The tattooed horsemen had charged through the bonfire, scattering it about, not putting it out exactly; rather, sending small fires burning here and there around the camp. Partially blinded in the cloud of sand raised by the pounding hooves of horses, the Americans (with the exception of Chamberlin, who was apparently cowering in his tent), were standing their ground, firing revolvers, occasionally picking off a warrior; but they were seriously outgunned.

Daniels caught a bullet in the left shoulder, but the tough bastard kept shooting as he spun and fell, killing the man who'd wounded him. Blasting away as best they could, Henderson and Burns dragged their wounded friend out of the line of fire.

O'Connell was at the outskirts of the camp now, ducking in and around the ruins, when a figure dashed from behind a rock pile and bumped right into him: Beni.

"Going somewhere?" O'Connell asked.

"Rick! I was just looking for you! To warn you, my friend!"

O'Connell grabbed onto Beni's sleeve and dragged him along, toward the battle, saying, "Let's make ourselves useful, shall we?"

"A small question, my friend—what is it you have against running away from a fight?"

"I don't know. Maybe the company I'd have to keep."

Staying low, they moved along a ridge of rocks and rubble, nearing the raid in progress; finally, O'Connell yanked Beni down behind the rubble pile.

Just beyond where they hid, a tall, angular-faced figure, flashing a golden scimitar, was galloping through the camp; he seemed to be the leader, cutting down the native diggers with a certain relish reserved for traitors. The diggers cried out as they died, their robes fluttering in the night like the wings of dying birds.

"Stay here with this," O'Connell told Beni, putting him in charge of the gunnysack arsenal. "Keep me reloaded."

"You can trust me, Rick!" Beni was blinking in rhythm to the gunshots beyond their protective rubble-pile barrier.

"Of course, I can't trust you. But ditch me, or run off with my weapons, and you better pray I get killed out there."

"Rick, you hurt me!"

"Exactly."

O'Connell peered up and over the barrier, waiting for the right moment, then—revolver clutched tight in his right hand—scrambled up on top of the rocks just as the Med-jai leader was riding by, and leaped out at him, tackling him, dragging him down off his horse, both men slamming to the ground, raising a cloud of dirt and sand and dust.

Both men adroitly got to their feet, wheeling toward each other, the Med-jai leader with his golden scimitar hiked high to slash his foe, O'Connell shooting the damn thing out of the warrior's hand. His next shot would have taken the bastard out, but another warrior on horseback charged between them, another scimitar slashing above him, narrowly missing his head. O'Connell fired up at the son of a bitch, blowing him off his saddle and into the next life.

But when O'Connell spun around to take out the Med-jai leader, the man was riding off. Drawing his other revolver, O'Connell stood ground, swiveling about, firing both weapons, shooting warriors out of their saddles, until he was out of ammunition. He dove in back of the rubble pile, where Beni waited with the gunnysack and ammunition. He was still behind there, reloading his revolvers, when a too distinctive explosion attracted his attention—the sound of his elephant gun discharging its deadly load!

O'Connell peered up above the rubble just in time to see a Med-jai rider blasted out of his saddle to take a twenty-foot ride into a collapsed wall, by Evelyn, who—lifted back off her feet by the recoil of the huge weapon—went flailing through the air herself, landing in a pretty pile in a dune. He was at once horrified by her presence and delighted by her spirit.

From here, O'Connell could see that Jonathan had joined the battle, too—and he couldn't help but feel a swell of pride for the Carnahans.

Jonathan had rounded up a group of diggers who had armed themselves with pistols; all Jonathan seemed to have was that little gambler's handgun of his—and the bottle of Glen Dooley tucked in his belt. But they were positioned down around the front-entry pylons, just inside the temple grounds, and as four Med-jai horsemen charged through, Jonathan's group fired, leaving four empty saddles.

But several Med-jai warriors were coming up over the temple walls, and Jonathan and the diggers were soon in the midst of brutal hand-to-hand combat.

Reloaded now, O'Connell—after throwing Beni a hard

stay put look—scurried around the rubble, hands filled with revolvers, on his way to help Jonathan.

O'Connell didn't make it that far.

Hearing hooves thundering up behind him, O'Connell whirled and that Med-jai leader was right above him, swinging that golden scimitar. O'Connell ducked, raised an arm instinctively, to protect his face, and the scimitar flicked the revolver from his hand; another swing of the blade, and the other gun was gone!

The hard-eyed, angular-faced figure looming above him smiled—partly in respect to a valiant fellow warrior, partly to gloat that O'Connell, who earlier had disarmed the Med-jai leader, had been similarly disarmed by him.

This moment of arrogance on the warrior's part bought O'Connell the time he needed: He dove over the rubble pile, where Beni held open the gunnysack like Santa allowing a child to choose a toy, and when O'Connell came running back over the rocks, he had a stick of dynamite in his hand.

Quickly he dipped the fuse of the dynamite into the nearest small fire, helpfully scattered by the warriors, and its fuse came alive, spitting sparks.

O'Connell stood before the Med-jai chieftain, looming on horseback, and held the hissing stick high.

"I hate to lose a fight," O'Connell said, grinning up crazily at the warrior, "but I'll settle for a draw."

The warrior's eyes locked with O'Connell's.

The fuse sizzled, shortening, making its journey toward a death for everyone in the camp.

The Med-jai leader thrust his scimitar toward O'Connell—a gesture, not an attack.

"Leave this place," the warrior said, in a deep, sandpapery voice. "Leave this place or die!"

O'Connell just looked at him. "That's kind of *my* point, isn't it?"

The warrior reared his steed back, and galloped off, crying out to the remaining Med-jai riders, who raced after him, vanishing into the night and the desert. In moments, only the dust of their hoofbeats remained—that, and the destruction they had wrought.

Beni looked up from behind the rubble pile. "You want to put that out, Rick? You made your point."

"Oh," O'Connell said, "yeah," and he plucked the fuse from the stick of dynamite.

Evelyn, covered in sand, came staggering up to him, looking very shaken indeed; he went quickly to her, held her close to him.

"Darling," he whispered. "Are you all right?"

She drew away from him, just a little, but not breaking their close embrace, perhaps surprised by this tender intimacy—O'Connell was surprised himself: It had just come out.

"Yes," she said. "I'm fine . . . now."

Henderson and Burns, disheveled but seemingly none the worse for wear, came stumbling up. Burns was bracing Daniels, whose shirt, at the shoulder, was a scarlet blotch, though the man revealed no pain whatsoever.

"You see," Daniels said through his teeth. "That proves it. Old Seti's fortune is under this goddamn sand!"

Henderson said, "It's got to be down there! Why else would these savages try to drive us off like this?"

O'Connell's eyes were searching the surrounding ridges of the valley. "These are desert nomads. They value water, not gold."

"There's no well here!" Burns said, cleaning his glasses on his shirt. "This place sure as hell ain't no oasis!"

"I know," O'Connell said. "That's what troubles me."

Dr. Chamberlin finally emerged from a tent, with a first-aid kit, and tended to Daniels.

Running a hand through his thatch of blond hair, Henderson, clearly embarrassed, said, "Listen, uh . . . thanks for pitchin' in."

"You'd do the same," O'Connell said, not at all sure of that.

"About before . . . today, down below . . . well. We shouldn't go wavin' weapons around at each other. We can be rivals without bein' enemies."

"Agreed."

Burns said, "Maybe at night, we should band together

124

. . . join forces. Maybe you people would like to camp with us.''

O'Connell glanced at Evelyn, who nodded. ''We'd like that,'' he said. ''Tomorrow we'll make the move.''

Evelyn was glancing about the overturned camp. ''Where's Jonathan? Has anyone seen my brother?''

No one had.

''We need to look for him,'' Evelyn said, worry creasing her brow as she clutched O'Connell's arm.

''You need any help?'' O'Connell asked the Americans. ''You have bodies to bury.''

''No,'' Henderson said, ''thanks. We'll manage—you did plenty, already.''

And Henderson offered his hand for O'Connell to shake, which he did.

O'Connell and Evelyn moved quickly through the moonlight-washed ruins, back to their camp, where the fire was dwindling, to find Jonathan's body sprawled out in its dimming light, vacant eyes staring at the sky.

''They've killed him!'' Evelyn cried. ''Oh my God in heaven!''

Jonathan blinked and stared up at his sister, goofily. ''I thought you were an atheist,'' he said, slurring drunkenly.

That was when O'Connell noticed the bottle of Glen Dooley, still tight in Jonathan's hand.

Half a bottle was left, and O'Connell shared the liquor with Evelyn, while Jonathan slept it off in his tent.

O'Connell had built the fire up, but the desert night was its usual bitterly cold self, and they sat close together, sharing warmth. She told him she wasn't a ''drinking girl'' and then proceeded to damn near drink him under the table, or anyway would have if they'd had a table. At one point, concerned—in the aftermath of the Med-jai raid—that she couldn't defend herself, she inveigled him into giving her impromptu boxing lessons.

She swung on him, landed in his arms, and they dropped to the sand together, cuddling rather drunkenly in the firelight. He offered her another drink from the chipped spout of the bottle.

"Unlike my brother, sir," she said rather grandly, "I know when to say no."

That was something a man in love didn't like to hear.

"I should be angry with you," he said, taking a swig.

"Why?"

"Risking your life like that. I told you to stay put."

She raised her eyebrows and slitted her eyes. "Who's in charge of this expedition, anyway?"

"Look, I understand why your brother's here—he's after riches. Anybody can make sense out of that. But why . . . ?"

"What's a rotten place like this doing in a nice girl like me?"

"Precisely."

A faint smile tickled her full lips; her voice became dreamy. "Egypt's in my blood. Don't you know who my father was?"

"Who?"

"Show you." She pulled on the chain around her neck, withdrawing from under the Bedouin gown a locket; she opened it to display the small photos of her handsome father and lovely mother, an Egyptian woman with her daughter's eyes and mouth. "Howard Carnahan. That is who my father was."

"I'm sorry . . . don't know the name. I'm just an ignorant American."

"But you're a soldier of fortune in Arabia, aren't you? Surely you've heard of the man who found King Tut's tomb . . . *one* of the men, anyway."

"Good lord . . . are your parents . . . ?"

"Dead," she said, with a forceful bob of her head. "Plane crash. And I don't believe it's a curse. Such tommyrot, such poppycock. Thirteen people have died, yes, but people die every day. Not because of a curse. Not because of fate . . ."

O'Connell was a tad blotto himself, but he wasn't fooled by the offhand, glib nature of her remarks.

"So you're continuing your father's work," he said. "Spitting in the eye of the King Tut curse."

"Put it that way if you like. I may not be an explorer,

126

like my father, or adventurer like you, Mr. O'Connell . . . but I'm exceedingly proud of what I am."

"And what, pray tell, is that?"

She slapped her chest, lifted her chin. "Why, I . . . am . . . a . . . *librarian*!"

He snorted a laugh. "You mean a drunk librarian."

She snuggled next to him. "How dare you say such a thing?" she cooed. "When are you going to kiss me again, anyway, Mr. O'Connell?"

"I'm not going to kiss you at all, unless you stop calling me 'Mr. O'Connell.' I told you—call me Rick."

"Why should I?"

"Because it's my name."

"Rick. Rick . . . kiss me, Rick."

And then she kissed him, and passed out in his arms with that same goofy expression her brother had worn. O'Connell looked at her with great fondness, holding her very close, and fell sound asleep wearing a smile almost as silly as hers.

·☾ 12 ☽·

Discoveries

With the dawn of a new day, the two expeditions returned to their respective sites underground, in the caverns and chambers of the City of the Dead. Four men, Hassan and three diggers, had died as a result of yesterday's attempts, not counting the five natives who'd been killed in the attack by Med-jai warriors; but that raid had only convinced the American group that abundant riches awaited them.

Accompanied by a mere trio of diggers now, the Americans returned to the base of the statue of Anubis. Over a breakfast of canned beans, they had decided that the booby trap that had reduced three men to steaming skeletons had (in Henderson's evocative phrase) "shot its wad"; that its supply of acid was exhausted.

Nonetheless, certain precautions were taken, specifically, the enforcing of the three turbaned natives, at gunpoint, to pry open the lid of the secret compartment.

No spray of death emerged, though when the heavy stone lid thunked to the floor, everybody jumped—except the seemingly unflappable Daniels, his wounded arm in a sling. Beni, who had protested returning to this site, suggesting they seek the pharaoh's treasure elsewhere in the underground maze, was huddling against a wall, praying in several languages.

Dr. Chamberlin stepped forward and, in their native language, bid the diggers to reach inside the secret compartment. This they did not want to do, but Chamberlin repeated his threat to invoke a withering curse of death upon them and their families, which was underscored by the three fortune hunters cocking their weapons, and the frightened diggers, faces beaded with sweat, reached within the dark, yawning chamber at the feet of the god.

They removed a wooden chest of exquisitely ornate workmanship, alive with lovely, colorful hieroglyphs, gold and black and blue and red. As the diggers carefully, fearfully, deposited the chest on the sandy floor, Chamberlin's eyes greedily drank in the vivid symbols: winged sun disks, griffins, squatting gods, falcon-headed Horus, jackal-headed Anubis . . .

. . . but as he knelt beside the chest, interpreting the symbols, reading the deadly story they told, the Egyptologist could feel the back of his neck tingling with dread, his heart racing, his throat, his mouth, turning dust dry.

"What is it?" Daniels demanded, punctuating his words with gestures of gun-in-hand. "Spill!"

His voice soft, somber, even ominous, Chamberlin spoke as his eyes stayed affixed to the hieroglyphs. "There appears to be a curse on this chest . . . a most monstrous curse."

"Curse my hairy ass," Daniels growled dismissively. "Does it say anything about the pharaoh's treasure?"

Chamberlin, still kneeling, looked up sharply at the three rough-hewn adventurers gathered around him, torches in one hand, guns in the other (but for the wounded Daniels, who settled for a gun). "Gentlemen . . . please. We must proceed with caution."

"Look, Doc," Henderson said, "I understand these ancient savages were pretty savvy joes—with their fancy booby traps and all. So we'll be careful. But spare us the mumbo jumbo."

"These were not savages," the Egyptologist said, touching the lid of the chest as if protecting it. "This was a civilization of great glory and accomplishment, existing thousands of years before Christ.''

"Write a book about it," Daniels said. "What's it say about the loot?"

"These are hallowed grounds, gentlemen. . . . Who are we to say that the beliefs of these people were any less valid than our own?"

Burns laughed. "I believe in gold and silver, Doc."

"That which was set forth in ancient times," the Egyptologist said, "could well be as strong today, as then."

Beni stepped forward, a tiny step, bowed his head, and folded his hands as he addressed Henderson. "Listen to him, *barat'm*. Beni is all for plunder, but we must be swift, cautious, clever. . . ."

"Yeah, yeah," Henderson said. "We're all shakin' in our shoes, and genuflectin' before this dog-headed god, all right? Now—what's the box *say*?"

Chamberlin did not have to look at the chest to remember the exact phrase, which he now repeated for his impulsive partners: " 'Death will come on swift wings to whomever defiles this chest.' "

A ghostly gust of wind came howling through the chamber, and the torches in the hands of Henderson and Burns nearly flickered out. The three diggers had finally had enough, guns or no guns: They threw their hands in the air, screamed bloody murder, and went scurrying away, disappearing into the labyrinth, babbling in their native tongues.

"Superstitious riffraff," Burns said.

"Really?" the Egyptologist asked. "You don't find it unusual, a gust of wind, underground?"

The three fortune hunters did seem shaken, even Daniels, which relieved Chamberlin; perhaps they'd come to their senses.

"I would advise we move on," Chamberlin said. "There is no reason to borrow trouble. As our guide indicates, we should investigate this underground city more thoroughly. We could round a corner, gentlemen, and enter a chamber littered with gold and jewels and precious objects."

"Open the box," Daniels snarled.

"The inscription on that 'box' goes on to say that there is a mummy here. . . ."

"We oughta find a lot of mummies, here, Doc," Henderson said.

"But this is an unusual mummy, my friends. He is described as 'the undead,' who—should he be brought to life—would be bound by sacred law to consummate the most appalling of all curses."

"Yeah, well," Henderson said, "we'll just be real careful not to bring any mummies back to life."

"Open the box, Doc," Daniels repeated.

"The undead mummy would kill all of those who participated in the opening of this chest," Chamberlin warned them. "He would assimilate our organs and fluids."

"You mean eat us?" Daniels asked, almost smiling, but not quite.

"Jeez," Henderson said, "sounds like he's worked up a real appetite, this mummy, bein' undead a couple thousand years."

"By eating the flesh of the 'defilers,'" Chamberlin continued, desperation coloring his voice now, "he will regenerate. And no longer will he be the undead, rather a plague upon this earth."

Wind rustled down the tunnels, whistling an eerie tune, torches again flickering.

Henderson said, "We didn't come all this way for nothin'. . . . Beni! Get your skinny ass up here."

Beni, who'd been doing his best to climb inside the chamber wall, smiled nervously, bowing, and saying, "The view is fine from this vantage point, thank you, *barat'm*."

"Get over here!"

Beni obeyed.

Henderson nodded toward the crowbars on the floor, dropped by the diggers. "Pick one up, and pry that baby open."

"No, *barat'm*!"

Henderson touched the nose of the revolver to Beni's. "Fine—I'm getting sick of canned food, anyway. It'd be a nice change to have some Hungarian goulash for lunch."

131

And then Beni was prying at the lid of the wooden chest, the Americans looking on—guns and torches in hand, keeping a safe distance, the Egyptologist cowering behind them.

The seal seemed about to break when Beni cried, "No . . . the curse . . . the curse!"

And Beni shoved Henderson into Daniels, who bowling-pinned into Burns, and the skinny little guide bolted away, disappearing from the chamber into the tunnels, his voice, echoing, *"The curse! The curse!"*

"Stupid superstitious little bastard," Daniels said, picking himself up.

Henderson, on his feet again, said to Chamberlin, "Is that chest likely to be booby-trapped? The truth!"

Chamberlin shook his head. "That would be a defilement of the object's sacredness. The 'booby trap,' as you put it, *is* the curse! My advice is not to . . ."

But Henderson had already jammed the crowbar's tip in the seam and began prying the chest open, the seal snapping, the lid popping open—*and an explosion of dust was discharged into the air!*

An impossible filthy cloud of it, a nasty vapor that enveloped the room and the men, left them coughing and disoriented and frightened, bumping into each other. . . .

But within a few terrifying minutes, the dust had settled, the foul ancient vapor dissipating, and Chamberlin was almost amused at the sight of the three Americans training their weapons on the opened chest—as if their brute force and firepower could have an effect on antiquity.

Still, they had survived, and Chamberlin's thirst for knowledge, and (truth be told) his own greed, overwhelmed his better instincts, and he had to see what was within that chest.

Slowly, even reverently, Chamberlin approached the beautiful box, and reached inside to lift out a large burlap bag, within which—obviously—was some big square object. Trembling with anticipation, slipping the protective burlap covering away, the Egyptologist withdrew a heavy brass-hinged book, exquisitely decorated with hieroglyphs carved by some ancient artisan from pure obsidian.

"I have read of this," Chamberlin said breathlessly. "I have heard of this—but no man of the modern age has, until this day, this moment, been sure that *The Book of the Dead* truly existed!"

"A book?" Daniels said, kicking at the sandy floor. "A goddamn book? That's what this fuss was about?"

"Ah, but gentlemen," Chamberlin said, running his fingers delicately across the carved surface of the volume's cover, "this is a most priceless treasure. . . ."

"I wouldn't give you a brass spittoon for the damn thing," Henderson growled, and kicked the chest with savage anger and frustration.

"Please, no!" the Egyptologist cried, but the damage was done.

If indeed it was damage: Through the splintered wood, a lower compartment had been revealed. Within were four jewel-encrusted canopic jars and a fifth, shattered mate.

Chamberlin shuddered, experiencing the giddy jolt of a cocktail of dread and elation: precious objects, these jars . . . but also the coda to the curse, the preserved entrails of a mummy.

Burns, eyes glittering behind his glasses, was grinning. "Jewels! *Now* we're gettin' somewhere."

Just as the raid last night had only fed the American contingent's lust for bounty, Evelyn Carnahan's thirst for knowledge, for discovery, for scholarship, had only surged.

Her thirst the evening before, however, was causing certain problems this morning, as work got under way at the granite sarcophagus that had fallen at their feet yesterday, like a gift from the gods. Evelyn—and, judging by their dark-circled eyes and sluggish demeanor, Jonathan and O'Connell, as well—was suffering from that most ignoble of maladies: a hangover.

At the moment, she was unfolding the puzzle box with a little difficulty, though she'd opened it before, numerous times, easy as pie. "I can't believe I let my defenses drop to such a sorry state that you two reprobates could get me tipsy."

133

"Don't blame me, Sis," Jonathan said. "I'd already passed out, like a true and proper drunkard."

"'Tipsy' doesn't quite cover it," O'Connell said. His eyes were bloodshot and his flesh a sickly gray. "You were drunk as a lord."

"Well!" Evelyn huffed, and glared at her brother.

Jonathan raised his hands in surrender; he looked even worse than O'Connell. "Don't ask me for vindication. I don't even remember being there."

"Neither do I," she said, "thank you very much."

"That's a shame," O'Connell said, with a hurt look that was obviously feigned. "Last night you said you'd remember it forever."

"I never!"

"Until last night." And he grinned at her.

Horrified, flushed with embarrassment, she fumbled with the box, and O'Connell reached out, took the box, and opened up its metal petals.

"Nothing happened," he said softly. "Except that you agreed to start calling me Rick."

Relieved, she smiled; then she was irritated by his teasing and said, "This couldn't be more serious. Now I want you two schoolboys to behave yourselves."

"Stand back," O'Connell said, and he inserted the box-turned-into-key into the large lock, which mirrored the box's unfolded shape, ducking down, keeping his back to the sarcophagus.

"Mr. O'Connell," Evelyn said, "I appreciate your concern, but there's no record of any sarcophagus itself being booby-trapped."

And Evelyn strode up and turned the key to the right, initiating a series of strange grinding noises, as the mechanism responded; and then a loud hiss indicated the breaking of an airtight seal.

All three of them backed away, glancing at each other with excitement and perhaps some anxiety—finding themselves facing no splashing acid bath, no thrusting steel spikes, no nasty surprises at all.

Soon, they were exercising their aching, morning-after

muscles by doing their best to slide the heavy granite lid off the sarcophagus, pushing, shoving, groaning; at first, they seemed not to be getting anywhere at all. But finally, the lid began to budge, only grudgingly, inch by inch.

"It'll be too heavy for us to lift off," she said, as they took a break, panting, passing a canteen around. "I'm afraid we'll have to shove it to the floor, and risk breaking it."

"It's that or our backs," Jonathan pointed out.

And their backs were what they put into their next joint effort, and suddenly the lid slid off its perch and went pitching off the sarcophagus onto the chamber floor with a loud, resounding *slam* that echoed through the chamber, as well as Evelyn's poor, hungover head. Beside her, O'Connell and Jonathan had reacted similarly—Jonathan covering his mouth, O'Connell his eyes, and with Evelyn covering her ears, the sound had made monkeys of them all.

Within the sarcophagus was a considerably less grand wooden coffin. She bid her two assistants to lift it out, which they did, and she could not have stared down at the ancient object, adorned only with cobwebs and dust, with more avid anticipation and tingling ecstasy if it were fashioned of solid gold.

"I've dreamed of this since I was a little girl," she said.

"You must have been a weird kid," O'Connell said, still kneeling by the coffin.

"Oh, indeed she was," Jonathan said, crouching at the other end of the thing, like a reluctant pallbearer.

She flashed them disgusted looks, and asked O'Connell for a rag, which he proffered, and she began brushing away the webs and dirt, clearing the coffin lid, looking for hieroglyphs. What she saw—or rather, what she didn't see—sent a chill up her spine.

"All the usual, sacred spells have been chiseled off!" she said, pointing this out to the two men.

"What's the significance of that?" O'Connell wondered.

"The hieroglyphs that would have protected the deceased within this coffin, accompanying him into the afterlife, have been systematically removed."

"So he *was* 'naughty,' " Jonathan said.

135

Evelyn nodded. "Apparently it was not enough that he be condemned in this life—they condemned him in the next, as well."

"Those ancient Egyptians sure were strict," O'Connell said.

"Yes, I'm all choked up for the poor blighter," Jonathan said. "Now—shall we look inside, and see if he's wearing a golden mask or silver jammies?"

Evelyn, who had given up on these two, was brushing off a large lock on the side of the coffin, which again mirrored the shape of the unfolded, puzzle-box petals. Following his sister's lead, Jonathan inserted the key-box and gave it a hard turn to the right.

Again, a hiss indicated an airtight seal's surrender, as it broke after centuries of concealment.

But this time a foul stench emanated from the cracked-open lid.

"Uggh!" Jonathan said, backing away, holding his nose. "This isn't by chance where you buried Warden Hassan, is it, O'Connell?"

Evelyn took several steps back, coughing, while O'Connell—one hand covering his nose and mouth—tried to open the lid with the other. Then he tried with both hands, putting everything he had into it.

"Damn thing's stuck," he said. "Caught on something. . . . Give me a hand, Jonathan."

Both men gave it their all, and the lid slowly began to give way.

"Don't stop now!" O'Connell said to Jonathan. "I think it's coming loose. . . ."

And the lid popped open!

But with the lid came the coffin's inhabitant, a hideous, maggot-infested, still-rotting corpse in black-stained oozing bandages, seemingly jumping up from within!

The brave American, the self-composed Englishwoman, and her dapper brother screamed like blithering idiots, scared witless.

And the mummy plopped back into his coffin.

O'Connell swallowed, then laughed nervously. "Some of

136

the bandages must've got caught or stuck to the lid or something.''

''Those bandages do look frightfully sticky at that,'' Jonathan said.

''There's something terribly wrong here,'' Evelyn said, stepping slowly toward the coffin, then peeking tentatively within, at the twisted, deformed mummy. ''I've never seen a mummy that looked remotely like this. . . . After three thousand years, he's still—''

''Moist?'' Jonathan offered.

''Actually, yes. Even in an air-sealed coffin, this is unheard of—he's still decomposing!''

O'Connell was examining the inside of the coffin lid. ''Take a gander,'' he said, pointing to traces of dried blood and deep scratches, dozens of them, on the inner lid. ''His fingernails did that.''

''My God,'' Evelyn said. ''He was . . . buried alive.''

''*Very* naughty,'' Jonathan said, quietly.

''Looks like he left us a message,'' O'Connell said, pointing out a cluster of crudely fashioned hieratics—in dried blood.

'' 'Death is only the beginning,' '' Evelyn translated.

Jonathan shivered, and O'Connell's and Evelyn's eyes locked.

''You planning to stay down here much longer?'' O'Connell asked her. ''I thought I might go get my gunnysack.''

·❧ 13 ❧·

Plague on Both Your Houses

Another starry amethyst night had descended upon the City of the Dead, but now the Carnahan suburb had merged into the American expedition's city of tents, where members of the rival teams gathered around one roaring campfire. The wary truce was matched by an uneasy calm, as rifles and revolvers lay near at hand, should the Med-jai welcoming committee decide to drop by again.

Arms folded, rather enjoying the chilly evening, Evelyn carried a small canvas bag by its drawstrings, like a kid with a sack of marbles, as she headed toward the campfire. Starting from her own small tent, she passed casually by the much larger tent which served as Dr. Chamberlin's headquarters.

The Egyptologist, wearing his sun-shielding pith helmet even in the moonlight, stood at a worktable arrayed with various artifacts gathered from below, including one jewel-encrusted canopic jar in perfect condition and another that was in pieces. Half a dozen turbaned diggers sat in the sand nearby like disciples awaiting the holy word from the mousy professor.

"Hello, Doctor," she said, as she passed, but Chamberlin did not respond.

This wasn't rudeness on the professor's part: He seemed wholly absorbed with the examination of a certain artifact—a book—a large, brass-hinged, obsidian volume with a strange, large lock on its face that was keeping Chamberlin from opening the thing.

Smiling privately, Evelyn strode to the campfire, sitting between her brother, Jonathan, and Rick O'Connell, who was perched next to his old Foreign Legion comrade, Beni. Both legionnaires were roasting scraggly meat on sticks, which was producing a rather pungent, even foul, aroma.

Jonathan sniffed the air. "Might I ask what that vile-smelling entrée might be?"

"It might be a rat," Beni said. "Best the desert has to offer."

"Want some of mine?" O'Connell asked. "Don't worry—it doesn't taste too much worse than it smells."

"No, thank you." Jonathan shuddered. "For a moment I thought our old friend Warden Hassan had returned from the dead."

Across the flittering flames, the adventurers from America—Henderson, Burns, and Daniels—were sitting together, talking quietly, all grins and high spirits. Like Chamberlin, each had a canopic jar, elaborately and valuably jeweled, and the men were turning the jars over and over in their hands, practically fondling the things.

Henderson held his jar up and grinned through the flames at Evelyn and O'Connell. "Miss Carnahan—you're an expert. What do you think this beauty will fetch on the collector's market?"

"My expertise is in the realm of scholarship," she said primly. "I'm afraid commerce is your department, Mr. Henderson."

"Beni tells us you kids found yourselves a mummy today," Burns said, flames dancing on the lenses of his wire-frames. "Congratulations."

O'Connell glanced irritably at Beni, who didn't acknowledge this small betrayal of confidence, focusing on how his rat-on-a-stick was doing.

"I hear he's nice and ripe," Burns added.

"Why don't you dry him out?" the stoic Daniels asked, offering a rare witticism. "We could use the firewood."

The fortune hunters bellowed with laughter, patting each other on the back, drunk with their good fortune.

Evelyn ignored this uncouth behavior and said to O'Connell, "I made another interesting discovery, after you and Jonathan went topside."

O'Connell frowned. "You didn't go wandering off into another chamber without us, did you?"

"Heavens no! This is something I found in our friend's coffin."

She emptied the canvas bag on the sandy ground before her, so both O'Connell and her brother could have a gander at her latest precious find: a pile of big, dusty bug exoskeletons.

Jonathan recoiled. "Those are nasty-looking devils *dead*! I'd hate to meet one that was wiggling."

"I should say," Evelyn replied. "These are legendary in their nastiness: scarabs—flesh eaters. They can stay alive for years, feasting on the flesh of a corpse. . . . Do you have an extra rat-ka-bob, Mr. O'Connell? I'm famished."

"I'll put one on the fire for you," O'Connell said, raising an eyebrow.

Jonathan was staring at the beetle exoskeletons, aghast. "Are you saying, dear sister, that those abhorrent creatures ate the flesh from that corpse of ours?"

"Yes . . . and no. I'm afraid, where our friend was concerned, he wasn't a corpse, when they started eating him."

Jonathan and O'Connell exchanged incredulous looks.

Evelyn, who had her own rat-on-a-stick now, courtesy of O'Connell, was holding it over the flames. "Our theory that he may have been . . . naughty . . . would appear to have some validity."

"You're saying he was not only buried alive," O'Connell said, "but whoever singled him out for that

140

honor also pitched in a handful of flesh-eating bugs? To munch him to death?"

She frowned, thoughtfully. "Rather more than a handful, I'd say."

"What could he have done to become so popular?" Jonathan wondered.

O'Connell smirked. "Maybe he got a little too frisky with the pharaoh's daughter."

"At the very least, I would say." Evelyn was turning her rat slowly over the flames. "From the evidence at hand, I would hazard an educated guess that our mummy suffered the worst of all ancient Egyptian curses—the *hom-dai*."

She explained to them that the *hom-dai* was reserved only for the most evil of blasphemers.

"The only doubt I have," she said, "is that scholarship indicates that this curse was never executed."

Now Jonathan smirked. "Well, our mummy friend was executed, all right."

"You mean, supposedly this famous curse," O'Connell said, "was never used? What was the point of it, then?"

She shrugged. "As a threat, a deterrent—as something that could be invoked, should anyone *really* misbehave. But the ancient Egyptians never used the curse—or so it is thought—because they were afraid to."

"Why on earth?" Jonathan asked. "Isn't it usually the person *being* cursed who should be afraid?"

Matter of factly, she told them, "It is written that should he who endures the torment of *hom-dai* ever arise from the dead, that entity would return as the bearer of the ten plagues."

"How many plagues?" O'Connell asked lightly, but Evelyn could see apprehension in his eyes.

Beni, nibbling his rat, had not seemed to be paying any attention to any of this; but suddenly he put in: "Like Moses and the pharaoh?"

"Just like Moses and the pharaoh," Evelyn said, nodding.

"Let's see how much Sunday school stayed with me," Jonathan said glibly, and began ticking off the plagues on

141

his fingers. "You have your frogs, your flies, your locusts . . . dear me, I'm stuck already."

"Hail," Burns said, from across the flames. "And fire."

"Sun turning black," Henderson added.

"Water turning to blood," Daniels said.

Seemed the Americans had been listening all along.

"Well, and then there's my personal favorite," Jonathan said, "boils and sores all about the body—always a crowd pleaser. . . . Can't anyone think of the other two?"

No one said anything; then some nervous laughter followed, but Evelyn could sense real trepidation among these brave fortune hunters. Men were such children.

She plucked the rat-on-a-stick from the fire, blew on it to cool it off, then nibbled at the warm meat.

"Really not half bad," she said, chipper.

Later, Evelyn—who had done her best to freshen for bed (she really was quite tired of wearing the Bedouin gown, which was frightfully wrinkled and dirty)—was walking past Dr. Chamberlin's tent, heading back to her own tent, when she noticed something interesting.

The professor was asleep on his pallet, on his side, one arm cradling the jeweled jar to his bosom, almost tenderly, his other arm and hand draped loosely over the large black ancient book.

She glanced about, noting that Chamberlin's loyal diggers were all asleep under the stars, hither and yon, beneath blankets. All concerned seemed sound asleep, and Chamberlin was snoring.

Moments later, Evelyn was sitting in the glow of the campfire, the big book in her hands.

"That's called stealing," someone said.

O'Connell crouched down beside her.

"I believe the word you used before was 'borrowing,' " she replied, referring to the archaeologist's tool kit he'd given her. "Be a dear and go get that puzzle box out of Jonathan's backpack, would you?"

O'Connell did.

Then she was inserting the key into the book's huge lock,

which shared its shape with those of the sarcophagus and coffin they'd opened.

"Is that the book you've been looking for?" O'Connell asked. "That sure isn't made of gold."

"It isn't *The Book of Amun Ra*, either—it's something else, every bit as precious."

"Yeah? What is it? King Tut's little black book?"

"I think this may be *The Book of the Dead*."

O'Connell frowned. "Dead? I don't like the sound of that. . . ."

"Don't be a ninny. What harm ever came from a book?"

And the librarian turned the big key.

The unlocking click seemed to echo through the night, and she looked around to see if anyone—in particular, Dr. Chamberlin—had been roused. All was quiet, except for the muffled rumble of men snoring, here and there.

Wind blew through the camp—not a gust, this time, more like the expulsion of bored breath by some giant in the sky—but the flames of the campfire shivered, as if they too felt the desert chill.

The two shared a nervous look, then Evelyn laughed. So did O'Connell, though not terribly convincingly. He moved close, putting a protective arm around her shoulder, though somehow she felt he was seeking the comfort of her closeness as much as offering the security of his.

Her eyes slowly scanned the exquisitely rendered hieroglyphs on the first page, lips moving as she read silently.

"So what is it?" he said, finally. "The Hamanaptra—phone book?"

" *'Amun kum ra. Amun kum dei.' "*

"I'm so glad I asked."

"It speaks of the night and of the day."

She began to read aloud, still to herself, but wanting to hear the words, compelled, somehow, to speak them . . .

(And she could not know, of course, that within the chamber where their mummy lay, uncovered in his coffin, alongside his granite sarcophagus, his ancient, putrescent flesh and bones stirring, his eyelids opening—Imhotep awoke with a jolt, staring into the darkness with empty sockets.)

143

... and so Evelyn Carnahan, earnest scholar that she was, hopelessly in love with the lore of ancient Egypt, devoted to the memory of her late celebrated father, continued to read the words that roused the mummy.

"No!" a voice screamed from behind her.

Someone else had been roused: Dr. Chamberlin.

"You must not not!" he shouted. "Cease!"

Like a teenager caught reading a forbidden novel after dark, Evelyn shut the book's cover as the Egyptologist ran toward her on stubby legs. She noted, rather absurdly, that he was not wearing his pith helmet for once. His hair, white and wispy, was standing straight up from sleeping on it . . . or maybe fright. . . .

Then, halfway to the campfire, Chamberlin froze in place, his eyes turning toward the desert behind him, as if he'd heard something.

He had, and soon so had Evelyn and O'Connell: a buzzing, building drone that was streaming in from the desert, as if a plane were swooping somewhere out there, only the sound was more piercing than that, and more of a whine.

Evelyn and O'Connell flew to their feet. In his tent nearby, Jonathan awoke with a start. The buzzing whine was building, like a siren. Over by the cluster of American tents, Beni stumbled out, clutching his stomach.

"Musta ate a bad rat," he mumbled, then his eyes widened as he perceived the growing drone coming in off the desert.

Henderson, Burns, and Daniels emerged from their tents, revolvers in hand, eyes wild, as the strange, unearthly drone grew louder and closer.

They all stood, in the flickering firelight, watching the darkness of the desert, confused, helpless, the Americans wondering aloud what the hell this could be.

And then what the hell it was became incredibly, dreadfully, apparent, as the living cloud of locusts descended upon the camp, enveloping everything and everyone. . . .

Clawing and pawing the air, Evelyn felt O'Connell's arm slip around her waist and he pulled her through the rain of wings, and they ran—Jonathan at their side—toward the crevice at the feet of Anubis. Frantically waving the bugs off as best they could, they raced to the shrine.

In the meantime, Beni and his American employers were running toward their own entrance to the underground, though Dr. Chamberlin—wearing a shroud of locusts—had retrieved *The Book of the Dead*, and stood asking the sky, "What have we done?"

Then, spitting out the locusts he'd just let into his mouth, Chamberlin followed the rest of his expedition into the underground.

O'Connell, Evelyn, and Jonathan had moved through the darkness of the now familiar embalming room into the tunnels, slowing down to slap at themselves and pick locusts out of their hair. O'Connell, who'd had the presence of mind to grab and bring along that gunnysack arsenal of his, lighted a kitchen match off his fingernail and set fire to the nub of a torch.

"I never saw so many goddamn grasshoppers in my life!" O'Connell said.

"Not grasshoppers," Evelyn said, doing her best to regain her composure, "locusts."

"That's one of the ten bloody plagues, isn't it?" Jonathan demanded of his sister, rather hysterically. "Locusts!"

"This is not a plague, Jonathan," she said calmly, plucking a locust from her ear, "it's a natural phenomenon—a generational phenomenon. Every so many years the locusts of this country have a population explosion and they all take flight. . . . They're probably gone by now, they'll have moved on."

Evelyn took a step back the way they'd come, and felt something squish under her sandal.

"Ick," she said. "I've stepped in something."

"Not *in* something," O'Connell said, frowning, lowering his torch. "*On* something."

The floor was covered in frogs—slimy, awful frogs!

Evelyn held back her scream, which allowed her to hear O'Connell asking, "Okay—so are the Egyptian frogs breeding, too? And did they fly here?"

Before she could answer (though what that answer would

have been is hard to say), the ground under them began to shake; the floor was covered with sand, and that sand began to swarm, not unlike the locusts above.

In the light of the torch, they witnessed the impossible: The sand gathered and grew into a mound, rising in front of them, like a man materializing; but it wasn't a man or sand, either.

From somewhere, perhaps up through cracks in the floor, they had come, and now they came spilling out of what had seemed to be a pile of sand, but was really a pile of them: *scarab beetles!*

Hundreds of them, chittering dung beetles boiling out of the sand to form a quick crawling army that moved toward them in a black, wriggling wave.

Evelyn screamed, and so did Jonathan, and even O'Connell, though he was actually forming the words: "Come on!"

And, his torch showing the way, he led them into a passageway, even as the scarab army advanced on them.

Elsewhere in the underground tunnels, the Americans had similarly moved away from the locusts into the darkness; but early on, racing down a passageway, Burns—initially leading the way—had lost his footing, his wire-rims slipping from his face, skittering across the rock floor and winding up in the path of the stampede of his comrades.

Without his glasses, Burns couldn't find his glasses, and even if he could have, they were crushed beyond use; and now he had lagged seriously behind. Without a torch, half blind anyway, he squinted toward the blurry figures up ahead of him, watched them vanish into the darkness of the tunnel.

"Wait!" he called. "Wait!"

But they either didn't hear him, or didn't care.

Burns did his best to navigate in the darkness, running one hand along the wall, holding the other out in front of him, groping. Up ahead was light, not the light of a torch, but moonlight filtering down through the crevice above. He moved toward the light, and suddenly he could make out something, someone: An indistinct figure had stepped out in front him, perhaps ten feet away.

"Daniels?" he asked. "Henderson, is that you?"

Burns staggered toward whoever it was, then tripped, stumbling forward, throwing his hands out in front of him, to stop himself, to brace himself against the figure.

But his hands sank in!

It was as if he'd pushed his palms into mud, foul sticky mud, and he yanked them out with an awful slurping sound, and even with his bad eyes, he could see that his hands were covered in a jellylike slime. His brain finally informed him that this was a living mummy standing before him, and the slime on his hands consisted of a soup of maggots and rotten flesh from a putrid chest cavity, and as Burns started to scream, a skeletal hand clamped down over his mouth, muffling the sound.

The noisy insects in pursuit, O'Connell led Evelyn and Jonathan down several tunnels which they had never before traversed, and soon they found themselves in a chamber with stairs carved into the stone, a tall narrow staircase leading up, which was the way the three headed.

The mass of scurrying, chittering scarabs apparently thought that was a fine idea, too, and stayed right on the heels of the humans.

Halfway up, on the left of the staircase, chiseled out of the wall, was a pedestal where some icon or urn had once stood. O'Connell leaped onto it, and Jonathan followed; a similar indentation was on the right, and Evelyn leaped onto it, and perched there like the statue of a goddess—a frightened one.

A moment after the trio had vacated those stairs for their respective roosts, the herd of insects clambered between them, scrambling on up the narrow stairs like a moving black carpet.

O'Connell and Jonathan watched until the insects were out of view.

Trembling, Jonathan sighed in relief. "Gone."

"Hell!" O'Connell said, looking past him. "So's Evelyn!"

The pedestal where she'd stood was empty.

·❈ 14 ❈·

Bringer of Death

O'Connell's fingers fumbled over the wall in the recess of the pedestal where Evelyn Carnahan had stood.

Just below, on the chamber floor, Jonathan, holding the torch, asked, "Anything?"

"Nothing—but there's got to be a goddamn hidden switch, or a trap door, or—"

Somebody screamed—not a woman, not Evelyn: a man. Several men, in fact, as scream layered upon scream came echoing down from the top of the stairway. O'Connell glanced at Jonathan in confusion, and—elephant gun in tow—hopped down from the pedestal and began to climb the stairs . . .

. . . and out of the darkness above came Henderson and Daniels, followed by several native diggers, and all of them, including the hardy Americans, were scrambling frantically down, spooked as hell, hurtling the stairs, two and three and four steps at a time, screaming their lungs out.

Henderson yelled down to O'Connell and Jonathan, "Out of the way, you sorry sons of bitches—run for your lives!"

And from behind these new arrivals, and above them, came that awful sound again, the hungry chittering of the herd of scarabs, making their inexorable way down the stairs in a wave of wriggling black.

Jonathan fell in with the running men, but one turbaned native tripped and fell, offering himself in unintentional sacrifice, flung across the bottom of the stairway. O'Connell turned to go back and help the man, but the beetles had already swarmed over the digger, covering him, consuming him, and the metallic music the beetles made seemed to intensify, to grow almost deafening, as in moments the creatures had reduced the poor bastard to a half-eaten corpse whose skeleton provided a stark white contrast to the black dung beetles devouring his flesh.

And now O'Connell—who was brave, but not stupid— ran, too, as the men darted into the catacombs, dividing up, disappearing into the darkness of various tunnels, taking advantage of the precious moments they had as the raucous army of insects finished their meal.

Evelyn found herself enveloped in darkness. She'd leaned back so hard against the wall behind the pedestal where she'd perched, the panel—like a trick door in a haunted house—had moved under the weight of her, pushing open, sending her tumbling backward, dumping her rudely onto the sandy floor of an adjacent chamber, and closing again behind her!

She called out, "Jonathan! Mr. O'Connell . . . Rick!"

But there was no response. So, shaking the sand out of her hair, she got to her feet and began tentatively feeling her way along the wall, her eyes trying to adjust to the dark. At least there were no scarabs in here, or locusts, or frogs. . . .

Rounding a corner, she entered a chamber where she was relieved to see moonlight filtering down in through a long crack in the ceiling, the last gasp of the crevice that granted entrance to this underground world. An even greater relief was the sight of one of the Americans—the one called Burns, she thought—his back to her, standing in the moonlight, head back, staring upward.

"Thank goodness," she said, approaching him. "I was just beginning to get worried. . . ."

As she neared him, she suddenly heard a sobbing, a whimpering.

Touching his shoulder, she asked, "Are you all right?"

And Burns careened around and stared at her with gory gaping sockets where his eyes had been, streaks of blood like tears streaming down his pain-distorted face.

Evelyn did what any self-respecting Englishwoman in that situation would do: She screamed like a banshee.

Moaning, Burns dropped to his knees, as if he were praying to her. Evelyn backed away, her scream subsiding into deep, hysterical breaths, and bumped into something, or someone, just behind her. She wheeled and looked into the slimy, bandaged face of the awakened mummy, who looked at her through freshly harvested, recently inserted eyeballs.

The mummy squinted at her—Burns's eyesight hadn't been the best, after all—and a decayed hand pawed the air.

"Anck-su-namun?" the mummy rasped at her.

Evelyn's reply was another bloodcurdling scream as the young woman backed into a wall and the mummy stumbled toward her, its skeletal legs shedding rotting bits of flesh, its slime-soaked bandages loose and oozing.

As the mummy closed in upon her, a walking nightmare in the moonlight-dabbed darkness, Evelyn edged down the wall, horror-struck. Beyond the mummy, in the shaft of moonlight, knelt Burns, and she cried out to him for help, and his response was to lower himself even further, as if he were bowing down to the mummy.

"Please!" Evelyn cried, as the mummy staggered toward her.

Burns looked up, with his blood-streaked, eyeless countenance, and opened his mouth, as if to reply to her, but he could only moan and gurgle, frothing blood—his tongue missing, ripped out!

As this appalling fact dawned upon her, Evelyn—still sliding along the wall in the semidarkness—saw the mummy stretching out his arms toward her, as if to embrace

151

her, and even under the filthy wrappings, his face seemed contorted with emotion.

"*Kadeesh pharos Anck-su-namun!*" the mummy cried, and she looked past the fetid lips, beyond the rotten teeth, to see the fresh tongue flapping there—Burns's tongue.

Almost paralyzed with shock, shivering with cold fear, Evelyn still managed to make her way along that wall—the mummy was moving slowly, shambling toward her, bandaged hands outstretched—and then she ran out of wall, and realized she was at the entrance of a tunnel.

Relieved, she turned and bumped into somebody, and screamed!

"Hey, take it easy," O'Connell said, taking her by the arm and moving her back toward the moonlit chamber. "Where have you been? This is no time for exploring. Let's get out of here, already—"

And that was when he looked beyond her and saw the tall creature in grimy bandages, with rotting flesh and exposed bone and glittering eyes, moving toward them.

"Jesus!" O'Connell said, grabbing Evelyn and pulling her close to him, then stepping in front of her, protectively.

This seemed to irritate the living mummy; that seemed to be a look of rage distorting the decaying face, and just as the mummy was lurching toward them, reinforcements arrived—unintentionally, but they arrived, as into the chamber burst Jonathan, Henderson, and Daniels, emerging from a tunnel behind the mummy, whose towering if deteriorating presence was highlighted by the moonlight.

The men skidded to a stop at this remarkable sight, and any exclamations of surprise caught in their throats as the dire consequences of their greed stood wrapped in filthy bandages before them, tottering, but menacing.

The mummy cast its newly acquired eyes about the room, taking in the grave robbers with loathing and scorn, looking from face to face, as if he were making an inventory, and wondering where to start. . . .

The mummy's borrowed eyes bore in on O'Connell, who stood protecting Evelyn, and He Who Shall Not Be Named unhinged his skeletal jaw, his nearly skinless mouth stretch-

152

ing to an inhuman size, as does a snake when devouring larger prey, and he emitted a primordial shriek that would have been loud enough to wake the dead, had the dead not wakened already.

This prompted screams from everyone else in the chamber, not just the young woman, but every brave man, including O'Connell, who—immediately embarrassed by his fearful behavior—shrieked right back mockingly at the mummy, and blasted the bastard with the elephant gun, a resounding explosion in the enclosed space that nearly shattered the eardrums of all concerned.

But it did much worse to the mummy, tossing it to the far wall like a rag doll, a limp pile of putrescent flesh and stained, mucky bandages, his ribcage half torn away, exposing the ooze and sludge of rancid organs within, leaking out.

No one, however, stayed around to take the mummy's pulse. O'Connell latched on to Evelyn's hand and pulled her into the darkness of the nearest tunnel, and she went along gladly, and the others followed after.

O'Connell's torch showing the way, they were soon in the embalming chamber beneath the crevice where the Carnahan expedition's dangling ropes provided an exit. They clambered up, stumbled out into the moonlight, sucking in the cold, fresh air of a night free of locusts now, though wind was whipping through the ruins, stirring sand, the campfire long since extinguished; and they huddled, disheveled, disheartened, in the shadow of the half-buried statue of Anubis.

From the darkness, through the stirring sand, emerged Med-jai warriors, on foot, rifles at the ready. O'Connell's weapon was empty, and around him the other men—those tough Americans included—were putting their hands in the air. Dr. Chamberlin, holding on to *The Book of the Dead*, was already the prisoner of one of the warriors, being dragged along on his knees.

The angular-faced leader stepped forward, wind tugging at his black robes like a child seeking attention. "Who did this? Who read from *The Book of the Dead*? Who invoked the sacred incantations?''

Evelyn took a step forward, chin high. ''I did. Evelyn Carnahan.''

''Carnahan,'' the Med-jai leader said, as if tasting the word, and finding its flavor unpleasant. ''I know of your father. . . .''

''My father was a great man.''

''Your father was a great fool. And his daughter has proven even more foolish than he who unleashed the curse of Tutankhamen upon the world.''

O'Connell stepped up beside Evelyn. ''Who are you?'' he demanded.

''I am called Ardeth Bay.'' The Med-jai leader's eyes narrowed as he regarded O'Connell. ''How are you known?''

''O'Connell.''

''You are the leader?''

Evelyn started to speak, but O'Connell, touching her arm, said, ''Yes.''

Ardeth Bay sighed dramatically. ''You were told to leave, or die. You refused. And now you may have killed us all—and many more. You have unleashed the evil we have held at bay for more than three thousand years.''

''Yeah, well maybe we 'unleashed' him,'' O'Connell said, nodding toward the crevice, ''but we stopped him, too. I let him have it with this.''

And O'Connell hefted the elephant gun.

Ardeth Bay's smile was like an unhealed wound in his face. ''No mortal weapon can kill this creature. He is not of this world.''

Two Med-jai warriors dragged Burns up. Slumping, barely conscious, the blood-spattered American stared at nothing out of the ghastly red holes where his eyes used to be.

Horrified and outraged by their friend's condition, Henderson and Daniels lunged forward, Henderson yelling, ''What did you bastards do to him?''

Daniels spat, ''Goddamn savages!''

154

Ardeth Bay backhanded Daniels with a casual viciousness, and Daniels fell to the sand, landing on his wounded arm-in-a-sling, and howling. Henderson seemed ready to act, but a warrior's rifle pointed at his head made him reconsider.

"We *helped* him, you fools," Ardeth Bay growled. "Saved him before the creature you unchained could finish his work. Your friend is a lucky man—he lost only his eyes and his tongue."

Henderson helped Daniels up. Evelyn was holding on to O'Connell's arm, not so proud now.

As if delivering a death blow with his golden scimitar, Ardeth Bay gestured forcefully yet dismissively at the group of infidels, saying, "Now leave! All of you! Quickly—before He Who Shall Not Be Named returns to finish you."

"Oh!" Jonathan said. "So you're not going to kill us, then?"

Evelyn glared at her brother.

"Killing you is no longer a remedy," Ardeth Bay said. "We must now go on the hunt, and find this creature—and find a way to kill *him*."

Leaving the cowering Egyptologist behind, and the slumped Daniels, too, the Med-jai warriors—robes flapping in the wind—strode toward the crevice near the shrine of Anubis.

"Ardeth Bay!" O'Connell called.

The Med-jai leader stopped, turning to look back.

"You're wasting your time," O'Connell insisted. "I told you—I already blew the bastard to Kingdom Come!"

Ardeth Bay's expression conveyed pity at first, then contempt, before settling into a somber mask, as he said, "Know this—He Who Shall Not Be Named is the Bringer of Death. He Who Shall Not Be Named does not eat, does not sleep, and does not stop until he has consumed the earth in pestilence and flame. . . . Allah be with us all."

Then the Med-jai were sliding down the ropes into the crevice.

O'Connell gathered the two expeditions, taking a head count, telling them, "We better break camp, what's left of it—and get going while the going's good. Say—where's Beni, anyway?''

After the locusts had driven them underground, Beni had broken away from the American expedition, at his first opportunity, and had hidden away in the darkest corner he could find. Sounds of screams echoing through the catacombs had not encouraged him to come out of his hiding place. But now things seemed quiet—the worst, apparently, was over—and Beni began to make his way back.

Moving cautiously, gun in hand, Beni crept around the base of the statue of Anubis, knowing the ropes dropped down the crevice by the Carnahan expedition were just one chamber over—moonlight seeping in from the start of the crevice above paved his way. Then he rounded the base and almost bumped into somebody.

Something.

Some*thing*.

Beni looked at the rotting mummy in the loose, slimy bandages, a mummy with a huge gaping hole in its side, as if a cannonball had blown through there, and for a moment wondered how this artifact had been propped up like this. Then the mummy took a step forward, and Beni screamed and raised his gun to fire, and a bony decomposing hand batted the gun from Beni's hand.

Beni backed up and found himself immediately cornered. Quivering with fear, he clutched at the chains around his neck, where symbols and icons from many faiths dangled; Beni was not a religious man, exactly, just hedging his bets. He held out a Christian crucifix, as if this were a vampire not a mummy, and uttered the opening phrases of the Lord's Prayer.

The mummy shambled forward, apparently not a Christian.

Beni fumbled with the other icons, trying to slow the mummy's progress: an Islamic sword and crescent moon, a Hindu Brama medallion, a small Buddhist Bodhisattva statue, blessing himself in Arabic, Hindi, Chinese, and even

Latin, just in case this crumbling monstrosity staggering toward him was Catholic.

The mummy's skeletal hand was outstretched, not to make the sign of the Cross, but to reach out for Beni's throat.

Weeping, hysterical, Beni displayed a Star of David and began to pray in Hebrew . . .

. . . and the mummy stopped, as if he'd taken root.

That was funny, Beni thought; he didn't look Jewish.

Nonetheless, that decaying hand had lowered, and those weirdly familiar eyes were staring at Beni, who blessed himself in Hebrew.

The mummy spoke, his voice a rumbling thing, echoing up like bubbling lava: "You speak the language of the slaves."

This was spoken in ancient Egyptian, and meant nothing to Beni, but the mummy's next words, in Hebrew, did: "I am Imhotep. . . . Serve me . . . and the rewards . . . will be bountiful."

The mummy clawed at himself, at his tattered bandages, and withdrew a small object, which he displayed to Beni, in a fetid palm crawling with squirming maggots: a jeweled fragment of the one canopic jar that had been discovered in a shattered state.

In Hebrew, the mummy asked, "Where are Anck-su-namun's sacred jars?"

And in Hebrew, Beni said, "I will help you find them."

Above ground, the two expeditions had broken camp, and loaded up their horses and their camels.

Henderson and Daniels helped their blinded friend up onto his horse, putting the reins in his hands, assuring him they would lead him. Burns said nothing, a living dead man in a saddle, but at least he didn't fall out of it.

O'Connell helped Evelyn up onto her camel. She was looking toward Dr. Chamberlin, saddled up, clutching *The Book of the Dead* to him as if it were a life preserver that would keep him afloat through the sea of the night and desert that awaited them.

"Let him keep the damn thing," O'Connell told her. "All we want now is our lives."

She swallowed, nodded, and said, "You're right . . . Rick."

He smiled at her. "Let's go back to civilization, Evelyn—our civilization."

And soon O'Connell and Jonathan were astride their camels, as well, heading out into the moonswept, windblown desert, ready to leave the ruins and riches of Hamanaptra gladly behind.

As they rode quickly away, they did not see—none of them—the skeletal hand punch up out of the sand, behind them, in the City of the Dead.

But they did hear the terrible, resounding shriek of the mummy, echoing across the sands, telling them that Ardeth Bay had been right: O'Connell's mortal weapon had not killed He Who Shall Not Be Named.

That they had indeed unleashed the Bringer of Death.

·❦ PART THREE ❦·

The Mummy's Revenge

Cairo—1925

·❮ 15 ❯·

Sanctuary

On the southernmost outskirts of Cairo squatted Fort Stack, named after Sir Lee Stack, the assassinated governor general of the Sudan. The mudbrick, courtyard affair reminded O'Connell of a cavalry outpost in the old American West. Great Britain had withdrawn, not long ago, from the actual governing of Egypt—Fuad the First was the elected king— but the British army remained in an advisory capacity.

It was to Fort Stack, where the Union Jack flapped lazily in the dry breeze, that the disheveled, dusty caravan of the combined Carnahan and American expeditions sought sanctuary from the blistering desert sun, not to mention assorted plagues and a resurrected mummy. After a three-day trek from oasis to oasis, they had trudged up to the front gate, displayed their various papers, and were granted admittance.

For two days, the members of the combined parties mostly slept, in the guest quarters of the fort; they had taken their meals in the officers' mess, at the generous invitation of the commandant, and the only time any of them had left the compound was to go to a nearby tavern whose clientele was largely off-duty soldiers.

On the second day, a steamer trunk of clothing had arrived for Evelyn, which she had dispatched Jonathan to bring from their home, accompanied by her white cat, Cleo. O'Connell had carried the trunk up the stairs to her second-floor quarters overlooking the courtyard while Evelyn carried and petted the purring animal.

Today, the third day, however, she had called O'Connell to her two-room quarters and—in the process of removing her clothing from the closet of the spare, military-style bedroom, and piling them back into the steamer trunk—announced that she was mounting a return expedition.

And O'Connell was invited.

He stood, dumbfounded, watching her parade from the closet to the trunk, her movements brisk and mannish, her attire the same—jodphurs, black boots, and a white blouse. All she needed was a cap and riding crop and a fox to chase.

"*Another* expedition?"

"Yes," she said crisply. "I'm arranging for a full team of diggers and this time we'll have proper equipment, and proper weapons . . ."

"Evelyn, I shot him with an elephant gun."

Her cat had crawled inside the trunk; she lifted the white animal out and placed some underthings within. "Now, I want you to find some brave, competent men, regular soldiers of fortune—"

"What do you call Henderson and that bunch? And you saw how well *they* fared! Listen, for all we know, that mummy is dead, or anyway dead again. . . . I blasted the bastard! Pardon my French."

She frowned at him. "You heard that terrible scream as we rode off!"

He followed her to the closet. "Maybe that was his death rattle, or maybe it was just the desert wind playing tricks on our ears."

"Fine." Dresses folded over her arm, she marched to the trunk and deposited them. "Then if the mummy is dead, why not return and properly excavate the site? We'd barely scratched the surface, you know."

"And risk the wrath of those Med-jai warriors again?"

She shrugged, heading back to the closet. "They had

162

every opportunity to do us ill, and they didn't.''

Watching her as she made the journey from closet to trunk and back again, O'Connell gestured melodramatically. ''Do you *really* think that walking dead man is going to come after us? It's been days, and where's the rest of his plagues? Have you noticed the sun turning black, or seen any water turn to blood? Can't say *I* have.''

Tucking some shoes away, she looked up, arching an eyebrow, a teacher explaining something to a particularly dim student. ''The curse is very specific—he will seek us out, if we don't seek him out. It's those who disturbed his slumber who—''

''I thought you didn't believe in curses.''

''I was wrong.''

''You now believe your parents died as a result of King Tut's curse?''

She paused, halfway between closet and trunk. ''I . . . I believe I do. You see, Mr. O'Connell, once a young woman has had a tête-à-tête with a walking, talking corpse, her outlook on life tends to change.''

He followed her along as she packed. ''All right, I understand all that, but no new expedition—why borrow trouble? Maybe you'd like to see Chicago; we'll go rowing on the lake. Or maybe you could give me a tour of London; I always wanted to see the clowns at Picadilly Circus.''

She gazed at him and the affection showed through. ''Rick . . . we can't run away from this.''

''Who's running away? I just don't see the point of running *back* to where we just barely escaped with our lives.''

Her expression turned firm, her voice, too. ''We woke him—and it's our responsibility to try to stop him.''

''*We* woke him?''

''All right—I woke him. And I intend to stop him. If you don't want to help me, well, that's your decision. . . . Cleo! Bad girl.''

The cat was in the trunk again.

''Listen,'' he said, ''I'm no coward, but you heard that Med-jai chief, Ardeth What's-It. . . . He said no mortal weapons can kill this thing.''

163

That stopped her, but only to mull over his words, as if he'd provided her telling food for thought. "Then perhaps we need to consider what would constitute an 'immortal weapon.' Perhaps another incantation in *The Book of the Dead.* . . ."

"I want no part of this." He went to the trunk and grabbed a handful of her clothes and marched back to the closet with them. "And I can't allow you to—"

"Allow? Who appointed you my guardian?"

Hanging her dresses back up in the closet, he said, "Evelyn, it's too goddamn dangerous."

"Rick . . . I need your help. Now that this creature has been reborn, his curse will spread, like a terrible infection. The mummy himself is the real plague, a plague that could destroy the entire world."

He snatched some underthings from the trunk and marched them to the chest of drawers. "That's not my problem."

She stepped in front of him. "Are you insane? It's everybody's problem!"

"I'm not insane—that's why I want no part of this. Look, I appreciate what you did for me, buying my freedom, saving my life. But the agreement was I'd take you to Hamanaptra. I did that, and I brought you back, too."

She snatched the underthings from him and marched them back to the trunk, and dropped them in. "Oh, and so what's the American term? We're 'square' now? We're 'even'?"

"I didn't say that. . . ."

Hands on her hips, chin high, she peered down her nose at him, in that familiar, infuriating way she had. "Is that what this has been to you, what *I've* been? A business arrangement?"

"Hey—you got a choice: Come with me, and leave this insanity behind; or hop a boat back to hell, and try to save the world."

"I've already booked passage, thank you."

"Fine," he said.

"Fine," she said.

He searched for just the right, telling remark, to really put her in her place, to state his case in a manner so articulately that later, upon reflection, she would just have to come around to his way of thinking.

"Fine!" he said, and slammed the door behind him.

Then he realized he had some of her underthings in one hand, opened the door, pitched them in, and went off to get drunk.

Within minutes, O'Connell was sitting at the bar in the dingy dive near the fort, where even in the middle of the afternoon, business was good. Within these mud walls, in the dim gas lighting, soldiers of His Majesty and ex-soldiers of His Majesty and soldiers of fortune mixed bad women and bad booze in search of good times. A ceiling fan stirred the stale air as O'Connell sat between Jonathan and an old friend of Jonathan's, Winston Havlock of the Royal Air Force, who'd been stationed here for years.

The walrus-mustached Havlock, his eyes nearly as bloodshot as his nose, was in fact the last of the RAF still assigned to Cairo. The "rest of the laddies," as he put it, had either died in the air and been buried in the sand, or been transferred to better duty. A fighter pilot who now served as a taxi for British officers, Havlock spent more time in the bag, these days, than in the air.

Ten minutes into a bottle of whiskey, Havlock was O'Connell's "old friend," as well.

"Rick, old sport," Winston said, "ever since the Great War ended, there's been nary a challenge worthy of men like us."

"You might be surprised," O'Connell told him.

"At times I wish I'd've gone down in a blaze of glory, like the other lads, 'stead of sitting around this foul watering hole, rotting from boredom and booze."

Jonathan was lifting a shot glass to his lips when Havlock reached out, plucked it from Jonathan's fingers and drank it down.

"Bloody hell, Winston!" Jonathan said. "What's the idea?"

"That rotgut's not worthy of you, lad," Havlock told

him, climbing off the stool, barely able to stand. "Never let it be said Winston Havlock was not willing to sacrifice for his friends."

"Thank you, ever so," Jonathan commented dryly.

The pilot slapped both O'Connell and Jonathan on the back, said, "Right-o, lads! It's back to the airfield with me."

And he staggered off.

O'Connell raised an eyebrow. "How would you like to have *him* as your pilot?"

"Winston's never really needed a plane to fly higher than a kite. Bartender!"

As O'Connell and Jonathan sipped their whiskey (Havlock was right: It was vile rotgut, at that), Henderson and Daniels sidled up to the bar. Daniels still had an arm in a sling and both men—though shaved and bathed, in fresh shirts and chinos—had a hangdog, bedraggled look.

"Well," Henderson sighed wearily, "we're all packed up. Booked a steamer to Alexandria, for tomorrow morning."

Jonathan, who was a little drunk, said, "Going back home to mummy?"

Henderson bared his teeth, and it wasn't a smile.

O'Connell touched Henderson's arm, gently, and said, "Don't mind him. He's just a fool."

"A bloody fool, I'll have you know," Jonathan insisted. "Sit down, gentlemen. My sister will buy you a drink."

Henderson took the stool next to O'Connell, but Daniels—who was scowling at Jonathan, as if trying to decide whether to brain him or not—just stood there.

Henderson said to O'Connell, "So—you think that walking maggot pile is really coming after us?"

"I don't know," O'Connell said. "Plague season seems to be over, anyway. Funny . . . now that we're away from that ungodly place, it's like it . . . never happened."

"Tell that to Burns," Daniels snapped, still just standing there.

O'Connell asked, "How is he?"

"How the hell do you think he is? He had his goddamn eyes and tongue ripped out. How would you be?"

And Daniels, shaking his head, stormed out of the tavern.

"Don't mind him," Henderson said, his turn to apologize for a friend's behavior. "It's just . . . hell, can you imagine? Your eyes, your tongue, torn out like pages from a goddamn book. If I was Burns, I'd feed myself the barrel of a gun."

"Maybe you can get him some help back in the States," O'Connell said, swirling whiskey in his shot glass.

"You ask me," Henderson said, "the only way to help the poor bastard is . . . kill him."

And Henderson threw back a shot glass of whiskey, then called for another.

Sunlight filtered in through the closed curtains, but the quarters inhabited by the third American—Burns—were dark. The fort had electric lighting, but those lights were off. Only those few rays of sun were available to dance on the precious jewels decorating the canopic jar that sat in the midst of a table like a centerpiece. The man staying in this spartanly furnished guest room was, after all, blind, sitting at that table in dark glasses.

He had heard a knock at his door, and bid whoever-it-was enter. And whoever-it-was had turned out to be Beni, his expedition's missing guide, who had somehow made his way back to Cairo, too. With Beni was an honored visitor who, informed of the valuable canopic jar, wished to make Burns an offer.

Or so Beni had hurriedly said.

And now, attended by Burns's turbaned native servant, the three men sat at the table—Burns, in white shirt and chinos, Beni in his black pajamalike apparel, and (as Beni had introduced him to Burns) Prince Imhotep, a tall presence in a dark hooded robe, his face covered in a white mask, sculpted to his features, eyes glittering out of almond-shaped holes.

But, of course, Burns could not see this strange, forbidding figure, and for the first time since his eyes and tongue had been taken from him, a small kindling of hope grew within him: a buyer for his artifact! Money to take home, in seeking aid, therapy, nursing, for his new deformities . . .

167

"So varee peased too mee choo," Burns said, by way of tongueless greeting. And the American, almost eagerly, thrust his hand out in the Western world's ritual of friendship and trust, the handshake—a ritual his visitor refused.

Beni said, "I'm sorry, Mr. Burns, but the prince's religion does not allow him to touch one beneath his station. A silly Eastern superstition, but we must honor it."

"Mah ahpaw-low-gees," Burns said.

The native servant poured tea for the group, but when Burns reached for his cup, he spilled it.

"Oooh!" Burns said. "Saw-ree. Eyes arn whaa they use taw be."

"The prince sympathizes with your loss of sight," Beni said, shooing the servant away, using a harsh look to send him from the room. "The eyes he's using aren't the best, either."

Long, tapering fingers reached for the canopic jar—the flesh of the hands bandaged, and strangely withered. Imhotep picked up the jar, and Beni rose, backing away.

"Mr. Burns," Beni continued, "the prince humbly thanks you for your hospitality ... not to mention your eyes."

"Mah ... eyes?"

"Oh, yes, and your tongue."

Confusion blurred into fear within the darkness that was the world Burns lived in.

Beni was saying, "But I am afraid we must ask you to contribute even more, sir. You see, the prince must consummate the curse that you and your friends have brought down upon yourselves."

Burns stood, seized by fear, stumbling backward, losing his way in this small room he'd memorized, as lost as if he were wandering in the desert. The only mercy Imhotep had granted him was ripping out his eyes, days before, which spared Burns from the horror of seeing the robed mummy remove his strange mask to reveal the hideous visage beneath: a skull whose flesh had rotted largely away, a gray grotesque mask-beneath-the-mask enlivened only by bright eyes and rotten teeth and a pink darting tongue.

In the dingy dive near the fort, three men seated at the bar—bound together by the adversity of the Hamanaptra adventure—raised shot glasses, clinking them together, in one last farewell drink.

"Good luck, fellas," Henderson said, and simultaneously he, O'Connell, and Jonathan threw back their shot glasses of whiskey . . . and then, just as simultaneously, spat the liquid back out, onto the sand-and-sawdust-covered floor.

Around them, other patrons were doing the same—spitting out their drinks onto the floor, onto tables, onto the bar—and everywhere the liquid glimmered red.

"Sweet Jesus!" Henderson said, rubbing his face with a hand, streaking his flesh scarlet.

"Blood," O'Connell whispered.

The floor of the tavern looked like the aftermath of a slaughter, a bloodbath. . . .

" 'And the rivers and waters of Egypt,' " Jonathan intoned, " 'went red . . . and were as blood.' "

A sick feeling clenched O'Connell's stomach—not the nausea of the taste of blood in his mouth, but the realization that if one of those plagues was suddenly here, then . . .

"He's gotta be here," O'Connell said.

"Who?" Jonathan asked.

"Who?" Henderson asked.

"The creature, you goddamn owls!" O'Connell growled, jumping off the stool, heading quickly for the door. "The mummy!"

As he ran out into what had been a sunny afternoon, O'Connell found—in this land where it rained perhaps once a year—a sky roiling with black clouds, flashing with lightning. Running across the road through the front gates into the compound, O'Connell spotted a spooked Evelyn, walking with some books in hand, her white cat tagging along, staying close.

Suddenly the sky thundered, startling Evelyn, and she dropped her handful of books; O'Connell grabbed her arm and she jumped like a scared cat—like the scared cat next to her, in fact.

"You were right," he told her, breathlessly. "It is my problem, too."

She frowned at him, trying to make sense of that, but before she could, a barrage of hail and fire hurtled from the sky, assaulting the courtyard like an air raid. O'Connell grabbed Evelyn, pulling her under the eaves, as a wooden trellis just in front of them caught fire.

And then the courtyard was filled with panic—soldiers, servants, camels, horses, running in every direction, the men doing their best to duck the baseball-size hail, dodging the fireballs, a few running to the central fountain to get buckets and start fighting the small fires that had broken out all around the fort.

O'Connell clutched Evelyn by the arms and spoke above the din of hysteria around them: "He's here! The mummy is here!"

An alarm caused by more than the maelstrom around them leaped like flames in her eyes. "Are you sure?"

A ball of fire crashed within inches of them.

"Call it a hunch," he told her.

Then, as abruptly as it had begun, the hail ceased; the fireballs abated. Only the whinnying of horses, braying of camels, and crackle of flames remained, and then those noises too settled and stopped and gave way to silence—a dead, unearthly silence.

The silence did not last long: A scream of pain and terror unlike anything O'Connell had ever heard—and in recent days, he'd heard a few—ripped the stillness like a sharp blade through thin fabric.

Right above them.

"Stay here!" O'Connell said, and raced up the open wooden stairway to the living quarters above; and, of course, Evelyn followed.

A turbaned servant, who'd gone in to check on his master, was in the process of running back out, wild-eyed, screaming, and when O'Connell entered the quarters of the blinded American, Burns, he immediately saw the man, what little was left of him, sprawled upon the floor: shriveled to a human husk, drained of its bodily liquids, organs sucked away as well.

O'Connell was suddenly aware of Evelyn's presence, because she had hugged him, as if holding on for dear life. Then a loud moaning emanating from the far side of the room, beyond the bed, by the window, drew their attention to a bandaged head-to-toe figure standing there, loosely draped in a dark robe.

The mummy was skeletal, at first. Then as the adventurer from Chicago and the librarian from Cairo held each other close, in an embrace of terror, the creature began—incredibly, challenging their eyes—to regenerate.

A powerful new musculature formed upon the bones, like raw red flowers blossoming; then a thick skin grew, forming over the rippling tendons. Missing bones, including the hole O'Connell had blown in the mummy's ribcage, renewed themselves, and yet this muscular figure was somehow still clearly a corpse, wrapped in bandages, skin sickly gray, as if hell had sent its best soldier to wage war on those above.

"Did you see that?" O'Connell whispered. "Or am I crazy?"

"Yes," she said.

And then the mummy stretched, as if he'd woken from a long nap.

"We do have a problem," O'Connell admitted.

The mummy was moving toward them, slowly, but with a renewed confidence; and his eyes were fixed upon Evelyn.

O'Connell yanked the revolver from under his left shoulder and trained it upon the creature. "You get one chance to stop."

But the mummy kept coming, and O'Connell blasted away, stepping in front of Evelyn, blocking her, emptying the gun into the creature, which didn't seem to mind at all, the bullets making entrance wounds but no blood welling out.

Behind O'Connell, Jonathan came running into the room, with Henderson and Daniels close on his heels. The three men froze in place, stunned by the sight of the new and improved mummy that O'Connell was emptying his other

171

revolver into now, to no apparent affect, as the thing closed in on him.

O'Connell pitched his guns to the floor, thinking, *What the hell*, and he threw the best right hook he had in him, smack into the mummy's face . . .

. . . *and his fist went through the flesh and bone and sank into the mummy's head, getting stuck deep within!*

O'Connell stared at the head into which his hand was sunk wrist deep, thinking, *That must've been a hell of a right hook!*, and yanked his hand back out, like he was pulling it from thick, sticky mud, making a similar *slurping* sound. Evelyn was screaming behind him—or was that Jonathan? Before all of their eyes, the mummy's face—the area that had come into contact with O'Connell's fist—quickly degenerated, every bit as fast as the mummy's body had regenerated minutes before, decaying down to the bone, as if O'Connell's hand had infected it.

The mummy roared with rage and grabbed onto O'Connell by the shoulders, as if to shake him. O'Connell grabbed one of the mummy's hands, but could not budge it and then he was hurled across the room, into Jonathan, Henderson, and Daniels, knocking them down like milk bottles at a carnival.

But the mummy's hand had touched O'Connell's flesh and that hand too began to shrivel and decay, as if it were O'Connell who were the plague.

As O'Connell dazedly pushed himself up into a sitting position, the mummy was closing in on Evelyn, backing her up against a wall, where she raised the back of a hand to her mouth, eyes wide with fright.

The mummy was smiling at her! He spoke softly, tenderly, in a language that O'Connell figured was ancient Egyptian. The goddamn monster was leaning in to kiss her!

O'Connell was on his feet, and ready to infect that bastard with his touch again, when Cleo, Evelyn's white cat, revealed its presence atop a dresser, hissing, showing its teeth, hair standing up on its arched back, interrupting this tender moment between corpse and damsel.

The mummy reared back, shrieking like a scared old woman.

Then the balcony doors blew open with a sudden gust of wind and—though those who witnessed it questioned, later, what exactly they'd seen—the mummy seemed to spin into a tiny twister of sand and wind and speed, whipping himself into nothing except a spiraling sandstorm that went swirling out the doors.

Gone.

Everyone stumbled toward the center of the room and huddled, like confused football players, seeking a quarterback.

"What did he say to you?" O'Connell asked her.

She was trembling. "He . . . he said, 'You saved me. I am grateful.'"

White with fear, Henderson said, "We're cursed . . . all of us . . . cursed."

And the hardbitten American stumbled over to the shriveled shell of his dead friend, and knelt beside him, and began to weep—whether for himself or Burns, no one knew, and certainly no one asked.

·❦ 16 ❦·

Strange Bedfellows

Evelyn knew of only one person who might provide them with the answers they needed to combat He Who Shall Not Be Named, that walking plague carrier who had performed unspeakable acts and dark magic in the room where Burns had died.

She had to admit that, to his credit, O'Connell did not display any silly masculine pride when it came time for her to step forward and take the initiative. He had dutifully followed her lead as she instructed Jonathan to bring his Dusenberg around (when her brother had gone to their house to fetch her steamer trunk, he had returned with the convertible) and the entire lot of them—O'Connell, Jonathan, Henderson, Daniels, and herself—had piled in and roared off from the fort to her old place of employment.

Returning to this familiar facility made an eerie homecoming for Evelyn. Their feet echoing off the marble floors of the Cairo museum, she led the men through the halls, past galleries displaying the coffins of ancient kings, and the mummified kings themselves, who seemed to watch them pass by. In all the many months she had worked here, Evelyn had never found these premises, well, spooky . . . but now that she had met a mummy, in the rotting flesh, the nature of this huge haunted house, this repository of grave robbing, finally sank in for her, and her skin crawled.

She was leading the little group—the men in their white shirts, holstered guns, and chinos looking like a safari seeking a wild beast to shoot (which wasn't far from the truth)— toward the curator's office at the back of the museum. But as they rounded a corner, in the gallery to the left, there stood Dr. Bey—and not alone.

The round little man with the round face, a red fez atop his oily thinning black hair, in his usual dark suit with string tie, was speaking to an unusual guest: an angular-faced figure in dark, flowing robes, from under which gleamed the handle of a golden scimitar . . .

. . . Ardeth Bay—the chieftain of the Med-jai warriors— standing tall, like a figure from a museum exhibit come to life.

"*You!*" everyone said, in an echoing chorus of surprise and outrage.

Revolvers flew into the hands of O'Connell, Henderson, and Daniels; but Ardeth Bay merely glowered at them, a scowl touched with a contemptuous smile.

The curator gestured to Evelyn and her contingent. "Miss Carnahan. Gentlemen." And he gestured to the Med-jai leader. "May I introduce Ardeth Bay . . . a guest from out of town."

"We've met," O'Connell snapped.

Evelyn stepped forward, facing her ex-boss. "What is he doing here?"

"Do you truly wish to know? Or would your impulsive American friends prefer to react as they always do? With swift, stupid violence, and no thought as to consequences whatsoever?"

And indeed the guns of the Americans were raised and trained upon the curator and the warrior, the tension in the air crackling.

Pieces fitted quickly into place within Evelyn's mind, and she said, "As opposed to your considered, astute violence, Dr. Bey?" She gestured to Ardeth Bay. "*You* told the

Med-jai that I possessed the puzzle box, the key. . . . *You* sent them to steal it from me—and kill me!''

"It was not my desire for you to die—and here you stand alive before me.''

"But if I had been killed, and the key box retrieved, that would have been an acceptable price to pay, I suppose?''

"Frankly, Miss Carnahan . . . yes. The life of one silly, headstrong, incompetent girl in trade for saving the world from what, in your religion, might be called Armageddon? Oh yes—yes and yes, a thousand times.''

O'Connell stepped forward, uncocking his revolver, returning it to his holster; he nodded to Henderson and Daniels and the men frowned, but lowered their guns—they did not, however, join O'Connell in holstering their weapons.

"I don't think threats or insults are productive, at this point,'' O'Connell said, in a reasonable, intelligent tone that surprised Evelyn. "The genie's out of the bottle, so to speak. Maybe we need to work together.''

Dr. Bey's smile was patronizing, his tiny mustache twitching. "Are you sure you wouldn't prefer just to shoot us?''

"I'm not saying that doesn't sound like a good time, pal.'' And O'Connell gave Ardeth Bay a nasty smile. "But I just saw my fist vanish into the skull of some walking dead 'thing.' So I'm willing to go on faith here, at least for a little ways.''

"You would not be capable of comprehending—''

"Hey. I saw a guy turn into a sandstorm and blow himself out the window. You might be surprised what I'd buy, at this point.''

The curator studied O'Connell's face, as if it were an inscription he was translating, and then Dr. Bey said, "Follow me,'' leading the group through the gallery, Ardeth Bay at his side.

As if a tour guide, the curator led them down a sun-dappled aisle under high skylights, past displays with which Evelyn was most familiar, splendid mummy caskets of fine woods, exquisitely carved and painted with pictures telling the stories of the lives of their occupants.

Dr. Bey was saying, "This is King Rameses, who went to school with Moses—the pharaoh who oppressed the Israelites, who set in motion the tyranny that would your bring your God to afflict Egypt with plagues."

The well-preserved, iron-jawed Rameses seemed to look back at them, the teeth in his black face as white as if they'd been brushed this morning.

"And this is Seti the First, father of Rameses—a great warrior, who built a canal from the Nile to the Red Sea."

On display with his chariot and sword, Seti was propped up in his casket, his black arms folded, his black head resting on yellow grave clothes, features peaceful.

The throne of Seti was nearby and the curator sat in it, crossing his legs casually. "As you can see, Seti sleeps well—unlike his faithless high priest, Imhotep, who successfully conspired with a traitorous wench to murder him. This is why Imhotep was buried alive."

"And cursed with the dreaded *hom-dai*," Evelyn whispered.

"My dear," the curator said, "we will make a scholar of you yet." He gestured toward Ardeth Bay, who stood beside the seated-in-the-throne curator like a faithful servant. "We are members of an ancient sect—"

"The Med-jai," Evelyn said.

"I am impressed. But I doubt you were aware, my dear, that this secret society had endured, pursuing its sacred mission down through these three thousand years. For all that time, the Med-jai have guarded the City of the Dead, protecting it from the desecration of grave robbers, in part . . . but also to protect the world from the living curse buried there. You see, we are sworn at manhood to do all in our power to prevent High Priest Imhotep from returning into this world. And for thirty-nine generations, we have prevailed."

"But now because of you," Ardeth Bay said, thrusting a finger at Evelyn, "we have failed."

Appalled, Evelyn said, "And this justifies killing innocent people?"

177

"To stop this creature," the warrior said, "I would gladly kill you now."

O'Connell stepped between them and said to the seated curator, "Let's just keep it friendly, okay, pops? You want to try to pin the blame-tail on some jackass, or do you want to help us stop this son of a bitch?"

Evelyn frowned at O'Connell, wondering if she'd just been insulted.

A small smile traced itself beneath the curator's mustache; he nodded. "I believe you are right . . . Mr. O'Connell, isn't it?"

"Yeah. You know, for instance—why was this big bad monster afraid of a little bitty kitty?"

"Cats are the guardians of the underworld. He Who Shall Not Be Named will fear these harmless animals until he is fully returned to his perfect state."

"Regenerating himself, you mean."

"Yes. Once he has . . . regenerated . . . he will fear nothing. And nothing will be able to stop him."

Daniels stepped forward, gesturing with his revolver at the curator. "I don't need this clown in a Masonic cap to tell me how this creep is doin' that! He's killing everybody who opened that chest! He's sucking all of us dry!"

"A very astute observation," the curator said, "from so unlearned a man."

O'Connell glanced sharply at Henderson, who nodded, and went over to settle his friend down.

Evelyn approached the throne-perched curator. "At Hamanaptra, Imhotep addressed me by an ancient name."

Alarmed, the curator asked, "What was that name?"

"Anck-su-namun."

The curator and the Med-jai chief exchanged dire looks.

O'Connell said, "I think the slimy bastard was about to try to kiss her, when that cat spooked him."

Nodding, absorbing this, Dr. Bey said, "That is the name of the mistress for the love of whom He Who Shall Not Be Named was cursed. Could it be, even after these three thousand years, even after suffering unending death, flesh eaten away by scarab beetles . . . that even now he loves her?"

"A love that spans the ages," Evelyn said. "How sad . . . how romantic. . . ."

"Are you kidding?" O'Connell said, wide-eyed.

Her brother was shaking his head, smirking at her.

Embarrassed, she looked away.

Ardeth Bay said, "He Who Shall Not Be Named will try to raise Anck-su-namun from the dead."

"Yeah," O'Connell said, "and how the hell will he manage that, exactly?"

"With a human sacrifice," the curator said. Then he nodded toward Evelyn. "And it would appear He Who Shall Not Be Named has chosen a subject."

Evelyn felt a sudden chill—and every eye in the room, including those of the dead pharaohs, upon her.

Jonathan made a clicking sound in his cheek. "Bad luck, Sis. Sometimes it just doesn't pay to be popular."

"Jesus," O'Connell breathed. "Just when I figured things couldn't get any worse . . ."

"On the contrary," Dr. Bey said. "This may give us the time we need to find a way to kill this evil creature."

"That's why we're here, doc," O'Connell said. "You're the expert—can we read some other incantation from that *Book of the Dead*?"

"Possibly—if it could be retrieved. But I know of nothing, either in ancient writings or modern scholarship, to confirm that assumption."

The gallery, lighted only by gas torches, had grown dark.

Looking upward, Ardeth Bay said, "His powers are growing."

Evelyn, and everyone else, looked at the ceiling, toward the skylights that until moments ago had been slanting rays of sun down into the gallery.

And they saw the sun as it moved into full eclipse, afternoon becoming midnight.

Driving through the streets of a confused Cairo, Jonathan, behind the wheel of his Dusenberg, said, " 'And he stretched forth his hands toward the heavens, and there was darkness throughout the land of Egypt.' "

"You must have learned more in Sunday school than you thought," O'Connell said, sitting at the rider's front-seat window, Evelyn squeezed between him and her brother, Henderson and an increasingly agitated Daniels in the backseat.

"There must be a way to stop him from regenerating," Evelyn said.

O'Connell sighed. "You heard what your old boss said. Once Imhotep's fully back in his prime, there's no stopping him."

As they drew up to the fort, they could see British soldiers marching along the parapets under a black sun.

"Days are getting shorter," Jonathan observed.

Soon they were assembled in the foyer of Evelyn's two-room guest quarters. Henderson and Daniels were slumped in chairs. She and her brother were pacing. O'Connell had gone out to do "a little snooping," he'd said. The door opened and the adventurer from Chicago stepped back inside.

Shutting the door behind him, O'Connell said, "My ol' buddy Beni was seen here today, with a tall stranger in Arab robes. According to Burns's servant, Beni and this stranger—who wore some kind of mask . . . went in there to talk 'business' with Burns."

"Beni was with the mummy?" Jonathan asked. "What would that little scoundrel be doing with—"

"Who exactly opened that chest?" Evelyn asked suddenly. "I want a precise list."

Henderson shrugged wearily. "Me and Daniels here—and poor Burns, of course, and, uh . . . Dr. Chamberlin. That's it."

"But not Beni?" O'Connell asked.

"Naw," Daniels said. "He ran out of there like a scared rabbit, 'fore we even opened the goddamned thing."

"A smart scared rabbit," Henderson said bitterly.

Evelyn planted her feet and faced the men. "We should include Dr. Chamberlin in our group. We need to all stay together . . . we're safer that way."

"I checked," O'Connell said. "He's not in his room.

Servant said our resident Egyptologist didn't sleep in his bed last night."

"Dr. Chamberlin had *The Book of the Dead*!" Evelyn said. "We need it, desperately!"

O'Connell shook his head "no." "I looked everywhere in his quarters. All of his things—cleared out."

"We have to find him," Evelyn said, "and bring him here, to the safety of this fort. . . ."

"It was real safe for Burns, wasn't it?" Daniels snorted.

"If the mummy finds him," Evelyn said, "and . . . does to him what he did to your friend, Mr. Burns . . . Imhotep will be that much closer to full regeneration."

"Chamberlin has an office in Cairo," Henderson said. "In the alleys of the bazaar section. Maybe he went back there."

"Okay," O'Connell said. He nodded toward the Americans. "You two come with me. Jonathan, you stay here with Evelyn, protect your sister."

"The hell with that!" Henderson said. "I'll give you the address—you go, if you want to! I'm not going anywhere."

Daniels said, "I'm not leaving this fort."

Evelyn charged right up to O'Connell, who it appeared *did* have an unhealthy dose of masculine pride after all, and said to him, "*I* am leading this expedition, thank you! I'm not some child whose well-being you consign to the nearest *male* adult!"

O'Connell shook his head, sighing, as if he were a poor, put-upon soul just trying to help.

Then he grabbed her by the arm and dragged her toward the open doorway to her bedroom, tossed her in, and slammed the door.

"You can't manhandle me like that!" she shouted, pulling on the doorknob. "You brute!"

On the other side of the door, she could hear O'Connell saying, "Jonathan—you have a key?"

"I believe so, old boy."

She yelled, "Jonathan, you traitor! Don't you dare help this—"

But then she heard the click of the lock.

And on the other side of the door, O'Connell was saying, "This door is never to be opened—understood? Nobody in, nobody out."

"Understood," Daniels said.

"Stand watch over her, or I'll come back and suck out your spleens myself, got it?"

"Yeah, yeah," Henderson said. "Here's that address . . ."

"Come on, Jonathan," O'Connell said.

She was trying the knob; it was locked, firmly locked, all right.

Jonathan's voice beyond the door was saying, "You know, I liked your first plan much better, old sod. Where I stayed here at the fort? I could, uh . . . reconnoiter . . . that is, should anyone be able to explain to me what that is, exactly."

"Come on," O'Connell said, and then their voices were gone as, so, presumably, were they.

She pounded and banged on the door for a while, yelling, but it did no good whatsoever, and she stomped over to the bed, threw herself onto it, folding her arms, cursing Rick O'Connell, fighting the fondness for him flowing through her.

The bazaars of Cairo consisted of winding narrow streets crowded with stores, every store a factory for the goods offered therein. O'Connell and Jonathan navigated the turbaned vendors, veiled women in black bombazine, naked children, donkey boys, and even the occasional tourist, and found their way to the glassmaker's shop above which Dr. Chamberlin kept his tiny office.

The door was unlocked; in fact, it was ajar. The Egyptologist wasn't in, but someone else was: Beni, in the process of ransacking the place, desk drawers emptied, bookcases asunder, piles of photos and files everywhere.

The skinny little knave had just slipped a silver watch into a black pajama pocket when O'Connell, followed by Jonathan, stepped inside the office to say, "Let me guess, Beni—misplace your principles?"

Beni bolted for an open window facing onto the street: It was only a one-story drop. O'Connell almost casually picked up the Egyptologist's desk chair, which had been flung over near the door, and pitched it into Beni's path.

Beni tripped and slammed into a wall, knocking off several framed pictures of Chamberlin at various desert digs.

"I'll be glad to help you look," O'Connell said cheerfully, walking over, picking up Beni by the back of the neck and lifting him, pushing him up against the wall.

Feet dangling, Beni smiled sickly and said, "Rick! I didn't notice it was you—my old friend!"

"Oh, but you have a new friend, don't you, Beni? You came back from the desert with him, right?"

Blinking, smiling desperately, Beni asked, "What friend? You're my only friend, Rick. You know I've always been picky about my associations."

O'Connell allowed Beni to slide down the wall to his feet; the little man sighed in relief, smoothing out his black shirt, then his eyes widened as a knife blade suddenly appeared in the hand of his "only friend."

Holding the sharp edge of the blade against Beni's neck, O'Connell said, softly, menacingly, "Why, Beni? What's in it for you? Why are you helping this monster?"

"I . . . I serve him only to save myself. Better to stand at the devil's right hand than to be in his path."

O'Connell sighed; that sounded like Beni, all right. "What are you doing in this office? What are you looking for?"

Even with a blade at his throat, Beni managed a single, harsh laugh. "Do you really think your small threats compare to what Imhotep could do?"

"Imhotep isn't here right now. Do you really think I won't slit your lying throat? What are you looking for, Beni?"

O'Connell pressed the blade harder, flesh whitening.

"The book, the book! That black book they found at the City of the Dead . . . Chamberlin had it. Imhotep wants it."

"Why?"

"I don't know! All I know is, he said it was worth its weight in gold!"

"Gold?" Jonathan said, interested in the sound of that.

"Spill, Beni," O'Connell said, applying more pressure to the blade. "What does he want with the thing?"

"I don't know, I tell you! Rick—come on. Don't do this . . ."

"Spill what you know, or I'll spill your blood. Choose."

"It's . . . it's something about bringing 'her' back from the dead . . . whoever 'her' is."

"And he needs the book to do that."

"The book, yes, the book, and, uh . . ."

" 'And, uh' what, Beni?"

"The girl. He needs your girl." Beni looked toward Jonathan. "His sister."

Jonathan frowned. "I say—he'll have to kill me first."

Beni shrugged. "He won't mind."

Outside, in the night that was afternoon, a shrill scream rose above the chatter of the bazaar like the howl of a wounded animal. O'Connell's eyes went to the window and he took just enough pressure off the blade at Beni's throat for the little bastard to knee him in the groin.

O'Connell doubled over as Beni scrambled past him, leaping out the window, sliding down an awning to freedom.

Jonathan helped O'Connell to his feet.

"Anybody ever tell you you're bad luck?" O'Connell asked Jonathan through gritted teeth.

"Almost everyone, old man . . . Shall we see what the commotion is about?"

Down in the bazaar, the scream had been followed by shouts and cries and murmurs of horror and concern.

At the window, O'Connell and Jonathan could see down the narrow street, not far, where the crowd had parted and a body lay sprawled. Though barely recognizable, and mostly so only by the pith helmet and khaki clothing, the shriveled corpse was clearly Dr. Chamberlin, on its side, another human husk.

And over the body hovered the robed figure of Imhotep, the black *Book of the Dead* already tucked under an arm like a big heavy schoolbook. He Who Shall Not Be Named was plucking the jewel-encrusted canopic jar from the withered fingers of the dead Egyptologist.

Somehow the mummy sensed the eyes that were upon him, and the creature looked suddenly, sharply up at O'Connell and Jonathan poised in the window. Imhotep had regenerated further, and the infectionlike wounds O'Connell had inflicted earlier had healed perfectly.

And the mummy stood, jaw seeming to unhinge, mouth opening to an impossible, inhuman size, and from within him, as if disgorging himself of them, a swarm of flies emerged, more like angry hornets, a black buzzing mass racing right at the window where O'Connell and Jonathan watched, stupefied spectators.

O'Connell slammed shut the shutter, Jonathan closing the one on his side of the window, too, and the flies flew into it, pummeling the wood. The two men could not see the flies, deflected at the window, turn as a group like precision fighter pilots and swoop down on the confused, frightened crowd in the bazaar below, sending them running, screaming, pawing and clawing at their hair.

Breathing hard, O'Connell asked, "That's another one of the plagues, right?"

"Right. But there's a few left."

"Oh that's nice to know."

"He has the book, old chum."

"Yes. Now all he needs is . . ."

"Evy!"

And they ran from the office.

185

·❮ 17 ❯·

Beauty and the Beast

Night had come unannounced, blending into the day of the black sun, with only the stars and moon to mark the difference. At Fort Stack, the guard had been tripled, soldiers walking the parapets, outlined against every turret; but their presence was little comfort to the two Americans holed up in the foyer of the Englishwoman's quarters.

"What's taking O'Connell so damn long to get back?" Daniels asked. Arm still in a sling, the dark, brooding Daniels sucked on a cigarette as he paced, occasionally looking out the window, which had a view of the road out in front of the fort, and the mud-brick tavern across the way, whose lights and music beckoned.

"Streets are probably clogged," Henderson said. "Probably spooked the local savages, havin' the sun turn black."

"Oh, and it didn't spook a Great White Hunter like you."

"I've witnessed stranger things, lately." The tow-headed expedition leader was seated in a chair near the door to the Carnahan girl's bedroom, holding his share of the Hamanaptra booty: a jeweled canopic jar. He turned it in his hands, admiring it, studying it, hoping the artifact would bring a price remotely worthy of what they'd been through.

"Hell with this," Daniels said, grinding his cigarette out in an ashtray on a table by the window. "I'm goin' over and have a drink."

"Why don't you bring me back a bottle, when you're done?"

"Bourbon?"

"Bourbon with a bourbon chaser."

Daniels nodded and headed out.

Henderson lit up a cigarette, letting it pull on his lungs, relaxing him. Smoke streaming out his nostrils, dragon-style, he fondled the jeweled jar, and for the first time he reflected on its antiquity, its beauty, not just its value.

A breeze drifted in the open window along with the sounds of flute and tambourine music from the tavern across the way, creating pleasant images of veiled belly dancers in Henderson's mind, filmy curtains fluttering, like the arms of a native girl gesturing seductively to him. Then the breeze blew colder—nights were so goddamn chilly here—and Henderson, the precious jar in his hands, rose to shut the window.

He gazed out at the lights of the tavern, the foreign music with its compelling rhythm calling to him. Maybe he'd go over and join Daniels; maybe he'd see if some wench was dancing to that exotic music. He glanced at the Carnahan girl's door, wondering if he dared leave her here alone for a few minutes. He was dying to get out of this prison. . . .

Then he turned to the window just as the breeze gained intensity. Even as he was reaching to shut the shutters, a tidal wave of sand blasted through the window, knocking him back, the jar tumbling from his fingers, unharmed, to the floor, as a swirling, whirling dervish of desert dust en-gulfed him, lifting him, sucking him into its cyclonelike fun-nel.

There in the foyer of Evelyn Carnahan's living quarters, while furniture looked mutely on, untouched by the storm in its midst, Henderson twirled within the sandstorm, spin-ning in a deadly pirouette, his screams quickly dying, choked off, as the life was sucked out of him. Then the sand drew away from what had been Henderson, and gathered in upon itself, taking a human shape, transforming into a further regenerated, dark-robed Imhotep, looming above the withered shell of the American.

As the mummy retrieved the jeweled jar, a scarab scurried from a cavity in his chest and scampered up into a hole in Imhotep's cheek; almost absentmindedly, the mummy chewed the scarab, swallowed, and then—hearing the moan of a woman—looked toward the closed bedroom door.

Imhotep stepped over the husk of Henderson and strode to that door, trying the knob, rattling it. He examined the door, as if considering whether to knock the thing down or not; perhaps he did not want to disturb her, unduly, for he decided to enter in a less tumultuous manner.

Within the bedroom, Evelyn slept restfully atop the covers; she did not wear bedclothes, rather a black, arm-baring dress with a heart-shaped, white-lace-trimmed bodice, comfortable enough to sleep in, but something she could leap from bed wearing for whatever the next dreadful stage of this ordeal might be. That mind-set explained the dreams she was caught up in, nearly delirious images of herself and O'Connell fleeing from the mummy across the ruins of the City of the Dead, only at times she was fleeing from Rick and holding on to the mummy's hand . . . it was all very troubling, which was why she was moaning, even crying out in her fitful sleep.

She was unaware of an image, just across the bedroom from her, far more troubling and bizarre than those she was currently conjuring from her subconscious. . . .

Sand was streaming in through her keyhole and down onto the floor, pouring like water from a spigot, making a small pile, then a larger one, like an hourglass got out of hand, until a mound, a dune, had formed, and when the sand had stopped streaming in, that dune, that mound, began to form itself, as if some invisible sculptor were fashioning a sand statue of a god, or a man, or in this case, something that was both and neither: He Who Shall Not Be Named— Imhotep.

Almost floating, in his dark robes, Imhotep went to the

beautiful young sleeping woman, and like the Prince waking Snow White, he knelt over her, whispering, "Anck-su-namun," and kissed her.

He paid no heed to sounds behind him—the bedroom door, its knob rattling, then the crashing, the pounding, as some mortal fool on the other side tried to bash it down.

Nor did Imhotep pay any heed to the result of his kissing the sleeping beauty, that her very flesh corrupted his, causing his lips and the skin around his mouth to decay, putrefy almost instantly, down to the bare, white bone, creating a ghastly skull-like grin as he looked down adoringly at the tossing and turning young woman.

The door burst open in an explosion of splintering wood, O'Connell shouldering through, stumbling to a frozen stop as he faced the remarkable, appalling tableau of the black-robed mummy bending over Evelyn, on her bed.

And, while the mummy's kiss had not woken her, the sound of O'Connell breaking her bedroom door down had served as an abrupt alarm clock going off, and she now looked up at the fetid face of the adoring mummy, leaning in to bestow her another kiss, and her lips parted, her lovely mouth widening as if to accept the tongue that had once belonged to the late Mr. Burns, and then a scream emerged from her so bloodchilling that even the mummy reared back.

And then Evelyn was sitting up, shoving him away, one hand slipping past the robe to the ancient bandaged flesh and sinking in, creating instant infection, immediate atrophy.

"Aren't you a little old for her, pal—like two or three thousand years?" O'Connell advanced on the creature, though his guns remained tucked in his shoulder holsters. "Get the hell away from my girl!"

Wheeling in anger, robes flowing, Imhotep scowled and growled at the intruder, teeth bared through rotting flesh.

O'Connell winced in disgust. "Whoa! Next time you're plannin' to kiss somebody, bring your lips."

The mummy raised his arms in attack, lurching toward O'Connell, who yelled, "Jonathan—now!"

And in the doorway, Evelyn's brother appeared, her white cat in his arms; Jonathan pitched the cat to O'Connell, fire-brigade style, and O'Connell tossed the little creature into the oncoming arms of the big creature, who instinctively caught it, reacting like a man who'd grabbed onto a bucket of hot coals.

The cat screeched, the mummy shrieked, in dreadful comic harmony. Imhotep dropped the animal and, clearly weakened, stumbled toward the window, which blew open, shutters rattling, and a gust of wind swept through.

And the mummy began to spin, to twirl, and before their wide eyes, which they soon covered as if caught in a sandstorm, whirled like a dervish into a funnel of sand, which blew and spewed out the window with incredible force, sucking and slamming shut the shutters behind him.

Not a grain of sand remained on the floor.

Jonathan entered, revolver in hand, trembling like an old man, and O'Connell rushed to Evelyn, taking her in his arms, as she looked away, rubbing the slime off her face with the back of a hand, reeling with revulsion.

O'Connell, an arm around Evelyn's shoulder, walked her into the foyer, with Jonathan following, just as Daniels entered, bottle of bourbon in hand.

Which he dropped, the bottle exploding into glass fragments and splashing liquid.

"God in heaven," Daniels said, gazing upon the withered corpse of his friend Henderson, "I'm next."

O'Connell grabbed the man by his good arm. "None of us is next if we can kill that bandaged son of a bitch. And I just stopped him with a goddamn kitty."

"Pity that famous gunnysack of yours isn't full of felines," Jonathan said dryly. "All *we* have are bullets."

Evelyn was staring down at the shriveled corpse of Henderson, but not in horror: She was thinking.

"You're both right," she said to O'Connell and her brother. "We can only battle this monster from antiquity with the weapons of antiquity . . . and I think I may know how to do that."

Within minutes, they were speeding down the streets of Cairo in the Dusenberg convertible, Jonathan behind the wheel, honking the horn to clear a path, Evelyn again squeezed between her brother and O'Connell. Daniels, sole survivor of the American party, sat in the backseat, with O'Connell's gunnysack arsenal; his face drawn in fear, the once stoic soldier of fortune was removing his sling, testing his arm, apparently thinking having two limbs might come in handy.

Though still shaken by the appearance of an amorous living mummy in her bedroom, Evelyn managed a small smile for O'Connell, asking teasingly, "So I'm your 'girl,' am I?"

"Aw, just tryin' to fluster that freak."

"Are you sure you weren't jealous?"

"What? That guy makes Frankenstein look like Valentino! When I kiss you, you won't be spittin' out bones and bandages."

"Shut up!" Daniels screamed from the backseat. "Shut up you, fools! We're all going to die if we don't do something!"

Evelyn looked back at him, not unkindly. "We're about to do something. Right now."

And indeed the massive Museum of Antiquities loomed ahead, palm trees out front swaying in the evening breeze, gas torches along its sandstone walls glowing and flickering in the night, Egyptian warrior statues standing tall, guarding the double front doors, where—moments later—Jonathan dropped his passengers.

The curator was expecting them—Evelyn had phoned ahead—and the round little man, still accompanied by Medjai chieftain Ardeth Bay, escorted Evelyn, O'Connell, and Daniels through the museum's vast atrium entryway with its impressive display of sarcophagi, boats, and enormous statues. Their footsteps echoing (Jonathan, who'd parked the car, catching up with them), they headed up the wide marble staircase, Evelyn lecturing the curator, for a change.

"According to the ancient lore," she was saying, "the black book found at Hamanaptra is said to bring the dead back to life."

"*The Book of the Dead*, yes," Dr. Bey said. "My un-

191

derstanding is that you read an incantation from that volume, which—''

''Yes, we've been over that quite thoroughly, haven't we?'' Evelyn's expression was a combination of a wince and a smile. ''But as a scholar, I tended to judge such things from an anthropological viewpoint. Such sorcery was something I was unwilling to believe.''

The curator's pursed smile made his tiny mustache wiggle. ''I take it you've revised your opinion.''

''Better believe it, buddy,'' O'Connell chimed in. ''Ask her how three-thousand-year-old breath smells.''

Evelyn gave O'Connell a quick, cross look, then said, ''Yes, well, what I'm thinking is that if that obsidian volume can restore life to the dead—''

''I get it!'' O'Connell snapped his fingers. ''That *gold* book you had us looking for!''

''Why, Rick,'' she said with surprise and pleasure, ''I believe you've hit on the answer, too.''

''Sure—if the black book brings 'em back, stands to reason that gold book can send 'em to hell again!''

''Quite,'' she said. ''That certainly would be consistent with the lore.''

Narrow-eyed, nodding, Ardeth Bay said, ''That might undo the damage you have done—and return He Who Shall Not Be Named to the grave.''

''Finally!'' Daniels said through his teeth, clenching a fist and shaking it.

They had reached a landing and paused there.

''An incantation from *The Book of Amun Ra*,'' the curator was saying. He'd been thinking this through. ''Yes. That might do it! But that priceless artifact has been high on the lists of those plundering the Valley of the Kings since the time of the pharaohs—from the grave robbers of antiquity, to the likes of your own father, Miss Carnahan.''

She shrugged. ''Well, maybe they didn't know where to look.''

O'Connell touched her arm. ''And you do?''

''Possibly. There's a display on the balcony that may hold the answer.''

And they moved onto the balcony to a glass-and-wood display case of fragments of stone tablets bearing various hieroglyphs; the curator—using a far more conventional key than a puzzle box—quickly opened the display case. In so doing, he seemed to unleash an eerie chanting. . . .

"What is that dreadful sound?" Jonathan asked.

"It's coming from outside," O'Connell said, nodding to the octagonal window that faced the parking lot.

The chanting was growing, and what exactly was being said became chillingly evident, and horrifying familiar: *"Im-ho-tep! Im-ho-tep! Im-ho-tep!"*

They gathered at the window and looked down at the crowd of people, in turbans and gowns, veils and dresses, rabble and well-to-do alike, even a few tourists mixed in with this native mob, pouring from the streets toward the museum, swarming like insects, some of them carrying torches.

"Jesus!" Daniels said. "What's wrong with them? They're like . . ."

"Zombies," O'Connell said.

"Im-ho-tep! Im-ho-tep! Im-ho-tep!"

"I say, what's a 'zombie,' old chap?" Jonathan asked, his eyes wide with the terrible sight below him, the milling, chanting multitude.

"The living dead," O'Connell said.

Daniels drew his revolver.

"West African voodoo cults," the curator put in.

"Look at their flesh," Ardeth Bay said.

Many of them were closer now, staggering like sleep-walkers, eyes wide and empty, their skin covered with hideous lesions.

"Boils and sores!" Jonathan said. "It's another plague!"

"Im-ho-tep! Im-ho-tep! Im-ho-tep!"

"And they don't look happy about it," O'Connell said.

"It has begun," Ardeth Bay said. "The end begins."

"You can give up if you want to," Evelyn said to the Med-jai warrior, then added sarcastically, "After all, you have been at this for three thousand years—perhaps it's time you took a break. But *we're* going to get to work—right, Dr. Bey?''

"Im-ho-tep! Im-ho-tep! Im-ho-tep!"

"Yes," the curator said. "As soon as I go down and lock the doors. . . ."

While the curator did that, Evelyn began sorting through the broken pieces of tablets, tossing precious relics aside like empty paper cups when they didn't give her what she sought.

"Im-ho-tep! Im-ho-tep! Im-ho-tep!"

"According to the Bembridge scholars," Evelyn said, entirely focused and seemingly unconcerned about the crazed crowd beyond these walls, "the golden *Book of Amun Ra* was hidden inside the statue of Anubis."

Daniels said, "But that's where we found the other book, that goddamn black book."

"Precisely," Evelyn said.

"Those Bembridge boys were mistaken when they spurned my sister," Jonathan said. "Maybe they were wrong about that, as well."

"Im-ho-tep! Im-ho-tep! Im-ho-tep!"

Daniels, pacing about with revolver in hand, said, "No offense, but your British reserve is giving me a royal pain. Can't you work a little faster?"

Evelyn's fingers were moving quickly across a large stone tablet. "My theory is that the Bembridge scholars confused the books, reversed where the two volumes were hidden. So if the black book was inside Anubis, then the gold book should be . . ."

"Im-ho-tep! Im-ho-tep! Im-ho-tep!"

"Evy," Jonathan said, "our American friend Mr. Daniels has a point—faster, dear, faster!"

"Patience is a virtue," she reminded her brother.

"So is breathing," O'Connell pointed out. He had a revolver in hand, too.

"Why don't I save us some time," Jonathan said, "and go get the car. Dr. Bey, is there a side door I can take?"

The curator gave Jonathan rapid instructions, pointing him toward a back stairway deeper inside the museum.

As Jonathan was about to scurry off, O'Connell said, "You think you can wade through those zombies?"

"Im-ho-tep! Im-ho-tep! Im-ho-tep!"

The sound of the mob throwing themselves against front doors resounded through the atrium; the little group on the balcony could easily see those doors from where they stood, the heavy wooden panels shuddering and swelling and giving. . . .

Jonathan patted O'Connell on the shoulder. "I don't see that I have much choice, chum! Meet you at the side door!"

And Evelyn's brother scurried off.

"Im-ho-tep! Im-ho-tep! Im-ho-tep!"

"Here it is!" Evelyn cried. "So much for the Bembridge scholars—the golden *Book of Amun Ra* is in the statue of Horus!"

"The statue of Horus," the curator said, frowning in thought, "should be located fifty kadams west of the Anubis statue."

"Oh Christ," O'Connell said, making a face. "You don't mean we have go back to the City of Dead?"

Ardeth Bay said, "Only if you want to destroy He Who Shall Not Be Named."

The front doors of the museum gave way, falling and echoing like giant timber, the front line of turbaned zombies pitching and tumbling in on top of the fallen doors, getting trampled by their bonkers brethren as the vocal mob, caught up in their frenzied trance, began streaming in, pouring into the gallery below, and reverberating up through the atrium came their crazed chanters' cry: *"Im-ho-tep! Im-ho-tep! Im-ho-tep!"*

"Trip back to Hamanaptra sounds swell right now," O'Connell said. "Let's go!"

And they ran in the direction Jonathan had gone.

·❮ 18 ❯·

Imhotep's Triumph

In his own view, Jonathan Carnahan was neither brave nor a coward; what he prided himself on was his resourcefulness, a certain quick-thinking adaptability, no matter how dire the situation.

But as Jonathan exited the museum into the parking lot, where the Dusenberg awaited, he found himself facing a situation so dire it challenged even his deep reserve of self-serving sufficiency: a splinter group of the crazed, drooling throng, which had otherwise swarmed the front of the museum, was staggering toward him, eyes wide and glazed, flesh blistered with sores and boils, arms outstretched like insane somnambulists.

A dozen of more of these zombies were bearing down upon him, chanting at the top of their lungs: *"Im-ho-tep! Im-ho-tep!"*

Whereupon Jonathan, skidding to a stop, bugged out his eyes, thrust his arms forward, turned, summoned some drool and intoned: *"Im-ho-tep! Im-ho-tep!"*

As the deranged chanters lurched on, heading toward the front of the museum, Jonathan pretended to join in, while actually marching in place.

"Im-ho-tep! Im-ho-tep!"

And when the lunatic cluster had moved on, Jonathan, wiping spittle from his face, shaking with fear, but giddy with his own ingenuity, sprinted to the Dusenberg, the only car in the lot, relieved to find it had not been overturned by the berserk horde. He fired up the convertible, hit the gas, and pulled a manic U-turn, drawing up alongside some bushes near the side door of the museum.

Interminable seconds slid by as Jonathan sat, the car's motor purring; he could hear that rabble within the museum, wreaking havoc, turning treasures to trash; windows on the second floor were shattering as precious artifacts were hurled heedlessly out. Heart racing, hands clammy on the steering wheel, Jonathan wondered how long he could stand to wait, how much time he could give his sister and the others to join him, knowing they might already lie twisted and bleeding and dead at the hands of that lesion-ravaged legion. . . .

"Im-ho-tep! Im-ho-tep!"

But Jonathan waited, summoning the courage and will-power from somewhere, and suddenly they came bursting out of that side door, O'Connell and his sister hand in hand, the curator and the Med-jai warrior with scimitars in their hands, with Daniels bringing up the rear, revolver at the ready. They jumped and piled into the convertible and Jonathan floored it, yanking the wheel around, tires squealing as they headed for the only way out, the front drive of the museum.

The squealing tires caught the attention of a rare member of the mob, one whose mind was clouded only by greed, not by Imhotep's spell: Beni.

Jonathan noticed the little scoundrel stepping out of the portal where the museum's front doors had been, Beni's face alive with recognition, as—seeing them as they fled in the Dusenberg—he called out, *"Imhotep! Imhotep!"*

Beni was not joining the chanters, either, but alerting his master.

And as the convertible peeled out of the drive, its passengers looked back with alarm at the sight of Imhotep, appearing in a shattered second-floor window of the museum, reaching out an arm as if from this distance he could pluck them from the vehicle.

O'Connell, in the front seat of the car, Evelyn between him and Jonathan, looked back sharply at Beni, pointing an accusing finger, yelling, "You'll get yours, you little bastard!"

Beni grinned nastily and waved good-bye. "See you soon, Rick! See you very soon!"

And in that second-floor window, Imhotep—his regeneration more nearly complete, most of the mummy wrappings having dropped away, revealing smooth brown flesh—again opened his mouth wide, jaw unhinging, emitting a horrific, primordial shriek that cut through Cairo like a demented siren.

"Jesus!" Daniels, in the backseat, where he sat between Ardeth Bay and the curator, was slinging a pouch containing the precious jeweled canopic jar on a strap over his shoulder. "What's the son of a bitch doing?"

"I think," O'Connell said, looking back toward the receding museum, where the mummy's disease-ridden disciples were suddenly streaming out of the front doors, in apparent pursuit of the Dusenberg, "he's giving his army new orders."

The plague had spread across the city, its inhabitants in the thrall of Imhotep, humans turned inhuman, sores and boils inflaming their bodies and their minds. Frantically, Jonathan sought streets free of the roaming crazies, with mixed success, losing any sense of direction, though O'Connell served as pilot, steering him toward the fort. This route took them down a narrow street in the bazaar section, a deserted artery that had the passengers in the Dusenberg trading tentative, relieved smiles. The worst was behind them, apparently.

But the worst was in fact right ahead of them, a gaggle of lunatics swarming out of alleyways and into the narrow tunnel of the street, blocking the way.

Jonathan slammed on his brakes, and the human roadblock began to press forward, charging at them, eyes wide, teeth bared in every pustule-pocked puss.

"Im-ho-tep! Im-ho-tep! Im-ho-tep! Im-ho-tep!"

"Back up, goddamnit!" Daniels screamed. "Back up!"

O'Connell—glancing back at a mass of madmen coming up behind them, wielding weapons now, knives, axes, picks, clubs—clutched Jonathan's arm. "No! Plow through the bastards!"

"Im-ho-tep! Im-ho-tep! Im-ho-tep!"

Jonathan hesitated, and O'Connell reached his foot over and punched the pedal, the convertible leaping forward, ramming into the herd, tossing them aside like roadkill, blood splashing the hood of the Dusenberg. Evelyn gasped and cried out in horror, but the murderous mass of deranged disciples gave not a thought to a few deaths among their numbers, and their corpses slowed the car's progress. Others of the crazed crowd clung onto the car, half a dozen turbaned madmen trying to clamber into the automobile as the group fought them back—O'Connell and Daniels firing their revolvers, then frantically reloading, the Med-jai warrior and the curator hacking away with scimitars, Evelyn just pushing them off, throwing them overboard. Even Jonathan was driving one-handed, shoving, elbowing the lunatics as best he could.

"Im-ho-tep! Im-ho-tep!"

But it was an impossible task, and Jonathan finally swerved, knocking into a row of stalls lining the street, baskets and bottles flying, the vehicle slowing as Imhotep's zombies clawed at the passengers, a pair of them latching on to Daniels and yanking him, screaming, out of the back.

"They've got Daniels!" O'Connell yelled.

Ardeth Bay was halfway over the back of the convertible, reaching out for him.

But there was no going back; the Dusenberg was swarmed with puss-oozing crazies and the remaining five passengers had their own waking nightmare to deal with. They did not witness what happened to Daniels . . .

. . . who managed to throw off the pair of zombies who'd torn him from the car, and tumbling across the pavement, came up shooting, blasting into the hideous teeming riffraff pressing in upon him, emptying his revolver into them, every bullet finding a target, curing insanity with death. But there was always another zombie to take the last one's place, and then his revolver's hammer was falling on one empty chamber after another, *click!, click!, click!...*

And yet the vacant-eyed, festering-faced crowd, surrounding him where he'd backed himself up against a wall, did not advance. They stood staring at him, like circling vultures, waiting for nature to take its course and provide them with supper....

And then the mob parted like the Red Sea and the mummy, regal in his black robe, walked through them as they very softly spoke the name of He Who Shall Not Be Named: *"Im-ho-tep! Im-ho-tep! Im-ho-tep! Im-ho-tep!"*

Daniels, who—in a soldier of fortune's life of risk taking and adventuring—had prided himself on his unflinching strength, his stoic courage, threw himself to his knees, whimpering in pitiful, prayerful submission to the towering high priest who stood reborn before him.

From the pouch, Daniels withdrew the jewel-encrusted jar, and held it up to Imhotep, an offering to a living god.

And Imhotep accepted the offering, nodding, smiling faintly, as if in thanks.

Daniels grinned up at him, nodding back, hope flooding through him: He had paid homage to Imhotep; he would be spared....

In the Dusenberg, Jonathan and his sister and O'Connell were still trying to plow through the sea of zombies when the bloodcurdling, death-rattling scream interrupted the mindless chanting of the boil-blistered battalion attacking them. The pause encouraged Jonathan to hit the gas hard again, and he charged through another series of stalls, swerving around the corner toward freedom. But instead they crashed headlong into a stone water fountain, fender crumpling, the convertible immobilized.

O'Connell grabbed Evelyn's hand, yelling, "Come on,

come on!," and the three of them leaped from the car . . .

. . . but there was nowhere to go.

They were encircled by the dead-eyed, ulcerated faces of Imhotep's zombie army. Panting, drooling, the former humans did not advance, poised though they were with weapons, just waiting to pounce.

Then, once again, the mob parted to allow its master to make his magisterial way to the fore, his flunky, Beni, following faithfully, like a dog.

Evelyn clutched O'Connell's arm, and gasped. "He's . . . he's like a god!"

Imhotep stood tall, handsome, perfect, the tanned luster returned to his skin from his toes to his shaved head, the bandages all having long since dropped away, majestic in his black robe, no signs anywhere of corrupted flesh, just smooth, rippling muscle. Not a dung-eating scarab beetle in sight.

"We are lost," Ardeth Bay said.

"He is fully regenerated," the curator whispered solemnly. "Now he must raise Anck-su-namun from the dead. That will be their beginning, and the end for all mankind."

"Not one to look on the bright side, are you?" Jonathan commented.

Imhotep—looking young and handsome, despite his three-thousand-some years—strode to Evelyn and stood before her, staring at her, his expression like stone, but his eyes intense.

"Keetah mi pharos, aja nilo, isirian," he said in a commanding baritone.

Beni stepped from behind his master to translate for Evelyn: "He wants you to come with him."

"For your information, you vile little man," Evelyn said to Beni, "what he said was, 'Come with me, my princess, it is time to make you mine for all eternity.' "

Imhotep took another step closer to Evelyn, who clutched O'Connell's hand.

But the mummy was offering his hand. *"Koontash dai na, aja nilo."*

201

Again, Beni translated: "Go with him and he will spare your friends."

Evelyn snapped, "Do you think I need you to interpret for me, you little weasel?"

The mob was chanting very softly now: "*Im-ho-tep . . . Im-ho-tep . . . Im-ho-tep . . . Im-ho-tep!*"

Imhotep stood tall, hands on hips, a powerful presence, smiling at his cornered quarry with the arrogance of the ages.

"Let me go with him," Evelyn whispered to O'Connell, trembling, eyes moist, but chin characteristically high. "You know where he'll take me. If he kills you now, you can't save me later, agreed?"

"Baby," he said tenderly, "you got more guts than sense."

"Yes. Well, your job is to see that they stay on the inside of me."

And Imhotep lurched forward, grabbed Evelyn by the wrist, and pulled her to him, locking an arm around her in a terrible embrace.

O'Connell lunged forward, but Ardeth Bay clutched him by the arms, holding him back, whispering, "Be calm— there is still time. He must take her to Hamanaptra to perform the ritual."

Imhotep grinned at Evelyn lustfully and kissed her cheek. This time the mummy's flesh did not deteriorate. Fully regenerated, he was immune now from the infection of a mortal's touch.

"If you let this beast turn me into a mummy, Rick O'Connell," Evelyn said, chin high, but crinkled with emotion, "you're the first one I'm coming after!"

Imhotep's gaze shifted to Jonathan, who was at O'Connell's side. It was as if the mummy sensed something, his nostrils flaring, as if picking up a scent. . . .

Then, with shocking speed and force, Imhotep reached out and ripped the side pocket loose from Jonathan's khaki jacket, revealing the golden puzzle box, which the mummy snatched, then handed to Beni.

"You might have asked," Jonathan said, as if mildly offended.

Imhotep sneered at them and, an arm around Evelyn's waist, withdrew into the opening the crowd had made.

"Goddamnit!" O'Connell yelled. "I can't take this—"

And as he tried to follow, O'Connell felt the steel-like bands that were Ardeth Bay's arms lock around him.

"No," the Med-jai warrior said. "We give him this small victory, and deny him his final triumph."

O'Connell was almost as crazed as the crowd around him, as he screamed, "Evelyn! No! *Evelyn* . . ."

Beni stepped in front of his incapacitated "friend," and bowed, saying, "Good-bye, Rick. I would say it has been nice knowing you, but you know Beni never lies. . . ."

Then Beni tagged after his master, who was dragging the struggling Evelyn along, and as the ranks of crazies closed, Imhotep's voice bellowed a command in ancient Egyptian . . .

. . . and the vultures began to close in for the kill.

"I say!" Jonathan said, blinking at the encroaching madmen. "The blighter lied to us!"

"Never trust a mummy," O'Connell said, already one step ahead, bending down and pulling open a cistern cover in the cobblestone road. "Come on!"

"What about my sister?" Jonathan said.

"If we can live through this," O'Connell said, "we can save her!"

O'Connell shoved Jonathan down into the rainwater tank. The Med-jai chieftain and the curator were slashing with their scimitars, holding the crowd at bay. O'Connell grabbed Ardeth Bay's arm, shoving him toward the hole.

"Get down there!" O'Connell said. "I need you!" Then O'Connell said, "Come on!" to the curator, who shook his head "no."

"One of us has to stay and fight," the curator said. "Then they will move on. They are not thinking creatures! Trust me . . . you must go and find a way to kill He Who Shall Not Be Named!"

Then Dr. Bey shoved O'Connell into the hole, pushing

203

the heavy stone lid into place, and returned to his task of hacking and slashing at the demented mob, which soon engulfed him.

Below, O'Connell held on to the lid handle with both hands, and all his strength, as the three men stood in three feet of rainwater. But no one above tried to open the lid: The curator apparently had been right. These were thinking men no longer, rather animals driven crazy by pain and sorcery. The sound of their footsteps and chanting soon abated.

O'Connell, Jonathan, and the Med-jai leader waited perhaps ten minutes before carefully, quietly emerging up onto an empty street, strewn with the bodies of the zombies they themselves had killed, and of course the tattered, trampled corpse of the curator, who'd given his life for theirs.

The bizarre bazaar thoroughfare was ghostly in its silence as the trio stumbled toward the battered Dusenberg, uncrumpled its fender, Jonathan getting behind the wheel, and starting it back up again.

And the trio of survivors rode away, undetered—battered, bruised, shaken, but united in their resolve to deny the mummy his final triumph.

·◖ 19 ◗·

Desert Storm

The headquarters of His Majesty's Royal Air Corps, located five miles beyond Fort Stack, had seen better days, a ramshackle ghost town of battered Quonset huts, with a single biplane—a threadbare veteran of the Great War—sitting like a neglected museum exhibit on a pothole-ridden, obstacle course of an asphalt runway, with no control tower to oversee a takeoff, unless you counted the looming dunes of the Sahara.

O'Connell—who had been driven here by Jonathan Carnahan in the bashed-in, steam-seeping Dusenberg, with the backseat company of the Med-jai warrior Ardeth Bay—was not encouraged; nor was he thrilled at the prospect of allowing himself to be piloted by one Winston Havlock, that walrus-mustached, walking (flying) death wish.

Yet here they all stood, dawn painting the desert even more golden, begging Havlock, in goggled aviator's cap and sand-dusted R.A.F. uniform, to take them to Hamanaptra.

Havlock was frowning in thought. "How does this matter effect His Majesty's Royal Air Corps?"

Gunnysack-arsenal strap in hand, O'Connell said, "The

creature we're chasing murdered two men at Fort Stack yesterday."

An eyebrow lifted over a bloodshot eye. "Creature? Interesting designation."

"Winston," Jonathan said, "we've witnessed bizarre events that we hesitate to even share with you—you might think we'd been drinking."

"I'd be disappointed in you, if you hadn't been." Winston put a hand on Jonathan's shoulder. "He's spirited your sister away, you say? Against her will?"

"Yes," Jonathan said.

"Egad man, that's kidnapping."

O'Connell closed his eyes; how had it come to this, his destiny in the hands of booze-soaked, over-aged British flyboy?

"Tell me," Winston said, and his eyes narrowed. "Would you call this mission . . . dangerous?"

"We'll be lucky to live through it," O'Connell admitted.

"Really?" Havlock beamed. "Now I am intrigued."

"Four of our men have died already," Jonathan said.

Havlock's smile made the tips of his walrus mustache point skyward. "This is a tempting challenge—save the damsel in distress, destroy the villain. . . ."

"And come away with his treasure," Jonathan added. "Let's not forget that."

Havlock straightened and gave them a snappy salute. "Captain Winston Havlock, at your service, gentlemen!"

O'Connell sighed, half in relief, half in despair.

Havlock began to trudge toward his plane on the torn-up tarmac. "Which of you gents intends to come along with me?"

"Well, all of us," O'Connell said, falling in alongside the briskly walking flier.

Havlock shook his head, "no," curtly. "Only have room for one."

Jonathan, having to work at it to keep up with the quick-striding Havlock, said, "That just won't do, Winston. All three of us will be needed—in addition to yourself, of course."

206

Havlock stopped abruptly and the others stumbled on ahead, then came to a clumsy stop themselves.

"Jonathan," Havlock said, pointing to the nearest Quonset hut, "I have a mission for you—you'll find a coil of rope hanging on a nail on the wall over the workbench."

"Rope?" Jonathan frowned. "What would that be for?"

Havlock shrugged. "Passengers, lad. Passengers."

Soon the biplane was high above the desert, creasing the sky at a dashing angle, which no doubt pleased the pilot, but frustrated two of his passengers. O'Connell, sitting in the gunner's seat, his back to Havlock, didn't mind; but Jonathan and Ardeth Bay apparently found the slant disconcerting, roped spread-eagled to either wing as they were. The apparently fearless Ardeth Bay had finally found something that scared him silly, a state he shared with Jonathan, who had been scared silly before, just not so thoroughly. . . .

"Are you all right?" O'Connell asked him.

Jonathan, belly down, looked over at O'Connell with wild eyes, wind whipping him, yelling above the engine noise, "Do I bloody well *look* 'all right'?"

O'Connell glanced over at Ardeth Bay, who was muttering a prayer in his native language.

From the cockpit came Havlock's jaunty call: "O'Connell! Take a look to your left, old chum!"

The tilt of the plane had been to give its pilot a better look at an unusual sight on the desert floor: A whirlwind of sand was gliding along, as if on a charted course.

"Sand devil!" Havlock said.

The wind the cyclone of sand was stirring was rocking the plane; Jonathan began to swear, colorfully, and Ardeth Bay's prayers could be heard above the engine's rumble.

"Is that unusual?" O'Connell yelled at the pilot.

"Never saw one like it! Never that big!"

O'Connell didn't like the sound of that, and he certainly didn't like the look of the "natural" occurrence. Was that the mummy down there? Traveling via supernatural sandstorm?

Then the whirling funnel began to dissipate, and suddenly O'Connell couldn't discern anything below, just a haze of floating sand.

"Go closer, Havlock!" O'Connell said. "I want a better look!"

"Righto!"

What O'Connell couldn't see from that height was the sand slowing to a stop, like a carousel nearing the end of its ride; and he also did not see two riders on that slackening carousel getting tossed rudely out and onto the waiting pillow of a dune.

Evelyn and Beni picked themselves up slowly, shaking sand out of their hair.

"What . . . what happened?" Evelyn asked groggily, dusting sand off her black dress.

Beni dug some grains out of one ear. "I don't remember. . . . Sand began swirling around us. . . ."

Evelyn pointed. "You mean like that?"

And just at the bottom of the dune, the swirling particles seemed to be condensing, shaping themselves, fashioning a statue of sand . . .

. . . a statue of Imhotep.

Beni clutched his various religious icons, gathered on a chain at his neck, and prayed in several languages. Evelyn, fascinated, watched as the sand seemed to transform, colors and textures appearing to shift and then hold, until finally He Who Shall Not Be Named stood before them: a dark, handsome man, shaved head gleaming, eyes gleaming, lordly in a black robe that left much of his hairless, muscular chest exposed.

"Oh my God," Evelyn said, though she wasn't referring to the admittedly impressive sight of Imhotep, as he walked up the slope of the dune toward her. She had just noticed the shape of a familiar landmark: the volcano that marked the entrance to the valley of the City of the Dead.

She looked at Beni. "We're back."

Beni shrugged. "The boss has plans for you, lady."

That was when the biplane swooped in for a closer look, its throbbing engine announcing its presence.

Evelyn looked up and beamed at the battered plane, knowing it was Rick—it *had* to be Rick!

Beni knew it, too, but he was smirking, shaking his head, muttering, "Doesn't that guy know when he's had enough?"

But Imhotep was taking it far worse than his servant: He scowled at the sky, and the handsome face turned grotesque, jaw unhinging to allow the mummy's mouth to again open wider than humanly possible, to emit a hideous shriek, a battle cry that rallied the sands themselves to his cause, a sheet of sand rising from the desert, millions of particles flying upward, into the path of the dipping biplane.

Evelyn ran toward Imhotep, who stood like a demented, self-satisfied genie, hands on hips, grinning up at his evil handiwork.

"No! You'll kill them!" she called. "Stop it!"

The mummy didn't acknowledge her with even a glance. Then she said the same thing—in ancient Egyptian.

And now Imhotep cast his gaze upon her, as she stood just a few feet from him, chin defiantly high, wind whipping her dress, and her hair.

"That is the object of the lesson," Imhotep told her, in the same tongue.

In the biplane, O'Connell—who had witnessed the fantastic sight of the desert virtually coming alive and rising up toward the biplane—was holding on for dear life. Havlock had thrown the throttle back, sending the plane into a steep dive, crying, "Hold on, men!"

Jonathan's reply was nonverbal—a scream interrupted only by the occasional intake of breath, before continuing on.

Ardeth Bay was screaming, too, but he seemed to be forming words, which were either more prayers or Arabic obscenities.

The biplane seemed to be heading straight into the dead funnel of the Hamanaptra volcano; then Havlock began a climb just as steep as his dive had been, swooping down into the valley beyond, as the sands swept into and buried the enormous volcano.

"Havlock!" O'Connell cried. "You are one hell of a pilot! You just faked out a sandstorm!"

"That's a first for me, lad!" Havlock yelled giddily.

But the wall of sand was arising, reshaping itself after its crash into the volcano, and chasing them; incredibly the sands seemed to be gathering into an image straight out of hell!

O'Connell was staring into a giant face formed in the cloud of sand—the face of Imhotep!

O'Connell, sitting in the gunner's position after all, latched on to the Lewis machine gun, cocked the bracket, and blasted away at the looming visage, which seemed to laugh as the bullets passed harmlessly through, a wide laughing mouth which seemed about to envelope the plane, as if to gulp it down, a little snack for the huge orifice. . . .

And then it did.

"Stop!" Evelyn screamed in English, seeing the plane swallowed into the cloud of sand. Then she repeated her appeal in ancient Egyptian.

But Imhotep seemed not to hear her, now; his eyes were almost closed, his brow tight as he gazed into the sand-obscured sky. He was lifting his arms, hands clenching and unclenching, as if the grains of sand were his orchestra and he their conductor.

Within the storm, the biplane was spiraling toward the earth, sucked downward in a whirlpool of sand, engine roar drowned out by the howling wind, over which the only thing that could be heard was the joint scream of terror from the men strapped onto the wings of the biplane. O'Connell, bracing himself for impact, thought he heard something else, from the pilot whose seat was back-to-back with his: laughter.

"Here I come, lads!" Havlock was yelling with maniacal glee. "Hold a place at the bar for Winston Havlock!"

Perhaps, O'Connell thought grimly, holding on to the sides of the plane, flying with a suicidal pilot had been less than an inspired idea. . . .

Pacing the desert floor, Evelyn, chest choked with despair, watched the wall of sand in the sky, knowing her friends were caught within, drowning in that dry sea. . . .

Whirling toward Imhotep, to curse him, she froze: The sight of him, standing there lost, *locked*, in concentration, told her what she must do.

She strode up to the handsome, unwrapped mummy and grabbed him by the arms and pulled him to her. She licked her lips and hooded her eyes and said, in ancient Egyptian, "I have been waiting for you, all these thousands of years, my love. What kept you?"

And she kissed him full on the lips.

Imhotep drew away, surprised; but as he gazed into Evelyn's face, his eyes softened and surprise turned to lust as he kissed her, deeply, hungrily . . .

. . . unaware that the wall of sand was collapsing from the sky, falling like a sheet of arid rain. The biplane—still spinning—emerged into a clear sky, and dropped down over a towering dune, into the Hamanaptra valley.

A blast of sand blew into the air—not Imhotep's work, but that of the biplane skidding to a stop. The sound of the crash landing alerted Imhotep to what had happened, woke him from his lustful reveries, told him that he had been tricked into breaking his concentration, and used by this twentieth-century wench, who—sneering at him—was pushing herself out of his arms, contemptuously, spitting disgustedly into the sand in rejection of his kiss.

Imhotep bellowed his rage as he backhanded her, knocking the woman to the sand; but she just sat up, sneering at him defiantly, wiping the blood from the corner of her mouth with the back of her hand.

Though the sand had slowed and softened the biplane's landing, it had flipped over and, like a bug on its back, skidded up atop a dune, in which the plane's nose burrowed.

O'Connell dropped out of the gunner's seat, onto the sand, hauling down his gunnysack, and leaned against the upside-down plane, catching his wind.

"Would I be imposing, terribly," a voice reasonably posed, "if I were to ask you to provide just a little help—*if it's not too much bloody trouble!*"

O'Connell glanced at Jonathan, looking at him with wide eyes from under the wing where he was still strapped on.

"A moment, Jonathan . . ."

"A moment!"

"I have to check Havlock. . . . This plane is precariously perched—feels like it could slide down that dune, nose under the sand, and I have to get him out of that cockpit!"

But when he went to check, O'Connell found Havlock slumped at the stick with a foolish smile under the walrus mustache, his neck broken—snapped on impact, apparently.

The biplane, however, was moving, or rather the sands under the plane were—caused by nature, not Imhotep, but dangerous nonetheless—and O'Connell quickly untied Jonathan. Ardeth Bay had managed to get his hands onto his scimitar and was able to cut himself free. The warrior took it upon himself to unfasten the Lewis machine gun from its mount, throwing the cartridge belt over his shoulder and hauling his prize away. Helping Jonathan, whose head was still reeling, O'Connell followed Ardeth Bay toward an outcropping of rocks.

The sand beneath their feet was shifting again, sinking under their feet, and the plane was moving, sliding down the slope of the dune, nose first.

They made it to the rocks, the ground solid enough to risk pausing, and from this vantage point they could see the biplane sliding down the dune and into a vortex of sand that sucked the ship and its brave pilot into an unmarked grave.

O'Connell took a deep breath, threw Havlock a quick salute, and nodded toward the ruins that lay sprawled across the desert before them.

The City of Dead had already claimed Winston Havlock; now, as they trudged toward Hamanaptra, they knew all too well who its next three permanent residents were likely to be.

·❨ 20 ❩·

Too Many Mummies

Under the blistering morning sun, the ruins of Hamanaptra lay scattered like a child's discarded building blocks. The lonely welcoming committee of stray, abandoned camels, subsisting on desert brush, still awaiting their dead masters, met O'Connell and his two companions at the periphery of the City of the Dead, the animals eyeing the newcomers hopefully.

No sign of the captive Evelyn, the monster Imhotep, or his sycophant Beni.

Somehow O'Connell knew that the mummy had beaten them here, that He Who Shall Not Be Named was already underground, preparing to raise his lover from the dead, at the expense of an innocent girl's life.

It was as if they had left this site hours ago, not days—the ropes still dangled into the crevice near the open shrine with the half-buried statue of Anubis. From his gunnysack, O'Connell removed several torches, their nubs presoaked with kerosene, kept one, and passed the others to Jonathan and Ardeth Bay, who was lugging the heavy Lewis machine gun.

Before they descended into the darkness, however,

O'Connell—using a compass—walked the ruins, according to the directions the late curator had given them: *"The statue of Horus should be located fifty kadams west of the Anubis statue."* At the base of the Horus statue should be a secret compartment with the gold *Book of Amun Ra*, which could banish Imhotep and save Evelyn. . . .

"All right," O'Connell said, standing on a small sand dune, under which—presumably—was the statue they sought. "Now we know the direction we have to head in."

And they dropped down into the embalming chamber—Jonathan's "mummy factory"—and, with O'Connell leading the way, lighted torch in hand, watching his compass, they began their underground trek through tunnels and caverns and chambers, toward the statue of Horus.

"Can you read from this gold book," O'Connell asked Jonathan, the group ducking low in a narrow passageway painted orange by their torches, "if we find it? Your sister may not be in any condition to."

"I've had some training," Jonathan said stiffly.

"Answer my question."

"I can definitely . . . possibly . . . read it."

"You can read ancient Egyptian."

"Yes. . . . Enough to order off the menu, anyway."

O'Connell winced; the fate of the woman he loved depended on the skills of her simp of a brother. It was enough to make him long for another ride with Winston Havlock. Then again, maybe they'd all be meeting up with Winston soon enough. . . .

Before long they were making their way down a winding narrow staircase, cut right into the face of the rock, heading into the dark depths of the underground city, a stairway that seemed endless, as if it might extend into hell itself.

But they finally reached the bottom and were moving across a sandy-surfaced floor, as O'Connell followed his compass.

After a while, O'Connell asked, "This statue—what the hell does this Horus look like? Lion head, ram head, dog head?"

"Falcon head, actually," Jonathan said. "Cute little fellow with a big beak."

That Jonathan had any Egyptology knowledge at all was reassuring to O'Connell, who pressed forward into the darkness. His torch soon revealed that he'd led his trusting little party to a dead end: a passageway which had caved in on itself.

"We need to go through here," O'Connell said, holding his torch close to the rock pile blocking the way. Looking carefully, he said, "I think it's navigable, just beyond this entrance. We need to start clearing this stuff away."

And they did, or at least two of them at a time did, as the quarters were cramped. On one of his breaks, Jonathan Carnahan noticed a grouping of jewels embedded in the nearby wall, glittering purple jewels arranged in the shape of a scarab.

Upon closer examination, Jonathan realized that the jewels were themselves shaped like those dreadful beetles whose skeletons had been discovered in Imhotep's coffin. As the late Warden Gad Hassan had been before him, Jonathan was ignorant of the relative worthlessness of such semiprecious stones, the purple quartz winking at him attractively, like the jewel in a belly dancer's navel.

With thumb and middle finger, Jonathan tested each stone, finally discovering one that seemed loose; he jiggled it, trying to free the scarab-shaped gem, and the object popped out. Dropping it into his palm, holding it there, Jonathan studied the stone, amazed to see the thing begin to glow, pulse with a light from within. Was something inside there? Something . . . wiggling?

"I say, lads," Jonathan said. "Take a break and look at this! It's quite remarkable. . . ."

And then the scarab stone showed Jonathan just how remarkable it was, breaking open on its own accord, like a nut breaking out of its shell, and suddenly a real beetle was wriggling from the quartz cocoon!

Yelping, Jonathan immediately tried to throw the thing off his palm, and the gemlike shuck went flying . . .

. . . but not the vicious dung beetle, which already had begun to burrow into, and under, his flesh!

"Dear God, help me!" Jonathan screamed, and he began to dance in pain.

Whirling from the rock pile, O'Connell recognized the frenzied tarantella immediately: The late warden had danced himself to death with those very steps. Jonathan threw off his khaki jacket and was clawing at his arm.

"Grab hold of him!" O'Connell commanded the Medjai warrior, and Ardeth Bay latched on to Jonathan from behind, gripping him around the waist.

Instinctively, O'Connell ripped the sleeve off Jonathan's shirt; something was burrowing up the poor bastard's arm, *you could see it*, right beneath the skin, like a bubble traveling up the bicep, as if on its way to his neck, where cords and veins bulged and throbbed!

"Scarab!" Jonathan shouted. "Beetle!"

If he hadn't been hysterical with pain already, Jonathan might have passed out at the sight of O'Connell whipping his knife off his belt, the blade flashing past Jonathan's bulging eyes.

And if Jonathan's screams had echoed throughout the cavern before, now they resounded, as O'Connell stopped the bug's progress with his blade, then cut the flesh in front of its path, and along one side, digging with the knife tip and flicking the dung beetle from its burrow onto the sandy floor in a splash of British blood.

The black bug was still hungry, however, and went skittering back toward Jonathan whose boot the bug was about to climb up on when O'Connell whipped out a revolver from under an arm and blew bastard away, turning it to jelly courtesy of a .38 slug as big as it was.

Having O'Connell's bullet cut so close to his foot drew a yelp from Jonathan, whose screams had already subsided to whimpers. He slid down the rocky wall to the sandy floor and sat there, moaning, while Ardeth Bay turned the discarded shirtsleeve into a bandage.

"It's not a bad wound," O'Connell said, having a look before the Med-jai warrior covered it up. "Just superficial."

Jonathan's lower lip was trembling as he sat there like a hurt, frightened child. "It . . . doesn't . . . doesn't bloody well *feel* superficial!"

"From now on, for God's sake, man," O'Connell said, "don't touch anything! Not a goddamn thing—keep your hands off the merchandise."

Jonathan swallowed and nodded numbly, then said, "O'Connell . . ."

"Yeah?"

"My, uh, future children and I thank you."

"We haven't lived through this day yet. You rest while we get this passage the rest of the way cleared."

Jonathan nodded again, and sat back, still breathing hard.

O'Connell and Ardeth Bay exchanged expressions, sharing silent knowledge that this little incident was only the smallest indication of trials, tribulations, and terrors to come.

And then they got back to work.

As O'Connell and his little crew had been descending down ropes into the embalming chamber near the statue of Anbuis, Evelyn Carnahan was already deep within the catacombs, the unwilling second of a three-person procession through the necropolis where, three-thousand-some years before, Imhotep and Anck-su-namun had died.

Skirts of her black gown flowing not unlike Imhotep's robe, Evelyn was not as frightened as she might have been, believing as she did that Imhotep viewed her as the reincarnation of his lover. She was already mentally rehearsing her lines, in ancient Egyptian, so that once he had performed whatever hocus-pocus he had in mind, she could pretend to be the reborn Anck-su-namun, and wait and watch for the right moment to escape.

Ahead of her Imhotep led the way, torch in one hand, the massive, brass-hinged, obsidian *Book of the Dead* in the other, as they approached a stone slab that served as a bridge over a moat of bubbling black detritus, a foul moat on the edges of which large, hairy rats scurried at the sound of the humans. But a pair of the beasts were not deterred by these intruders, as they were busy feasting on one of their own, a smaller, deceased rat.

"That's what happens to little vermin like you," she said over her shoulder to Beni, who was holding his revolver on her.

Beni just laughed at her, then glanced where she was looking and saw the cannibal rats munching on their smaller crony, and blanched.

"You pride yourself on a familiarity with many religions, don't you, Beni?"

They were crossing the stone bridge now.

"Keeping moving!" Beni said, nudging the base of her spine with the nose of the revolver.

"Well then, I'm sure you're familiar with the Buddhist concept of karma. Your kind pays, Beni—they always pay."

"Sure they do." Beni laughed. Then quietly he asked rhetorically, "They do?"

Moving farther into the catacombs, the group reached a deep, ampitheaterlike chamber, whose walls were cavelike, but whose sandstone floor was as smooth and perfect as any temple's. A steep staircase, carved in the rock face, emptied into this place. Though cobwebs draped the chamber—which was soon tinted orange as Imhotep glided about the vast room in his black robe, lighting ancient torches mounted on the walls—its stark majesty was inescapable. Statues of Anubis lurked here and there, icons and other precious objects perched on pedestals and mantels, and—most imposingly—a weird altar of heavy dark stone took centerstage. The altar was exquisitely decorated with winged scarabs, cobra heads, and rams' horns, and as the daughter of Howard Carnahan, Evelyn could not help being overwhelmed by its dark beauty.

Yet to the hostage of a reborn mummy, this sacrificial altar was less than reassuring.

It was then that the echoes of O'Connell's scarab-slaying gunshot, reverberating through the catacombs, reached the ears of Imhotep, his guest, and his servant.

The high priest scowled at the sound, even as Evelyn

brightened, knowing that Rick, and rescue, had to be close at hand. Hope flooded through her—the man she loved, and her brother, had survived that crash landing into the sand, she just knew it!

But Imhotep's coldly handsome features were etched with rage. On the altar lay a shattered canopic jar, which (if Evelyn was not mistaken, quickly scanning its fragmented hieroglyphs) contained the crusted remains of some vital organ of Anck-su-namun—probably her heart.

He held in his open palm the decayed remains of the organ—yes, her heart—and gazed upon the desiccated tissue with somber, respectful adoration.

Then he closed his fist, crushing the heart to powder.

Evelyn gasped, shuddered. Beni smirked at her, the way a schoolboy smirks at a skittish schoolgirl.

Black robes sweeping behind him, Imhotep strode to a wall of the chamber, holding the massive *Book of the Dead* open in one hand like a hymnal, reading from it, reciting an ancient incantation from its obsidian pages. Then he blew into his hand, with the force of a small gale, scattering the dust upon the wall . . .

. . . *which began to squirm, as things within it came alive!*

Beni gasped, shuddered. Evelyn might have smirked at him for his amazed fear had she not been clutched by the same emotion.

From behind the crumbling walls, in two tiny avalanches, came two living mummies—not handsome and lordly, like Imhotep, but the good old-fashioned brand of living mummy: horrific-looking, bandaged-wrapped, putrid, rotting corpses.

They stumbled toward Imhotep, unsure of their footing—it had been a while since they'd walked, after all—and bowed before him. He spoke to them in ancient Egyptian.

"My God," Evelyn whispered. "They're his priests! His long-dead priests!"

Beni, who had a revolver in one hand, was clutching his various religious icons with the other, praying silently in one language after another.

Then the mummies—surer footed now—marched off down a passageway.

Evelyn's heart sank: Imhotep had dispatched these creatures to attack the intruders—Rick, her brother, and the Med-jai chieftain.

Face tight with self-satisfaction, Imhotep strutted to the altar and began to reach within his flowing robes; one at a time, almost magically, as if making them materialize, he produced from hidden pockets the remaining four jeweled canopic jars, setting them tenderly upon the table that was the black altar. As he arranged them in a row along the altar top, Imhotep spoke not in ancient Egyptian, but in Hebrew.

This struck Evelyn as curious, until she realized he was perhaps avoiding his own language because he knew she understood it. Hebrew—the language of the slaves, after all—was a tongue he and Beni shared.

"What's he saying?" Evelyn demanded of Beni.

"Oh, and now you want Beni to translate? Well, I'll tell you: Prince Imhotep is pleased to have won your heart."

She sneered a bit. "Maybe he shouldn't flatter himself; maybe it's already taken."

Imhotep, still arranging the jeweled jars, continued on in Hebrew, his voice echoing through the chamber.

Beni listened, then smiled as he said to Evelyn, "Perhaps you shouldn't flatter *yourself*. You see, he also wants your brain, your liver, your kidneys, and . . . how do you say . . . those ropy slimy things in your sweet tummy?"

Though chilled by the revelation that Imhotep viewed her not as the reincarnation of his lost love, but as an appropriate human sacrifice, she managed to say, drolly, "They're called intestines, you dreadful little man."

"Ah yes! He wants those, too—all of you. What's the American expression? The works."

And, chin high, she called out to Imhotep in his own language, "So you only want me for my body? How like a man."

Imhotep strode to her, showing how high a chin could really be held, and he grinned at her, looked her up and down in the most demeaning fashion.

And then he backhanded her, a blow so savage, so hard, that she was unconscious before she, and her black gown, pooled on the sandy floor.

Beni, taken aback by the viciousness of the blow, looked timidly toward his master, who commanded him in Hebrew to carry the woman to the altar, which Beni—straining his weak back—somehow accomplished. He even arranged her gown, smoothing it out, covering her legs, giving her some modesty even as his fingers glided over her curves.

Evelyn was unaware of any of this, and was not awake to see Imhotep turn to walk off toward an adjoining mausoleum chamber, seeking the last element required for this ancient procedure. But the high priest was interrupted by the sound of more gunshots echoing out of the labyrinth.

Frowning, he quickly returned to the altar, reached a hand into another of the jeweled canopic jars, filling his palm with his late lover's liver and crushed the crusty decayed organ into dust. Hastily, he read a passage from *The Book of the Dead*, which lay open at the end of the altar at Evelyn's sandaled feet; and he blew another controlled gale across his palm, sending the dust swirling into and down a passageway.

In ancient Egyptian, Imhotep thundered, "Kill them! Kill them all! And I bid you bring me *The Book of Amun Ra!*"

Then Imhotep stormed into the adjacent mausoleum chamber, leaving Beni alone with the unconscious Evelyn.

Beni, shaken by Imhotep's escalating violence, not to mention mummies crawling out of a wall and coming to life, decided to take this opportunity to scurry out of there, into the darkness, with the other rats.

A few minutes earlier, O'Connell and his two companions had been moving through the cleared passageway when he spotted a crevice in the wall, just big enough for a man to squeeze through. Holding his torch to the crevice, he saw something glitter within.

Checking his compass, O'Connell looked back into the stubbly face of Ardeth Bay, Jonathan dragging behind him, and said, "This tunnel's taking us off course. I think there's a chamber nextdoor, which might get us back on track.''

Ardeth Bay, showing no strain from lugging the heavy machine gun, nodded his agreement to this strategy, and O'Connell, taking the gunnysack off his shoulder, handed it, and his torch, to the warrior.

Edging through, O'Connell dropped to the floor of the chamber. Without his torch, he was enveloped in darkness—almost. A shaft of light, shooting through a small hole in the ceiling, was hitting the wall, high up, right next to an oval object. Squinting, O'Connell wondered: *Is that what I think it is?*

He withdrew a revolver from a shoulder holster and aimed, precisely, up through the darkness, firing, catching the pedestal of what turned out to be, as he had guessed and hoped, another of those mirror disks. His shot moved the mirror into the path of the shaft of light, which reflected off other disks high above them, turning on the ancient lighting system, saturating the chamber with reflective light.

Reflective light, was right: Light was bouncing here and there off golden surfaces, off glittering jewels, gilded statues, ebony ivory-inlaid furniture, an array of treasures, overflowing, unimaginable treasures, shining, sparkling before him.

Within moments, after Ardeth Bay had handed down the gunnysack arsenal, the warrior and Evelyn's brother had dropped down into the chamber—and their mouths had dropped open, too.

"Seti's riches," Ardeth Bay uttered.

"Egad," Jonathan burbled, "it's all the wealth of Egypt, stuffed into one chamber! It's a bloody fortune! . . . I say, what's that peculiar odor?''

And the three men turned to look away from the piled treasure, taking in the rest of the chamber, seeing where one of several passageways that fed into this place had provided entry to a pair of filthy, bandage-wrapped mummies who seemed unhappy by the intrusion of these outsiders, and shambled toward them with arms outstretched.

"I'm gonna take a wild guess," O'Connell said, slowly

reaching into his gunnysack for the elephant gun, "and say that's mummy rot."

"The priests of Imhotep," Ardeth Bay intoned somberly. "Returned from the dead to do his foul bidding!"

"Foul is right," O'Connell said, and blasted away with the elephant gun, smoke and flame shooting from its snout, blowing the upper torso off the mummy at the right. Pumping the gun, a huge spent cartridge flying out, O'Connell fired again, taking the top half of the other malodorous mummy clean off, as well.

The loud reports echoed in the chamber, and as the smoke cleared, O'Connell gasped at the most bizarre sight he'd been subjected to yet: The lower halves of both mummies were walking toward him, undeterred, legs stumbling forward!

And then the goddamn blown-off upper torsos of the two creatures stirred, and started crawling toward the three men, who were backing up in amazed horror.

"The hell with this!" O'Connell snarled, and reloaded and blasted, and reloaded and blasted, and reloaded and blasted, turning the sons of bitches into mummy powder. A few mummy fragments were still squirming, and, grimacing, O'Connell went around and squashed them with his boot, like big ugly bugs.

Jonathan had backed into a golden throne, where he was sitting, stunned. "You don't see that every day," he admitted.

The floor beneath their feet began to rumble, and a hand punched up through, bursting the stone.

"That, either!" O'Connell said, reloading.

Then two more mummies had crawled up out of the ground, skull faces grinning, bandages drooping, their foul stench filling the chamber as they lumbered toward the three outsiders.

Jonathan, sitting in his throne, eyes wide, asked, "I don't suppose anyone thought to bring a bag of cats!"

Then the things were coming out of everywhere, the floor, the walls, even up out of the piles of gold and jewels, disgusting, reeking creatures, grinning skull-faced monsters whose grasping, clawing arms reached out for them, and only the slowness of the attackers' staggering gait gave O'Connell's party a prayer.

Backed up against the wall, O'Connell said to Ardeth Bay, "Let's welcome these sons of bitches to the twentieth century!"

And he helped Ardeth Bay position the Lewis gun, and thread in the ammunition belt. Then the Med-jai warrior opened fire with the machine gun as O'Connell pumped and fired away with the massive elephant gun, pulverizing the mummies with their firepower, while Jonathan did his Wild West best with a revolver in either hand, shattering mummy kneecaps, exploding skulls.

But the mummies just kept coming, crawling from around and beneath and everywhere, and O'Connell and his cohorts, weapons in hand, dashed out of the chamber into the passageway, O'Connell yelling, "Go! Go! Go!"

They did not see Beni enter from another passageway, to eye the scattered mummy fragments, some of which twitched with the resiliency of the undead. But Beni overcame any fear or revulsion with the sight of all that wonderful, beautiful plunder.

Laughing, Beni fell backward into a pile of jewels and gold baubles and lolled about, as if bathing in the booty.

Within the labyrinth, where at least no mummies were emerging from walls, the O'Connell crew raced, often running backward, to fire at the oncoming, relentless horde of mummies.

"I'm out!" Ardeth Bay yelled, the mighty Lewis gun finally falling silent.

With no compass in hand, no idea where the hell they were going, other than away from those mummies, O'Connell led Ardeth Bay and Jonathan through a passageway and around a corner and into a small chamber where a falcon-headed statue loomed over a claustrophobic domain.

"Horus, old boy!" Jonathan said, summoning a mildly crazed smile. "Hello!"

"We're cornered," O'Connell said.

Mummies, more mummies than the mind could imagine,

were plodding down the passageway toward them.

Reaching into his gunnysack, O'Connell withdrew a stick of dynamite, saying, "This may cave us in, too, but it's all we've got," and struck a match off the stubbly cheek of Ardeth Bay, who winced but didn't complain.

Then O'Connell lit the fuse, pitched the dynamite down the passageway, yelling, "Hit the deck!"

Which he and the warrior and Jonathan did.

When the explosion had stopped echoing, and the dust had begun settling, they got to their feet, brushing themselves off as they looked at the beautiful sight of the sealed-off passageway, clogged with rock and dirt.

"If there's anything left of those bastards," O'Connell said, "let's see them dig through *that*."

"Please, Richard," Jonathan said. "Let's not give the opposition any ideas."

A way out still remained: another dark, narrow passageway. O'Connell gestured toward it, with his torch.

"Jonathan, stand watch—if you see anybody coming down the tunnel in full-body bandages, point it out, would you?"

"Righto."

To Ardeth Bay, O'Connell said, "Now—let's see if we can find, and open, that secret compartment," nodding toward the base of the statue, "and find that gold book. . . ."

O'Connell did not make the connection that the diggers who'd died, in a acid-spray booby trap, had done so in a similar attempt.

So, thinking he had nothing to worry about except the occasional murderous mummy, O'Connell headed for the base of the statue of Horus, where he and Ardeth Bay soon found the outline of the compartment, detecting its seams, and began doing their best to pry it loose with crowbars from the gunnysack.

·❦ 21 ❧·

The Mummy's Bride

Evelyn awoke abruptly, as if from a horrible nightmare, realizing with startling clarity that she had woken to a reality worse than any dream her subconscious might fashion for her. She knew, at once, that she'd been laid out atop that sacrificial altar in Imhotep's vast chamber; she was aware, instantly, that she was bound to the thing, arms pulled up, hands over her head, her wrists shackled by ancient chains—her ankles, too.

But Evelyn was a strong woman, not physically perhaps, but mentally; she prided herself on an ability to summon intellect over emotion. As she stared up at the cavern ceiling so high above, she buttressed herself, knowing that Rick was nearby, that he would rescue her. She had faith that this man she had come to love, whom she had seen outwit and outfight anything that had been thrown in his path so far, would prevail. Even though she knew that Imhotep had summoned by sorcery the undead mummies of his bygone priests, she believed, she had to believe, that Rick would save her.

And so she determined she would show Imhotep no fear, she would not give him the pleasure of her pain. There would be no concessions to girlish fright, she assured herself, and then she glanced to her left into the rotted face of a corpse placed beside her on the altar, and screamed her lungs out.

When her shrieks had subsided, and reason settled back in, Evelyn noticed the headdress on the shriveled, mummified carcass beside her, the sheer, skimpy, feminine garb, and knew: *Her companion was the corpse of Anck-su-namun!*

Evelyn looked away from the gray grinning face of Pharaoh Seti's late mistress, and pulled at her chains, struggling against them, hoping beyond hope that the metal had lost its tensile strength over these thousands of years. As she made this futile effort, she became aware of a faint, ominous chanting in a dialect of ancient Egyptian her scholarship could not penetrate.

The chanting grew louder, but no more understandable, until she saw the shambling shapes emerging from the darkness into the orange glow of the chamber: *more of Imhotep's undead priests—shuffling toward her!*

Soon they had surrounded her, bodies swaying, or trying to, the awkwardness of their ancient bones denying their grotesque choreography any grace. And then she realized that this was not some unknown ancient Egyptian dialect at all: She was unable to understand the words because these bandaged-draped, rancid chanters lacked tongues, in every case, and jaws and even mouths in many others.

She smiled; she laughed.

It was funny. So horrific was it, that she found it just dreadfully funny, and—unaware how close she was teetering to madness—she accidentally glanced, again, into the face of the grinning corpse beside her, as if looking in a laughing mirror, and it snapped her back to reality: ghastly, horrible, unimaginable reality . . . but reality.

Alongside her—on the opposite side from the withered corpse of Anck-su-namun—had been arranged, in a perfect row, the jewel-encrusted canopic jars, including the broken one. Now the swaying mummified priests made a path and Imhotep stepped through, princely in his dark flowing robes, the formidable *Book of the Dead* propped open in one hand, as if featherlight. The high priest seemed to reach a hand toward Evelyn, and she recoiled . . . but instead he tenderly touched the decayed cheek of his long-dead love.

Imhotep began to read from *The Book of the Dead*. She could not see, from where she lay restrained on the altar, the eerie results of his utterances; but she heard the strange sound, as if an immense broth were being brought to a boil. She could never have guessed that the fetid black bog, whose pools formed a sort of moat around the chamber at its periphery, had begun to seethe and gurgle, to churn and burn and foam and fume.

She could not see the black sludge, like a living being, slip up over its boundaries and slither across the ampitheater floor, coating it, oozing around the bony, bandaged feet of the droning mummy choir, and the sandaled feet of Imhotep himself, as he intoned the incantation from *The Book of the Dead*.

But she did see, to her wide-eyed amazement, to her mind-numbing horror, the ooze slipping up and in and over and out of the canopic jars beside her!

Not knowing whether to cry or laugh or scream, she did nothing, nothing but watch in bewilderment and dread as the slime crossed over her, warm and bubbling, drifting across her as if she were a beach and it were the tide, sliding over the hills and valleys of her and onto the deteriorated corpse of the concubine, enveloping the gray husk, turning it black, like a shining ebony statue . . . and the the liquid seemed to be sucked down inside the corpse, disappearing into every available portal—eye sockets, mouth, gaps between ribs—every black drop of it.

That was when Anck-su-namun's mouth opened, and gasped for air.

Evelyn's mouth opened, too—in a scream so loud, so spine-chillingly shrill, that even Imhotep was momentarily taken aback, pausing in his recitation.

Even the mummy of Anck-su-namun, in the process of returning to life beside her, turned to gaze with empty eye sockets at Evelyn, who struggled wildly at her bonds, trying to will herself off that sacrificial slab, as Imhotep held the wide-hilted, swordlike sacrificial knife high above her, directly over her heart.

"With your death," Imhotep said, in his ancient language, which Evelyn understood painfully well, "Anck-su-namun shall live. . . . And together we will be an invincible plague upon this sorry world!"

And above her, the serpent's tooth sharpness of the knife's point, poised to strike, caught the flickering light of torches and winked at her, as if this were all some awful joke.

Minutes before, in the small chamber where the statue of Horus reigned, O'Connell and Ardeth Bay—both hunkered down, digging away at the seams of the secret compartment at the statue's base—had managed to pry the panel loose. It seemed just ready to give. . . .

"Okay," O'Connell said, breathing hard, resting for just a moment, "at the count of three, let's both put our backs into it, and the son of a buck should pop right off. . . ."

Ardeth Bay, also catching his breath, nodded.

"One," O'Connell said. "Two . . ."

"Company's coming!" Jonathan yelled.

O'Connell and the Med-jai warrior joined Jonathan at the mouth of the passageway, down which could be seen a contingent of rotting mummies, lumbering toward them in that too familiar, shambling but resolute way. . . .

Ardeth Bay grabbed the elephant gun, scooping up a handful of shells from the gunnysack, saying, "Keep digging! Get the book!"

O'Connell, working with Jonathan now, returned to the statue's base; crowbars inserted, they again pried at the seams, as from the passageway echoed the thunderous reports of the elephant gun. Jonathan, white with fear, paused to look toward the mouth of the tunnel, down which Ardeth Bay was making a stand against the oncoming horde of undead.

"Keep at it!" O'Connell said. "We've almost got it,

now! Let's pull together, Johnny boy, on the count of three. . . . One . . . two . . . *shit!*"

O'Connell gazed down in terror at the skeletal hand clutching his ankle, a mummy's hand that had burst up out of the sandy floor.

Jonathan, backing away, holding the crowbar like a weapon now, shouted, "Oh my God—they're everywhere!"

And indeed, like terrible flowers blossoming, hands were shoving up through the dirt-and-sand floor, and then a garden of corpses was crawling up out of the ground, their bandaged bodies filthy, their bony fingers grasping.

O'Connell swung the crowbar like a bat and cut through the rib cage of the oncoming mummy, but didn't stop the creature, who shoved O'Connell violently away from where he'd been working at the statue's base. As O'Connell got to his feet, the mummy blocked the way, as if wanting to keep him from the base of the statue, where another of the bandaged bastards seemed intent to go, as if on a mission, bending at the base of Horus . . . and suddenly O'Connell knew: *Imhotep had sent these creatures not just to kill the intruders, but to bring back* The Book of Amun Ra!

Another of the dingy devils had Jonathan by the throat, lifting him up off the ground, strangling him, keeping him away from the secret compartment.

And that third mummy grasped the seam of the compartment and, with incredible force, yanked back on the panel, pulling it free, and shooting a stream of acid, spraying out, drenching him and his buddy, who had been blocking O'Connell's path, both mummies sizzling and smoking like sausages on a grill. Even the monster choking Jonathan got spritzed by the scalding stuff, all across the back of him, and he—and the other two—went stumbling about in a steaming stupor, the withered, dried flesh melting off their bones, until their skeletons collapsed like pickup-sticks and began to liquefy into an unspeakable ooze.

The one who'd been strangling Jonathan, however, who hadn't been as doused to death as thoroughly as his brethren, crawled across the floor and slid into one of the holes they'd emerged from . . . but the damn thing latched a bony hand

230

on to O'Connell's gunnysack and dragged it down with him!

A single stick of dynamite had spilled out—otherwise, their arsenal was gone.

"Damn!" O'Connell spat.

From the passageway came the continuing thunder of Ardeth Bay's elephant gun; but the warrior would be out of ammo soon, O'Connell knew. He scurried to the base of the statue, the compartment now open, and called over to Jonathan, who was massaging his throat, breath heaving like a runner after the big race.

They knelt and withdrew from the compartment an ornate wooden chest, its craftsmanship exquisite, colorfully adorned with hieroglyphs.

"Could this bloody thing be booby-trapped as well?" Jonathan asked, wide-eyed.

The boom of the elephant gun echoed down the passageway.

"Yes," O'Connell said, "but we don't have time to care."

And he stuck his crowbar's tip into the seam and pried the lid off, snapping the airtight seal, popping the box open.

Within was a heavy burlap bag that obviously concealed a large object. O'Connell and Jonathan exchanged anxious looks, then the elephant gun boomed again and O'Connell snatched the bagged object from the box, and slipped the burlap covering off, exposing the brass-hinged volume, the golden twin of *The Book of the Dead*.

"*The Book of Amun Ra*," Jonathan breathed.

"Hell, it's bigger than the Chicago phone book," O'Connell said, hefting the volume.

"*Save the woman!*" came Ardeth Bay's voice, from the passageway. "*Kill the creature!*"

O'Connell and Jonathan scrambled to the tunnel's mouth and, not very far down at all, Ardeth Bay—out of cartridges—was swinging the empty elephant gun at the mass of mummies like Davy Crockett at the Alamo.

Then the moldy monsters had overrun him, trampling the brave warrior, and were swarming toward the small chamber of Horus.

231

O'Connell lit his final precious ingot of dynamite, looked about him, found the farthest wall, and flung the sizzling stick.

"That's the last one!" he said, pulling Jonathan down with him, hitting the deck. "We need some luck!"

The wall blew, debris collapsing, and, as the smoke cleared, a tunnel beyond beckoned. Just as mummies began to pile into the chamber, O'Connell and Jonathan scrambled through the opening and into the passageway, running for dear life, knowing that the one thing these lumbering undead monstrosities lacked was speed.

They cut down a passageway, then another, and another, just guessing, and almost ran through an archway. But O'Connell—having heard a bizarre, indecipherable sound, a sort of muffled, mumbled chanting emanating from beyond that portal—braced himself against the wall and stopped both of them from going on through.

Gingerly, O'Connell peered around the archway and took in a sight so stunning in its appalling scope and splendor that his mind could barely grasp what his eyes reported to him. . . .

At the bottom of an enormous stairway carved into the face of the rock, in the cavernous ampitheater below, dyed by the blue-orange patina of torches, surrounded by idols and icons of an ancient religion, Evelyn lay bound upon an altar as a clumsily swaying chorus of rotting mummies undulated in a circle around her; and next to her, on one side, were arranged the glittering jeweled canopic jars, while on her other side lay a rotted mummy—Anck-su-namun, O'Connell would wager!

And approaching her, sacrificial dagger in one hand, was He Who Shall Not Be Named—the regenerated mummy himself, Imhotep.

Jonathan was also peeking at this terrible tableau.

"My poor dear sister," he uttered, as if about to cry.

"Stiff upper lip, Johnny," O'Connell said, eyeing an adjoining passageway, which took a steep downward path. "Announce yourself. Attract some attention. . . . I'm gonna find a back door in!"

And as Evelyn struggled, unwilling to close her eyes and admit defeat, rather staring defiantly up at the dagger raised over her heart, Imhotep used his free hand to touch her cheek, almost affectionately, not unlike the gesture he'd made to the corpse of his beloved.

"You receive a rare honor," the reborn mummy told her. "You will not die—you will live within Anck-su-namun. And she will be reborn, your heart beating within her breast."

"Good news, Evy!" a familiar voice called out, from high above—higher than the knife blade. "I've found it!"

And she turned and looked and there, way at the top of those stairs, was her wonderful, foolish brother, brandishing the golden *Book of Amun Ra*.

The spell broken, at least momentarily, Imhotep stepped away from the altar, robes swirling, to look up at the intruder.

"Open the book, Jonathan!" she yelled. "That's the only way to stop him!"

Imhotep returned to the altar just long enough to gently place the sacrificial knife near the canopic jars, then quickly moved toward the staircase, and Jonathan.

"He's coming after you, Jonathan!" she screamed. "Open the book—kill him!"

At the top of the stairs, Jonathan was very well aware of the dark-eyed, bald-headed reborn high priest moving up toward him; but he wasn't having any luck at all getting the damned book open.

And he suddenly knew why: The volume had that same indentation on its face indicating the need for a very specific key.

"I need the bloody puzzle box to open this!" he yelled.

Imhotep was halfway up those stairs now.

"It's tucked away in his robes!" she called, straining helplessly at her shackles.

"What do I do, Evy?" he called back. The handsome creature climbing the steps was grinning up at him, dark eyes hypnotic, coming closer, closer. "What in hell do I do?"

And, as Jonathan panicked, ducking back through the doorway into the passageway, she called, "Don't read the inscription! It's a curse against defilement!"

But all Jonathan heard, frantically stumbling down the tunnel path O'Connell had taken earlier, were three of her words: ". . . read the inscription!"

And, thinking he was obeying his sister's orders, Jonathan—with his meager command of ancient Egyptian—did his best to translate the legend on the cover.

"*Keetash*-something," Jonathan mumbled, as he ran, heavy book in his hands, "*naraba*-something or other . . ."

Evelyn, unaware that her brother was misguidedly, fumblingly trying to unleash a curse upon them, felt a surge of relief as she saw Rick O'Connell come charging at the circle of high-priest mummies surrounding her, with a huge sword in his hand, procured apparently from one of the many statues on the fringes of the huge chamber.

Swinging the sword, he cut one of the mummies in two, and then swung it around and sank the flat edge of its blade into the chain that shackled her right wrist, making a satisfying *clang* as it snapped the ancient metal.

The mummy priests didn't seem to notice that one of their group had been cleaved in two, and made no attempt to interrupt O'Connell's efforts as he skirted the altar and flung the big sword's blade into the chain at the shackle at her left wrist, with another resounding *clang*.

Evelyn sat up, exhilarated by the taste of freedom.

Imhotep, nearing the top of the stairway, heard this commotion, and, as he turned to take in the sight of O'Connell rescuing Evelyn, froze in fury.

Imhotep bellowed a command in ancient Egyptian, which Evelyn knew all too well translated into: "Kill the intruder!"

And just as O'Connell slung the blade into the chain shackling her left foot, the mummies began attacking him with their rotting, clawing hands. The bastards were all over him, trying to rip him apart with their bony fingers, shred-

234

ding his shirt, carving bloody trails in his flesh. He swung his sword, taking off heads, arms, legs, chopping them to mummy kindling, but also elbowing and kicking at them, and with a final hacking blow of the blade he severed the chain at her right ankle.

He pulled her off the altar, arm around her waist, both of them breathing hard, nostrils flaring like racehorses crossing a finish line, and his eyes locked with Evelyn's. They grinned at each other in fierce animal pride and even lust and, in that moment, without a word promised each other everything.

It was at that instant of triumph that Jonathan stumbled through a passageway into the ampitheater, crossing a slab of stone bridging the black bog, and Evelyn heard her brother utter the last deadly words of an ancient curse.

"Rasheem . . . ooloo . . . Kashka!" Jonathan read from the gold book's cover, ever so proud of himself.

"Jonathan!" Evelyn cried, aghast. "What have you done?"

"What *has* he done?" O'Connell asked, arm still around her waist, massacred mummies scattered at his feet.

And a pair of huge doors threw themselves open from the adjacent mausoleum, the echo booming through the vast chamber like cannon fire. The sound of marching feet, the metallic clanking, seemed to announce . . . soldiers?

Midway on the staircase, Imhotep stood with arms folded, and again called to Evelyn's mind a self-satisfied genie, as he threw his bald head back, laughing a resounding laugh.

Ten soldiers, ten of Pharaoh Seti's best, bravest men, marched through that double doorway into the ampitheater, in shields and skirts and headdresses, spears and swords at the ready.

Soldiers of death.

Mummies.

"Oops," Jonathan said.

·❰ 22 ❱·

Army of Darkness

The ten soldiers of death came to a stop just beyond the double doors, standing at attention, like any good military unit, awaiting their orders. In front of them burbled the black bog over which one of those narrow stone slabs served as a bridge, just across from which, at the base of the altar, stood O'Connell, his arm still tucked protectively around Evelyn's waist.

"And here I thought your brother couldn't read ancient Egyptian," O'Connell said to her.

Imhotep was striding down that stairway, pointing at O'Connell and Evelyn, bellowing a command in his native tongue.

Evelyn said, "He's ordering them to—"

"I think I got that," O'Connell said, letting go of her, moving in front of her, holding the thick heavy hilt of the sword in both hands.

In perfect unison, the soldier mummies marched toward the fetid moat, as if they going to wade right in . . . then leaped across it—fully fifteen feet!—landing perfectly, as a unit, and began to march toward the two young lovers.

"Do something, Jonathan!" O'Connell called to his

friend, on the other side of the vast chamber. "You're the one with the book!"

"Bloody hell!" Jonathan cried, pacing along an edge of the moat. "I don't know what to do!"

"Finish the inscription!" Evelyn yelled to her brother. "If you complete it, you should gain control over them!"

"Really?" Jonathan said, gazing at the golden cover. "Well, then, I'll give it a go."

"Yeah," O'Connell said tightly, "why don't you?" He was backing up as the ten mummies moved toward him, their shields and swords and other weapons poised for battle.

Evelyn, just behind him, was backing up also, as the mummy soldiers fanned out in front of them, readying for attack.

Not expecting an assault from the rear, she let out a startled cry as a hand clutched her shoulder, and spun the startled Evelyn around, where she could see that sacrificial dagger raised high above her once again.

Not by Imhotep—he stood at the bottom of the stairway now, a general guiding his troops.

No, this knife was clutched in a skeletal hand, the hand of the rotted, revived corpse of Anck-su-namun herself!

They had not seen the hideous mummy in the filmy, feminine garb slip from the altar, steady herself on ancient bony legs, and pick up that sacrificial blade. Now, it would seem, Anck-su-namun had taken her regeneration into her own hands, and—though no eyes could be seen in those sunken sockets in that gray skull face—the pharaoh's concubine was having no trouble "seeing" Evelyn, at whose heart she swung the dagger.

Evelyn leaped back, bumping into O'Connell, the mistress mummy's blade missing by a fraction of an inch. O'Connell's already amazed expression managed to be even more astounded by this new player in the deadly game.

"You gotta stop her, baby," O'Connell said, squaring off with the advancing soldiers. "She may have the knife, but you got the weight advantage."

"Just what a girl wants to hear," Evelyn said, moving away from the advancing Anck-su-namun.

And O'Connell turned back, sword at the ready, to face the ten dead soldiers, who lifted their shields and screeched at him in a hideous battle cry.

O'Connell screeched back at them, and waved his sword, even as Evelyn bolted toward various statues and idols, where she could lead the lady mummy on a merry chase.

Imhotep called out a command, and five of the dead soldiers, again acting as one, leaped over O'Connell's head and landed nimbly on the altar. Now O'Connell had mummy soldiers in front of him, and behind him; there was only one thing to do—run like hell! Run like hell toward the sidelines. . . .

Across the chamber, Jonathan, moving along the edge of the moat, kicking skulls and skeletal fragments from his path into the black stew, was staring into the face of the gold book, trying his best to interpret the hieroglyphs, muttering, "*Hootash im . . . Hootash immmmm . . .* something or other, goddamnit!"

"Hurry up, Jonathan!" Evelyn called, as she played a deadly game of ring-around-the-rosie with the knife-wielding mummy of Anck-su-namun, circling a statue of Anubis.

Jonathan was unaware that Imhotep—content that his soldiers were in pursuit of O'Connell—was moving leisurely, but inexorably across the ampitheater toward him.

"I can't make out this last bloody symbol," Jonathan said.

"Hurry!" Evelyn said, ducking a jab from Anck-su-namun's blade, and scurrying toward another idol. "He's coming! Imhotep's . . ."

But Evelyn had no time for conversation, even when it might save her brother, because Anck-su-namun was bearing down on her. Somewhere in the back of her mind she knew she was destroying a precious relic of antiquity, as she pushed a vase on a pedestal into the mummy's path, where it shattered, creating an obstacle that bought Evelyn a few precious seconds.

With the soldier mummies on his heels, O'Connell raced across the chamber toward a rope secured to a post, just to the left of the yawning stairway; the rope stretched high above, to a pulley that held a big metal cage that had no doubt once been an instrument of torture. Right now it promised escape, temporary escape, at least. . . .

O'Connell swung the sword, severing the rope, and—with mummy soldiers nipping at his heels—grabbed hold and was yanked up and away so quickly that even though one of the mummies managed a supernatural fifteen-foot leap in pursuit of him, the bony bastard missed him and plastered himself against the wall like a bug on a windscreen. Simultaneously, the huge weighted cage on the other end of the rope came slamming down from the ceiling and, in an echoing crash, smashed another of the soldiers to dust.

Swinging like Tarzan, O'Connell nimbly leaped from the rope to the landing at the top of the tall stairway. He was not about to abandon Evelyn, but with the soldiers down there, at the bottom of the stairs, they might in their automaton-minded way follow him up that long distance, buying him time while he ducked around through the passageway and came in the back door, to save Evelyn. . . .

This plan in mind, he bolted into the passageway, and was about halfway to his destination when he almost ran headlong into the damn things, those goddamned soldier mummies! Imhotep had apparently seen through O'Connell's strategy, and sent his undead troops charging up this rear route, to get him.

Turning on his heels, O'Connell ran back the way he'd come, flew through the archway, and took the stairs two and three at a time, figuring the dead soldiers were right behind him—never dreaming that they'd race out of the archway and, defying gravity, walk down the walls, like spiders, and up on the ceiling above him.

When he got to the bottom of the stairs, O'Connell whirled, sword in hand, ready to do battle—but the soldiers weren't there! Hearing something clank in back of him, he turned quickly to see the undead bastards dropping from the ceiling and lining up behind him, shields up, weapons raised, ready to attack.

So, what the hell—he attacked *them*, wading into the

bandaged brigade, sword flashing and slashing, thrusting the blade into the trunk of the closest mummy and hurling him into the nearby bog, which splashed blackly, hungrily receiving this offering.

Dueling with another of the mummies, maneuvering the creature toward the slime pit, O'Connell brought his sword back to deliver what he hoped would be a telling blow, and unknowingly jammed it into and through the skull of another of the devils, who'd been coming up behind him with a battle axe. As he followed through with his swing, O'Connell was startled to find a detached head on the blade, but he hit his opponent just the same, with both the sword and the skull, shoving the soldier mummy into the voracious bog, even as the now-headless attacker, still lugging his battle axe, tottered into the muck on his own disoriented accord.

Two more soldiers rushed up to take the place of their fallen compatriots and O'Connell plucked a torch from a wall mount and jammed it into the face of the nearest mummy; apparently those ancient bandages were highly flammable, because the soldier of death burst into flame, a head-to-toe human torch, or anyway inhuman torch. O'Connell kicked the blazing bastard in the stomach, shoving him into his comrade, who similarly ignited, both of them doing a frantic flaming ballet before tumbling into the slime pit, which put out their fire but sucked them under, the bog burping bubbles.

Four of the mummy military remained. Parrying the blows of their blades, ducking the thrusts of spears, O'Connell held his own, until he again found himself at the foot of the stone staircase, and soon was slashing away with the big sword as he climbed, backward, the four skull-faced soldiers skulking up after him.

He kicked the shield of one, which sent the mummy toppling into two more mummies, all three taking a tumble from either side of the open stairway, onto the stone floor. But they sprang back onto their feet, as if that fall were nothing, while O'Connell fought their remaining comrade, sword to sword. With a vicious sideways swipe, O'Connell took the bastard's legs literally out from under him, dropping him to his bony knees. This success was undermined by the other three mummies making another of those supernatural leaps for a sprightly landing on the steps just above and behind O'Connell.

Swinging around with the sword ready to cleave, O'Connell felt a shield slap his body and send him tumbling back over the shortened torso of the mummy behind him, pitching down the stairs, toppling, losing his sword on the way to the hard stone floor.

And now, unarmed, he looked up at the grinning skull faces of three military mummies, advancing upon him down those stairs with their shields up and their swords high.

In the meantime, Jonathan, finally noticing Imhotep stalking him, continued skirting the edges of the black moat, doing his best to translate the remaining symbols of the inscription. On the move, he called out to his sister, who was fleeing Anck-su-namun's mummy, that sacrificial knife jabbing and hacking away as Evelyn weaved in and around any barrier she could find. Right now they were back at the altar, circling the thing, playing a lethal round of tag.

Jonathan, now engaged in a similar lethal game with Imhotep, called to his sister, "What's the Anck symbol that has two squiggly lines above it, a bird and a stork?"

"*Ahmenophus!*" Evelyn called, and stumbled.

This allowed the mummified Anck-su-namun, who was growing surer-footed by the second, to close the gap, reaching out a withered hand and grasping Evelyn by her throat; the skeletal fingers had incredible force, even as desiccated flesh peeled from the hand. The mummy turned Evelyn's face toward her own, and Evelyn, already growing faint, air cut off by the viselike grip, found herself staring into the grinning skull mask of a once beautiful woman, whose other hand held high the sacrificial blade.

As the same time, O'Connell was on his back, scrambling awkwardly on his hands and heels, like a crab, looking up at the three mummy soldiers whose swords swung back, then swung down . . .

. . . just as Jonathan was saying, *"Hootash im Ahmeno-phus!"*

And the dead soldiers froze, their blades halting an inch from the stunned O'Connell's face.

Then the mummified trio, in unison, stood upright, turning to face Jonathan at the outskirts of the chamber, where he'd been hopping around, playing keepaway, Imhotep slowly closing in.

Jonathan recoiled at this attention, and said to the dead soldiers, "Don't look at *me*!"

But Evelyn, choking under the fingers of Anck-su-namun, called out, "Ca . . . ca . . . *command* them!"

Jonathan, eyes wide at the scrape Evelyn was in, looked at his soldiers, pointed at his sister, and yelled, *"Fa-hooshka Anck-su-namun!"*

The soldier mummies turned, and marched toward Anck-su-namun. Imhotep, seeing this, quickened his stride, and closed in on Jonathan.

Help was on the way, the mummies marching, but Evelyn saw the wrinkled corpse bracing to deliver the death blow with the blade, and the Englishwoman summoned whatever strength she had left to throw a right cross into the gray, shrunken face, taking teeth and knocking off rotten flesh, Anck-su-namun stumbling back.

Then the soldier mummies were upon Anck-su-namun, carving and cleaving, the would-be bride of Imhotep hissing her rage and hacking back at them with the sacrificial knife, but quickly falling to the floor, cut to ribbons by the three flailing blades.

"Anck-su-namun!" Imhotep shrieked, as if he were the one suffering the pain, and as Jonathan frantically scrambled away, the High Priest of Osiris was after him.

Still reeling, Evelyn, picking herself up from the floor near the base of the altar, gasping for breath, watched in horror as Imhotep grabbed her brother by the throat, just as the mummy of Anck-su-namun had done to her.

"Rick!" she cried, moving toward her brother. "Help him! Help Jonathan!"

O'Connell, getting to his feet, had witnessed Imhotep's

assault on Jonathan, too, and he ran to recover his sword, watching as the high priest lifted Evelyn's brother up and off the ground as if Jonathan were weightless, pinning him against a wall. Sword in hand now, O'Connell raced across a stone-slab bridge over the bog, dashing toward where Jonathan struggled pitifully, Imhotep's robes flapping like black wings, as the regenerated mummy choked his prey with one hand while, with the other, snatched the gold *Book of Amun Ra* from Jonathan's grasp, as if removing a dangerous toy from a child's fingers.

And then O'Connell was there, swinging the big blade like a scythe, chopping off Imhotep's right arm like a tree branch, the limb thudding to the floor with *The Book of Amun Ra* still clutched in its dead hand.

Imhotep dropped Jonathan, who slid down the wall, clutching at his throat, making a gurgling sound; but He Who Shall Not Be Named—who whirled to cast a ferocious stare upon O'Connell—registered no fear, no pain, or for that matter blood: Where the dismembered limb had been sliced away, the rot of a decayed mummy showed within.

Imhotep might look human on the outside, but within he was still a desiccated corpse.

"Let's see how tough you are one-handed." O'Connell grinned at the monster, hefting the sword with a two-handed grasp.

Imhotep's remaining arm shot out and grabbed O'Connell by the shirt and hurled him into a pillar, across the black moat, twenty feet away.

Hitting the stone pillar hard, feeling a rib crack, O'Connell cried out in pain, bouncing to the equally hard floor, where he felt another rib crack. Pushing up, groaning, pain lancing through him, O'Connell saw Imhotep striding toward him, black robes swirling, scowling, his remaining arm outstretched, fist clenched.

Okay, so the bastard was left-handed. . . .

Dazed, O'Connell staggered to his feet, looked drunkenly for his sword, which he'd lost on the trip to the pillar, and Imhotep was closing in on him as Evelyn's voice called out, "Keep him busy!"

"See what I can do," O'Connell said, and Imhotep slung his remaining arm, like a club, across O'Connell's chest, and sent the American spinning through the air, crashing into the floor, near the altar, with an echoing slam. O'Connell did his best to get to his feet, but his knees were buckling. . . .

Evelyn was at her brother's side, bending over him, surprised to see him smiling, if somewhat dementedly.

"What . . . ?" she began.

Jonathan, breathing hard, held up the puzzle box. "Got it," he said, clearly proud that he had mustered his pickpocket skills in the midst of being strangled by a living mummy.

"Get the book," she ordered her brother, as she deftly opened the puzzle box, petals unfolding into the large, unusual key.

"You won't be needing this," Jonathan told the severed arm, as he lifted the golden *Book of Amun Ra* from its lifeless fingers.

And over by the altar, the regal, unstoppable Imhotep— eyes burning with rage—approached the barely conscious O'Connell, who was having trouble just staying on his feet, and clutched him by the throat, a deadly grip cutting off his air, lifting him off the ground.

Evelyn, kneeling over the book which Jonathan propped up in his hands, worked the key in the lock, and the golden volume opened with a hiss. Her brother held the book while Evelyn quickly turned the heavy golden pages, looking for the incantation, eyes racing over hieroglyphs, translating at record speed. . . .

O'Connell, held high in the grip of the mummy's hand, hung limp, like clothes on a line, was barely conscious, as an evilly grinning Imhotep spoke to him in ancient Egyptian. Evelyn was too busy to translate, but O'Connell—groggy as he was—felt he'd gotten the drift.

"I'm afraid your boyfriend's finished," Jonathan said glumly.

"Never," she said, then called out to him, "Hold on, Rick! Hold on!"

244

But it was Imhotep who was holding on, to O'Connell's throat, and now the mummy began to not just hold him there, but to tighten his steel fingers into a stranglehold. Coughing, choking, O'Connell's body swayed, and so did his mind, in out and of consciousness. . . .

It was like being back at the Cairo prison, with that noose around his neck, tightening, his feet kicking helplessly, the world turning red, then black. . . . Maybe this had all been a dream, some final nightmare flashing through his last living moments, and he was still on that gallows, just another deserter from the Foreign Legion, hanging, dying. . . .

And Evelyn stood, reading from the book her brother held open for her, and faced He Who Shall Be Named, as he strangled the man she loved, and in a loud, firm voice intoned: *"Kadeesh mal!"*

Imhotep froze, easing the grip on O'Connell's throat, but still holding him high, and glared at Evelyn.

But there was more than just rage in that glare: fear. There was fear.

"Kadeesh mal!" she cried, voice echoing off the ceiling. *"Pared oos! Pared oos!"*

Tossing O'Connell aside, discarding him, Imhotep pivoted and stared at Evelyn and his expression was no longer regal, nor enraged: Terror was etched there, sheer terror, as surely as the hieroglyphs were etched upon that golden page from which she'd spelled his doom.

As O'Connell, coughing, weaving, got to his feet, Imhotep turned and stared at the yawning stairway. Through the archway came a sudden, strong gust of wind; but this chill breeze, whipping Imhotep's robes and Evelyn's gown, had not been summoned by the mummy.

Evelyn Carnahan, who until recently had not believed in curses, had unleashed this wind, this curse. . . .

Through a vortex of wind emerged a black chariot, or a vision of one, as it seemed at once misty and transparent, and yet distinct and somehow real, charging down the stairs, neither the wheels driving the chariot nor the hooves of the two black horses pulling it ever touching the stone, hurtling down the steps nonetheless, with a jackal-headed driver—Anubis, a god who had apparently come to discipline a headstrong high priest.

Imhotep stood, facing this vision, with arms outstretched, a posture as close to surrender as possible for this proud man, and the chariot plowed right through him, circling through the vast chamber, dragging a black, semitransparent image of Imhotep behind—though the man himself still stood there, slumped. Evelyn could only wonder: *Was that ghostlike vision, taken captive by this phantasm of Anubis, Imhotep's soul?*

Wind still whipping them, Evelyn and Jonathan took a quick step back. Though it was only partly visible, this horse-drawn black chariot was making a thunderous racket, and they instinctively got out of its way.

And Jonathan, holding the golden book, tripped, taking a fall, accidentally pitching *The Book of Amun Ra* into the black slime. As the gleaming volume sunk below the burbling surface, sinking into the black putrescence, Evelyn felt nothing, though her brother looked about to cry.

The chariot charged back up the staircase, Anubis whipping his steeds, dragging that black, misty image of Imhotep, reaching out yearningly, helplessly toward the physical form that was left behind.

And that physical form, Imhotep, the mummy who looked like a man, ran after his departing soul, hurtling up the stairs after it; but the chariot returned to the swirling winds from which it came and, in an eyeblink, disappeared.

Turning, his robes swirling, Imhotep dashed down the stairs. His soul may have been gone, but the rage was still here, his eyes burning with it, teeth clenched in the tanned face.

And he was striding right toward O'Connell.

The American, who had managed to find his sword, braced himself—O'Connell may have not have lost his soul, but he was battered, pulsing with pain, and could only wonder if he had another battle left in him on this strange endless day.

From just behind him, O'Connell heard the voice of the woman he loved.

"Don't let him scare you, darling," she said, and hearing her call him that made him smile, even in these circumstances. "He's only human."

And as Imhotep neared him, hand poised in that familiar viselike grip, O'Connell swung the blade of the sword up and into the mummy—deep, hard, right through the son of a bitch.

Imhotep's eyes widened in surprise and pain. Wincing, he looked down at the sword impaling him, touched his stomach, and brought back a hand stained red.

"Tell him he finally got his wish," O'Connell said, speaking to Evelyn, but spitting the words into Imhotep's face. "Tell him he's a man again."

And Evelyn translated, shouting the words defiantly, and when O'Connell saw them register in the bastard's eyes, he yanked the blade free, and shoved He Who Shall Be One Dead Sorry Son of a Bitch into the black bog.

Evelyn came up beside O'Connell, slipping an arm around his waist, and Jonathan came up along his other side.

"Good show, Rick," Jonathan said. "Never doubted you for a moment."

Imhotep was taking his time sinking, the black slime drawing him down almost lovingly, and he stared up at those who'd defeated him, flushed with princely, arrogant defiance, almost smiling.

Then his head was sucked under by the simmering blackness.

"Is it finally over?" Jonathan asked.

And as if in reply, Imhotep's shaved head bobbed to the surface and he sneered at the victors, shouting out one last phrase in his ancient tongue. Then the slime pulled him under and he was, at last, truly, gone.

"What did he say?" O'Connell asked her.

Evelyn's expression had a haunted blankness; she turned almost mechanically to say to him, "He said, 'Death is only the beginning.' "

·❮ 23 ❯·

The Shifting Sands

While men and mummies clashed in the vast ampitheater, the rats of Hamanaptra scurried about the perimeter, going on about their business, unconcerned about eternal life or undying loves, scavengers concentrating only on their own immediate well-being, their own narrow little existences.

Beni was no exception.

The sounds of battle echoing through the labyrinths of the City of the Dead had meant only one thing to the little thief: The others were preoccupied, leaving him to scurry about, gathering from the treasure chambers of Pharaoh Seti the First (Beni had discovered several more) the precious jewels and golden artifacts, which he stuffed into saddlebags he'd appropriated from the various stray camels that wandered about the ruins.

And while O'Connell, his girlfriend, and her stupid brother waged their hopeless war against the mighty Imhotep, the shrewd Beni made trip after trip, carrying the glittering booty up through the stairway in the temple, which the American expedition had uncovered. Rounding up, and tying up, three camels, Beni began piling the saddlebags onto the backs of the beasts; then he would scamper back down into the underground world, return to one of several treasure chambers and load up more saddlebags. Though any one of the chambers held a king's ransom and more, Beni was flitting from one treasure room to another, looking for the smaller, more easily transported items: golden baubles, statuettes, loose jewels.

By the time the sounds of battle had died down, an exhausted Beni knew he would have to hurry, as Imhotep (he assumed the high priest would triumph over the mere mortals) came looking for his slave. So, despite his reluctance at leaving so much precious treasure behind, Beni knew this would have to be his last trip.

So he made sure he packed plenty of plunder into these last saddlebags, slinging one of them over an ornate golden staff that jutted from the wall like a fancy coatrack. Leaning against the wall, catching his breath, Beni heard a loud grinding, as if stone was rubbing against stone.

Not liking the sound of that, Beni reached for the saddlebags, slung onto the golden staff, and noticed that the weight of the heavily laden bags had pushed the staff down.

Backing away, startled, chilled with fear, Beni wondered if he'd accidentally pulled a lever. . . .

The answer to that question was immediate: The hissing of pouring sand, thousands of pounds of it, filled his ears as, all around him, the walls of the treasure chamber began to lower, to sink into the ground . . . but the floor was staying put!

Abandoning the saddlebags, grabbing a torch, Beni scrambled out through a lowering doorway and into the tunnels, finding the walls sinking there as well, bringing the ceiling down, down, down; soon he was crouching, crawling along, more than ever like a rat, though even a trained rodent might not have been able to duplicate Beni's feat of lighting the way with a torch in his teeth. . . .

Moments after Imhotep's slimy farewell, O'Connell, Evelyn, and Jonathan—standing at the edge of the bog—had also heard the rumbling of stones, the hissing of sand.

Immediately, they all knew something was terribly

wrong, though Evelyn assumed it had to do with the demise of He Who Shall Not Be Named.

"Dear God," she said. "Remember the legend?"

Jonathan, his Egyptology skills honed now, said, with some alarm, "That the pharaohs rigged Hamanaptra to slide under the dunes, at the flick of a switch?"

O'Connell didn't need to hear any more expert opinions on this subject—the gnashing of stone against stone, the sizzle of sand raining in, had the last word.

The high walls around them trembling, visibly sinking, O'Connell yelled, "Come on!" grabbing Evelyn's hand and she followed his lead, Jonathan tagging after. They raced across the stone slab over the black slime, past the trio of soldier mummies—frozen in place, awaiting a next command that would never come—and hustled past sinking pillars through a descending doorway.

As they scurried through the tunnels, ducking down as the ceiling lowered, sand began pouring in, sliding down the walls in a dry torrent, turning the air dusty.

"Cover your mouth!" O'Connell cried, then took his own advice.

Evelyn was right behind him, her brother bringing up the rear. Ceiling dropping inch by inexorable inch, they were bent in half now, like old people with terrible backaches, and it was harder than hell to run that way; but they did. They did.

Soon they had tumbled through half a doorway into the treasure chamber, that first one where O'Connell, Jonathan and the Med-jai warrior had fought the mummies.

Evelyn skidded to a stop, her eyes wide with wonder, taking in the piles of glittering jeweled artifacts, the ebony furnishings, the golden idols.

But O'Connell was taking in the sinking walls, and the sand piling in, sliding relentlessly down the walls. The sound of the lowering stone was thunderous, deafening; the world was collapsing around them and they had to find a way out, a path to some other world. . . .

He grabbed her hand and yanked her along, dragging her

250

through mounds of treasure, striding through the precious stuff toward a sinking doorway. . . .

"Rick!" a familiar voice called—too familiar.

As they waded through riches, O'Connell glanced back to see Beni entering the chamber, on his hands and knees.

"Come on!" O'Connell called to him.

Then Beni joined their escape party, just behind Jonathan when the four darted through the descending doorway, finding themselves at the bottom of a stairway, walls lowering, ceiling coming down. At the top of the stairs was an archway that had already lost half its height. It was perhaps at four feet now.

O'Connell bolted up the stairs, two and three at a time, Jonathan and Evelyn kept close pace behind him, that doorway sliding down, lowering like a slow-motion guillotine.

O'Connell dove through, spun around, Jonathan diving past his sister through the narrow gap. Evelyn crawled through, but got pinned by the lowering arch, catching her above the feminine flare of her hips. She cried out, eyes wide with terror, but O'Connell grabbed both her arms and pulled with everything he had, and yanked her through.

Then Beni's frightened face could be seen through the tiny gap remaining.

"Rick! My friend!"

Beni stuck his hand through and O'Connell grabbed on, pulling; but it was evident there wasn't enough room, and as the archway dropped down farther, Beni snatched his arm back before it got cut off.

The archway thudded to the floor, sealing Beni in.

Evelyn and Jonathan stared at the vanished doorway, aghast.

"No saving him now," O'Connell said, shaking his head. "Keep going!"

Crouching now, crawling, they made their way down a tunnel, sand racing down the walls. O'Connell had found his compass and, holding it and the torch in one hand as he crept along, did his best to guide his little group toward the preparation chamber where awaited, presumably, their ropes dangling from pillars. He only hoped that when they got there, the pillars would still be above ground!

When they entered the preparation chamber, on hands and knees, they discovered, to their relief and surprise, that the floor had risen, or anyway the sands had sunk, to where they were within a few feet of the surface. O'Connell used his locked hands as a step-up for both Evelyn and Jonathan, and then Jonathan reached a hand down for O'Connell, helping him out.

Then they were racing through the ruins, the shrine walls, pillars, pylons, all sinking into the sands, the ground disappearing behind them, Hamanaptra crumbling, collapsing around them in a rumbling underground earthquake. Up ahead a trio of camels were racing frantically as well, charging through the gate, as the pylons slipped under the sand. When the camels slowed on the stone ramp outside the gate, O'Connell, Evelyn, and Jonathan caught up with the beasts, O'Connell and Jonathan claiming two of them, climbing aboard, O'Connell pulling Evelyn up with him, onto the back of the animal. The camels, who apparently were glad to have their masters back, *any* masters—were easily handled.

And as they raced toward the desert, the remaining ruins crashed down behind them in a great cloud of sand and dust, billowing like the smoke of some immense explosion.

Several minutes later, they slowed, and paused, and looked back, but nothing could be seen yet—the cloud of sand was too broad, too concealing.

"Afraid your friend got left behind," Jonathan said to O'Connell.

"Beni wasn't anybody's friend," O'Connell said, feeling a twinge, nonetheless.

"Dreadful little man," Evelyn said, from behind O'Connell, arms hugging his waist. "But I wouldn't wish that on even a scoundrel like him."

"He always found someone to take advantage of," O'Connell said.

"Well," Jonathan said, "he's on his own now."

• • •

Not quite.

As the ceiling lowered, Beni had scrambled on his hands and knees down the stairs, and into the treasure chamber, torch still burning, albeit weakly. The walls had stopped lowering; though sand still streamed in, and the chamber was a mere four feet high, the ceiling was not coming down to squash him like a damned bug. No.

On his knees, Beni fanned the torch about and surveyed his domain, his glittering, golden, jeweled domain . . . but every doorway was below ground. He was trapped.

But he would find a way, Beni would find a way: He always did. The immediate problem was the air—it was bad, weak, and his torch was diminishing, fading. He sat on a pile of jewels and rested, brain buzzing, trying to think, scheming. . . .

Then he heard something: a scratching—no, not a scratching, more a—chittering.

In one corner, a scarab beetle seemed to stare at him, talking to him in its noisy, chitter-chatter fashion. Beni knew all too well what even a single one of these vicious dung beetles could do to a man, to his flesh.

Then the beetle scurried toward him, and Beni backed away. "Shoo! Shoo!" he said, waving his flickering torch at the thing.

That was when the torch went out, which was just as well, because seeing the dozens, perhaps hundreds, maybe thousands of scarab beetles boil up out from under the piles of treasure might have driven Beni completely mad, perhaps two or three seconds sooner.

In the darkness, the screams of the little thief rose above the chittering of the hungry bugs as Beni, not exactly on his own, met the other inhabitants of his domain.

From a high dune, dismounted from their waiting camels, O'Connell, Evelyn, and Jonathan watched as the dust cloud finally cleared, allowing them to witness the aftermath of the imploding sands, one final bizarre view to add to their large collection: the volcano itself sinking, rumbling as if some eruption underground might have caused the disappearance of the City of the Dead, the valley itself gone, nothing remaining but the timeless shifting sands of the Sahara.

A hand slammed down upon Jonathan's shoulder, and he yelped in surprise, O'Connell and Evelyn turned, startled, too, as if someone had said, "Boo."

Ardeth Bay, battered but alive, the classic image of an Arab warrior wrapped in dark robes, rode high on a camel of his own appropriation.

"I'd be pleased to see you alive," Jonathan said, breathing hard, "if you hadn't scared the bloody hell out of me."

"That was not my intention," Ardeth Bay said, with a little bow.

"How did you fight all those mummies?" O'Connell asked.

"How did you?" Ardeth Bay asked with a smile, one hand resting on his golden scimitar. "Perhaps one day we can share our stories . . . but now we must part—after I offer my humble thanks and the eternal respect of my people, and myself."

"Any time." O'Connell grinned.

"That's all well and good," Jonathan said, "but the priceless treasures we sought seem to have slipped under the bloody Sahara."

"Why don't you come back to Cairo with us?" Evelyn said.

"The city is not my place," the warrior said. "I have work to do."

"What work?" O'Connell asked.

"I must return to my people. The Med-jai again must guard these sands—so that He Who Shall Not Be Named remains under them."

"I don't think he'll be comin' back," O'Connell said, cocky.

But Evelyn didn't seem so sure. "Imhotep's last words were, 'Death is only the beginning.' I don't think keeping an eye on this area is such a bad idea."

Ardeth Bay bowed again, said, "May Allah always smile down upon you," and he galloped off.

"Allah smiles." Jonathan smirked. "I thought he believed in those ancient gods." He was kicking at the sands, irritated.

O'Connell put a hand on Jonathan's shoulder. "What's bothering you, buddy? We rescued the damsel, defeated the villain, didn't we?"

"Yes, but what about the bloody treasure? Allah can smile on my aching backside. I'd take a handful of gold over a smile, any day."

"Not me," O'Connell said, as he gazed into the beaming face of Jonathan's beautiful sister, the desert breeze ruffling her black gown, mussing her long brown tresses.

Then O'Connell, who was the hero after all, swept the damsel into his arms and kissed her, deeply, passionately; and she kissed him back the very same way, wrapping her arms around him, not seeming at all like a librarian, even if the coming days would find her appointed the first female curator in the history of the Cairo Museum of Antiquities.

"Posh," Jonathan said, quite disgusted with both of them, climbing onto his camel.

The kiss lasted forever, and then another of similar duration followed; but finally O'Connell slung himself onto one of the camels, pulling Evelyn up behind him, where she clutched his waist, cuddling, cooing, making her brother sick to his stomach.

O'Connell, from his camel, looked over at Jonathan on his and grinned, and suddenly Jonathan grinned back at his American friend.

"I guess it was quite an adventure, at that," Jonathan said.

"Beats getting hanged at the Cairo prison," O'Connell said.

Eyes locked, sharing identical grins, the two men slapped the reins of their camels and, together, shouted, *"Tuk-tuk-tuk!"*

And as they rode off into a beautiful red-and-purple sunset, toward the nearest Bedouin oasis, the three adventurers were unaware that beneath the closed flaps of the saddlebags slung over the backs of their camels awaited the gold and jewels of a pharaoh's treasure, bequeathed to them unwittingly by the latest resident of the City of the Dead.

A Tip of the Pith Helmet

As a fan since childhood of the Universal monster movies, I was delighted to have the opportunity to write the novel version of Stephen Sommers's lively update of this classic tale.

I would like to cite several reference works, in particular two accounts that were contemporary with the modern sections of this novel: *Cairo to Kisumu* (1925) by Frank G. Carpenter, and *Illustrated Africa—North, Tropical, South* (1925) by William D. Boyce.

Other books consulted, in an effort to provide color and accurate background, include *Ancient Egypt: Discovering Its Splendors* (1978), National Geographic Society; *Ancient Lives: Daily Life in the Egypt of the Pharaohs* (1984), John Romer; *The Curse of the Pharaohs* (1975), Philipp Vandenberg (translated by Thomas Weyr); *Egypt: Land of the Pharaohs* (1992), Editors of Time-Life Books; *Everyday Life in Ancient Egypt* (1994), Nathaniel Harris; *The French Foreign Legion* (1973), Nigel Thomas; *The Egyptians* (1997), John and Louise James; *Howard Carter Before Tutankhamun* (1992), Nicholas Reeves and John H. Taylor; *The Mystery of the Pyramids* (1979), Humphrey Evans; *Mummies and*

Magic: The Funerary Arts of Ancient Egypt (1988), Sue D'Auria, Peter Lacovara and Catharine H. Roehrig; *People of the Nile: Everyday Life in Ancient Egypt* (1982), John Romer; *The Pharaohs* (1981), Lionel Casson; *The Time Traveller Book of Pharaohs and Pyramids* (1977), Tony Allan, assisted by Vivienne Henry; and *Wonderful Things: The Discovery of Tutankhamun's Tomb* (1976), The Metropolitan Museum of Art (photographs by Harry Burton).

Cindy Chang of Universal Studios provided excellent, timely support for this project and I am grateful to her. Thanks also to my agent, Dominick Abel; and of course to my wife, writer Barbara Collins, who helped me survive this perilous expedition.

Max Allan Collins has earned an unprecedented eight Private Eye Writers of America "Shamus" nominations for his "Nathan Heller" historical thrillers, winning twice (*True Detective*, 1983, and *Stolen Away*, 1991).

A Mystery Writers of America "Edgar" nominee in both fiction and nonfiction categories, Collins has been hailed as "the Renaissance man of mystery fiction." His credits include four suspense-novel series, film criticism, short fiction, songwriting, trading-card sets, and movie/TV tie-in novels, including such international bestsellers as *In the Line of Fire*, *Air Force One*, and *Saving Private Ryan*.

He scripted the internationally syndicated comic strip *Dick Tracy* from 1977 to 1993, is cocreator of the comic-book features *Ms. Tree* and *Mike Danger*, and has written the *Batman* comic book and newspaper strip.

Working as an independent filmmaker in his native Iowa, he wrote, directed, and executive-produced the 1996 suspense film *Mommy*, starring Patty McCormack; he performed the same duties for a sequel, *Mommy's Day*, released in 1997. The recipient of a record three Iowa Motion Picture Awards for screenwriting, he also wrote *The Expert*, a 1995 HBO World Premiere film. He recently wrote and directed a documentary, *Mike Hammer's Mickey Spillane*.

Collins lives in Muscatine, Iowa, with his wife, writer Barbara Collins, and their teenage son, Nathan.